"Is there still hope for us, Lily?"

"Honestly? I don't know." She turned away then. "St. Louis is everything I thought I wanted. Until you."

Caleb knelt in front of Lily, hoping against hope that she would hear and respond to the urgent call of his heart. He picked up her hands and held them in his, seeking in her astonishing blue eyes the response he longed for. "Dearest Lily, I ask you before God to become my wife. I pledge you my undying love."

Her eyes filled with tears, Lily shook her head back and forth, gripping his hand tightly. She opened her mouth to speak, but no sound came. Adrift, Caleb could only stand, draw her to her feet and enfold her in his arms. Her slight body trembled in his embrace and muffled sobs gave evidence of her distress. Finally she stepped away and gazed at him with such love he feared ever forgetting this moment. A glimmer of hope. That was all he needed....

LAURA ABBOT

Growing up in Kansas City, Missouri, Laura Abbot was deeply influenced by her favorite literary character, Jo from *Little Women*. *If only,* Laura thought, *I could write stories, too.* Many years later, after a twenty-five-year career as a high-school English teacher and independent school administrator, Laura's ambition was unexpectedly realized. When she and her husband took early retirement and built their dream home on Beaver Lake outside of Eureka Springs, Arkansas, he bought her a new computer and uttered these life-changing words: "You always said you wanted to write. Now sit down and *do* it!" Happily, she sold her first attempt to Harlequin Superromance, a success followed by more sales to the same line.

Other professional credentials include serving as an educational consultant and speaker. Active in her church, Laura is a licensed lay preacher. Her great blessing, however, is her children—all productive, caring adults and parents—who have given her eleven remarkable, resilient (but who's prejudiced?) grandchildren, including at least three who show talent in writing and may pursue it as a career. Jo March, look what you started!

Laura enjoys corresponding with readers. Please write her at LauraAbbot@msn.com.

Into the Wilderness

LAURA ABBOT

For Jeannie,
I hope you will enjoy the Kansas setting. This new genre has been both a challenge and a blessing.
With much love,
Laura Abbot

HARLEQUIN® LOVE INSPIRED® HISTORICAL

LOVE INSPIRED BOOKS

ISBN-13: 978-0-373-82974-3

INTO THE WILDERNESS

www.LoveInspiredBooks.com

Printed in U.S.A.

I am about to do a new thing; now it springs forth, do you not perceive it? I will make a way in the wilderness and rivers in the desert.
—*Isaiah* 43:19

To Paula Eykelhof, editor extraordinaire,
with gratitude for her encouragement,
guidance and enduring belief in me.

Chapter One

Fort Larned, Kansas
March, 1869

Lily Kellogg stood before her mother's small grave marker, oblivious to the raw spring chill. *Mathilda Louise Kellogg, b. 1820, d. 1868. Beloved wife and mother.* From these few words, who would discern the bravery and compassion of the woman buried there? Or how quickly she had succumbed to the influenza that swept through the fort a few short months ago, despite the heroic efforts of Lily's father, the post surgeon.

Once again Lily asked the familiar questions. *Is this ultimately what we amount to? A few facts etched in cold stone? Do we rest for eternity beneath a blanket of grass battered by wind, sleet and snow, subject to infestation by creatures both crawling and flying?* Standing there motherless, she struggled to believe in a merciful God.

Too late she thought of the questions she should have asked her mother, but hadn't, and the family stories she should remember, but couldn't. Yet she knew her mother had loved her, as she had loved her father, brother and sister. In part, she blamed this isolated place for her mother's death. If only they had remained in Iowa, living with her maternal grandparents as they had while her father served in the Union Army. When the conflict ended and her father elected to remain in the military, her mother, not without misgivings, had insisted that she, Lily and Lily's older sister, Rose, accompany him to this remote fort on the Kansas plains. Her mother had loved fine things and had assumed she would always live in the familiarity of the town where she grew up and in comfortable proximity to her well-to-do parents.

Since her death, Lily had harbored a painful question: Would Mama still be alive if the family had stayed in Iowa? She cast a baleful glance at the headstone. It all came down to choices, and her mother, a faithful wife, had chosen to follow her husband. Now that Mathilda was gone, Lily knew her father depended even more upon his daughters and worried whether Fort Larned was a suitable home for two unmarried women, one twenty-one and the other twenty-four.

Gazing at the gray clouds scudding overhead, Lily permitted herself a moment of self-pity. She tried not to complain and to trust in God's plan for her. But surely her destiny lay someplace else—in a city lively with creativity and dedicated to progress. Blinking back tears, she laid her hand gently on the grave marker.

The clatter of mounted horses interrupted her reverie. The arrival of new troops was no novelty, and, like others before them, these soldiers deserved a welcome. Gathering her cloak around her, she waved. Their leader glanced in her direction, smiled and lifted his hat.

Whether it was his erect posture astride the black horse, his light brown curls blowing in the wind or his engaging smile that caused her heart to skip a beat, she couldn't say. Perhaps it was his air of confidence, the hint of mischief in his smile or his fleeting resemblance to the brother she had lost in the war that moved her. She turned away. *He is just another officer,* she reminded herself. Just another officer.

Dismayed by her spontaneous reaction to the man, Lily hurried toward home. No good could come from idle speculation about the new captain, handsome or not, and no such man could ever derail the exciting future she planned for herself.

When Lily returned to their quarters attached to the hospital, her sister met her at the door. "You look chilled. Come warm yourself by the fire." Rose gathered Lily's cloak and hung it on the hook in the entryway. "I've brewed some tea." She bustled to the stove to fetch it while Lily settled in the rocker in front of the hearth, grateful for her sister's solicitude. Rose, always a steadying influence, had moved effortlessly into her mother's homemaking role.

Her ample body swathed in an apron, Rose handed Lily her tea and sat on the bench across from her. "Did you see the new troops arrive?"

"Yes. They're fortunate to be assigned to this modern post, rather than one of the more primitive ones."

"And we are fortunate to have received an invitation from Major and Mrs. Hurlburt to dine with them and the newly arrived captain."

"How thoughtful." Ordinarily Lily would have been delighted by such a welcome invitation from the fort's commander and his wife. Yet she was suddenly overcome with uncharacteristic shyness. The possibility of acquaintance with the new captain should not so unnerve her.

Rose leaned forward. "I'm wearing my apple-green. What will you choose?" They smiled in concert, knowing full well that aside from their few everyday dresses and recently discarded mourning clothes, they had only two Sunday gowns. "You look best in the lilac," Rose ventured. "Do wear it."

"Why are you so bent on how I look?"

Rose took a sip of tea. "You know I will not leave Papa. I am a homebody. But you? It's time to consider romance. Past time. If a dashing cavalryman is to sweep anyone off her feet, it is you, dear Lily."

"Such a prospect! To follow some man from post to post, never having a true home of one's own."

"That's what Mama did," Rose gently reminded her.

"Yes, but though she never complained to us, I always thought Mama acted more from loyalty than from enthusiasm. Remember when we first arrived here? How she would purse her lips and shake her head with resignation?" Lily squared her shoulders. "I have bigger dreams than living at assorted military establishments."

"Ah, yes. Your dreams." Rose's sigh spoke volumes.

"You just wait. I am determined to seek another path. Mother always planned for one or both of us to visit Aunt Lavinia in St. Louis if she offered to take us under her wing. Think what we could learn there! What we could see! Libraries, museums, theaters—all just waiting for us." She glowed with the possibilities. "As for courtship, surely there are plenty of men of intellect and substance in the city." She glanced around the room. "Whatever happens, my future is not in an isolated place like this."

"Lily, if leaving is truly what you desire, I hope it happens even if I would sorely miss you. Mama recognized our different talents and temperaments. She knew you, not I, would thrive in a more sophisticated environment than rural Iowa or this fort. If Aunt Lavinia's invitation comes, you are the one to go."

Lily set down her cup and stretched her feet toward the fire. "Imagine," she said breathlessly. "St. Louis."

Lavinia, her mother's only sister, had married well. Henry Dupree had made a fortune in commerce and doted upon his wife, whose only apparent regret was that she was childless. She had begged Mathilda not to marry Ezra Kellogg, appalled that her sister would settle for being the wife of a small-town doctor. Then the war changed even that, and Lavinia had made no secret of her disappointment at finding Mathilda doomed to the itinerant life of an army surgeon's wife. Lavinia's letters following their mother's death had even intimated that she blamed Ezra for the influenza that had cruelly taken her sister.

Through the years, Lavinia had corresponded regularly, delighting her nieces with the wonders of St. Louis and the gaiety of her social calendar. Lily pored over the back issues of *Godey's Lady's Book* their aunt sent them. Transfixed by illustrations of the latest styles, she could picture herself dancing in the arms of a sophisticated city man at some fashionable soiree. Although she realized she was indulging in romantic fantasy, such daydreams alleviated the loneliness of her existence on the prairie.

Living among men of all ages and stations was not easy. Some ogled, some were crude and others were helpful, going out of their way to assist the surgeon and his household. Tonight she would meet another in a long string of officers, most of whom were either too forward or disdainful of women. Few viewed females as intellectual beings or appreciated a well-read woman. Why should this newly arrived captain be an exception?

Rose gathered their teacups. "We are due at the Hurlburts' home at six o'clock."

"Will Papa join us?"

"No, a serious case at the hospital requires his attention."

Lily seized on the excuse. She often served as her father's nurse. "Perhaps I am needed there."

"Papa said to assure you this was a delicate matter best handled by men."

Later as she and Rose walked toward officers' row, Lily wished her father's case had required her assistance. Then she could have avoided testing the giddy feelings of anticipation occasioned by the thought of meeting the new captain.

Captain Caleb Montgomery held up his arm to halt the cavalry troops behind him. From his vantage point on a small rise, he surveyed the endless expanse of Kansas prairie, barren except for cottonwood trees bordering a sluggish stream, which he took to be the Pawnee Fork of the Arkansas River. In the distance, neatly laid out in a rectangle, were the buildings of Fort Larned, his final duty post before mustering out of the army.

Behind him lay the wagon ruts of the Santa Fe Trail. Protecting it from Indians and renegades was a far cry from the havoc of clashing Union and Reb forces, but that war was over. However, it never left the minds of those who had fought it as he had. Nor would he ever forget the recent heartless attack on Black Kettle and his people at the Washita River in Indian Territory. Both his innocence and the lure of adventure had been lost long ago, obliterated by the bloodshed he had witnessed. Only twenty-seven, he felt much older, seasoned by the harsh reality of "man's inhumanity to man," as the poet Robert Burns so aptly put it. Duty and honor remained, but did little to compensate for recurring nightmares. Pushing aside such grim thoughts, he spurred his horse and men toward the fort.

Approaching the compound, he spotted the figure of

a woman standing in silhouette against the weak March sun. Tall and slender, she seemed oblivious to their approach. Only as they rode closer did he notice she stood in a cemetery, her eyes fixed on a small headstone. Caleb wondered whose grave she visited and what heartache might be represented by that solitary marker. He had seen many such markers, and, alas, too many comrades buried in nameless graves amid the confusion of battle. At the sound of the troops' approach, the woman faced them, then lifted her hand in greeting.

Doffing his hat, Caleb turned in his saddle to observe her more closely. She was fair-skinned, and tendrils of honey-hued hair escaped her bonnet. He was seized by an impulse to make her smile, to ease her burden of grief. He grunted. A foolish thought.

Entering the fort, Caleb was struck by the breadth of the parade ground and the height of the flagpole in its center. He drew his men into file for the approach of the commanding officer, Major Robert Hurlburt, who strode toward them. Caleb dismounted and saluted. "Captain Montgomery reporting for duty, sir."

The post commander returned the salute, then smiled broadly as he extended a hand. "Welcome to Fort Larned." He nodded at the soldier standing at his elbow. "Sergeant Major, show the men to the stables and then get them settled in the barracks." He clapped a hand on Caleb's shoulder. "Officers' quarters are over there." He pointed to a row of new houses on the west edge of the parade ground. "My wife and I would be pleased to have you dine with us this evening."

"It would be an honor, sir."

Before relinquishing the reins of his horse to a hostler, Caleb stepped forward and stroked the animal's nose. "Good job, Bucephalus."

The major regarded the horse. "Bucephalus? A noble enough steed for Alexander the Great. I hope his namesake has served you well."

"He's one of the finest, sir," Caleb said without going into detail about his affection for the horse, which had been with him through many fearsome engagements.

Following the major across the parade ground, Caleb commented on the fort's modern buildings, which had recently replaced more temporary structures.

Hurlburt nodded. "It is a fine facility. Better than most we've both seen, no doubt."

The major left him at the bachelor officers' quarters to get settled. Caleb was weary, not just from his travels but from military life, as well. Since enlisting at eighteen after the attack on Fort Sumter, he'd known nothing else. He mentally counted his few remaining months of service, eager to begin the next chapter in his life.

He unpacked quickly, ambivalent—thanks to his exhaustion—about dining at the major's home, but duty called and he would welcome a home-cooked meal. After washing up, he lathered his face then picked up his razor. Some of his fellow officers prided themselves on luxuriant beards and drooping mustaches. Caleb regarded such practices as peacockery and preferred to be clean shaven. Scraping the blade over his three-days' growth, he pondered the end of his military career. There were things he would miss—the physical challenges, the sense of accomplishment when missions went well and the camaraderie of his fellow soldiers; but he would never miss the thunder of cannons, the tumult of gunfire or the otherworldly, agonizing cries as bullet or ball ended a life. It was time to settle in one place, to put down roots.

Donning his best uniform, he made his way next door to the post commander's home, an impressive dwelling with a wide front porch overlooking the parade ground. Major Hurlburt greeted him and drew him into the parlor. "Captain, may I present my wife, Effie."

Caleb bowed slightly. "An honor, ma'am."

Mrs. Hurlburt was a plump, middle-aged woman with rosy cheeks, frizzy red hair and mischievous eyes. "Hurly and I are delighted to meet you."

Hurly? Her use of a pet name for her husband defied the customary formality of such occasions.

Noting the surprise he had been unsuccessful in concealing, she laughed. "I know, I know. We're supposed to observe stiff conventions. So silly. We are all in a strange place, thrust together by circumstance. Within my home, I will do as I please. Hurly can follow protocol elsewhere." She laid a hand on Caleb's sleeve. "I hope I haven't shocked you."

Caleb glanced at the major, whose eyes were fixed fondly on his wife. "No, indeed. I shall happily abide by the rules of this house."

Major Hurlburt moved to a sideboard. "Brandy, Captain? Tea?"

"I'd prefer tea, sir." While the major prepared his own drink and poured the tea, Caleb studied the room, furnished with a Persian rug, two settees, an armchair, a library table and a small piano. Several watercolor landscapes and embroidered samplers adorned the walls. The decor was tasteful but confining after his months in the field.

The major handed Caleb his cup, but before he could sit down, a knock sounded at the door. While Hurlburt went to answer, Effie said delightedly, "This will be the Misses Kellogg. Regrettably their father, our post surgeon, has duties which prevent him from joining us."

Feminine chatter filled the entry hall as the major took

the ladies' cloaks. A sturdily built young woman with pale skin and freckles entered the parlor first. "Permit me to introduce Miss Rose Kellogg," the major said before turning to the second woman. "And her sister, Lily."

From her erect posture and demeanor, Caleb recognized Lily immediately—the woman in the cemetery. Close up, her flawless skin, the thick blond hair coiled on her head and her wide blue eyes rendered him tongue-tied. When had he last seen such a lovely female? Then, recovering his voice, he said, "Miss Rose, Miss Lily, the pleasure is mine."

Was it his imagination, or did a faint blush suffuse the latter's face? Before he could make that determination, the major seated the ladies and offered them tea.

Effie motioned for Caleb to sit beside her while the major served the Kellogg sisters. "Tell us, Captain, what brings you to Fort Larned?"

Although Caleb was certain she already knew, he briefly recounted his experience subduing marauding Indian tribes.

Rose leaned forward. "Did you also see service in the recent war?"

"I did, miss." He had no desire to elaborate.

Lily, apparently sensing his discomfort, deftly changed the subject. "That's history. I am interested in your opinion of Fort Larned."

Until they adjourned to the dining room, he offered his initial impressions of the place and then listened as the others told him about the recent rebuilding. Effie, in particular, put everyone at ease with her gently humorous comments and informality. Clearly the major was satisfied to let her hold sway at home, just as he controlled the fort.

At dinner, Caleb had the good fortune to be seated directly across from Lily Kellogg. He hoped his perusal of her wasn't too obvious, but it was difficult to keep his eyes averted. The delicacy of her features was at odds with the self-composed figure he'd seen in the cemetery. She was both dazzling and enigmatic.

Effie seemed determined to direct questions to him, but he noticed her slyly studying Lily while he answered. He had a familiar sinking sensation. He was in the hands of a skillful matchmaker. If he wasn't bound by social niceties, he could save Effie Hurlburt the trouble. Looking at Lily Kellogg was one thing; entanglement, quite another. He had learned that lesson from bitter experience.

Buttering a slice of bread, the major commented that he was sorry about Ezra Kellogg's absence from the table. "A fine doctor he is. During the outbreak of typhus late last fall, he performed valiantly, keeping our mortality rate low."

"He's very skilled," Effie agreed. "As is his most proficient nurse." She smiled at Lily, who bowed her head modestly.

"I do what I can."

"Sister, you are a marvel," Rose said. "Few of us could do what you do."

Lily looked up. "When you find something interesting and fulfilling, it isn't work." Caleb watched her eyes light up. "Learning about the human body and how to control and treat disease is fascinating. If only…" Her voice trailed off.

Caleb suspected she'd been about to say "If only women could be doctors," but no one else picked up on the thought. To spare her the awkward moment, Caleb said, "May I ask how you began nursing?"

The young woman set down her fork. "Before she died, my mother attended women in childbirth. I was curious, and she began to teach me. Then when she was ill, we—"

she nodded at her sister "—helped nurse her, and I discovered I had a gift. Our father is often shorthanded or in the process of training inexperienced enlisted men, so I assist him as I can."

"A regular Florence Nightingale she is," Effie said, beaming approval.

"Miss Nightingale is an idol of mine, but I would never venture to compare myself to her."

"The nurses I observed during the war performed invaluable services," Caleb said, recalling painfully the field hospitals he had visited. "It is important work, and I commend you."

The conversation then turned to the latest rumors about a railroad to be built to replace the Santa Fe Trail. "The railroad is only the beginning of a new era, I suspect," the major observed. "With such progress, we will no doubt experience many changes."

"Not the least of which is moving to the parlor for coffee." The major's wife rose to her feet. "And perhaps Miss Lily will honor us with a selection on the pianoforte."

Caleb smiled inwardly. Miss Lily Kellogg seemed to be a woman of myriad and contradictory talents. He didn't want to be intrigued by her, but even fatigued as he was, the prospect of learning more about her kept him alert. A half hour later, after further conversation and two pleasing piano pieces, the major asked him to escort the Kellogg sisters home.

Outside, clouds played tag with a nearly full moon. The light-colored stones of the buildings shifted and glowed as shadows came and went. From the enlisted men's barracks came sounds of revelry. It was nearly time for taps, so as they proceeded across the parade ground, the noises gradually subsided. At the door of the small house adjoining the hospital, Caleb took each of the ladies' hands by turn. "Miss Rose, Miss Lily. Good night." His gaze caught Lily's. "Thank you for an evening I will long remember."

"Good night, Captain," the women said in unison before disappearing inside.

Caleb strolled back across the parade ground, reaching his quarters just as the bugler sounded taps. As they often did, the haunting notes recalled other nights, other encampments. Deeply moved, he lingered on the porch, taking in the fort, the surrounding countryside, the limitless sky. Feelings he hadn't experienced in a long time, if ever, came over him. Part longing, part mystery, part promise—all centered in the disturbing sense that it wasn't by accident God had put Lily Kellogg in his path.

Sighing wearily, he regained control of his thoughts. He would need to be on his guard. A woman had hurt him once, and he never wanted to feel that vulnerable again. No matter the provocation.

Chapter Two

Sunlight filtering through the windows of the post hospital the next morning brought an illusion of cheer to the convalescing patients. Lily moved among the beds, changing a bandage here and wiping a fevered brow there. Only after she had checked all the patients did she pause at the bedside of a young man who had been kicked by a horse, suffering painful bruises and a concussion. Taking his hand, she gently called his name.

The man stirred, then groaned. Lily spoke louder. "Benjamin, tell me where you are."

His eyes fluttered before focusing on her. "In heaven?"

"Try again. Where are you?"

The hint of a smile teased his lips. "Just joshin,' Miss Lily. Hospital. I'm in the hospital." Then just before he fell back to sleep, he mumbled, "Clumsy nag of a horse."

Across the room lay a cook, scalded by a pot of boiling soup, his hands mittened in gauze. She made her way to him. "I have time now, Timothy, to write that letter for you."

She retrieved paper, pen and the lap board and listened as he dictated his message. "Tell me mum I am dandy. Say

I had a bit of an accident, but that I'll be cooking again before she even gets this letter. Ask her to write."

Lily had seen the burns on his hands and doubted he'd be cooking anytime soon. She prayed he would be spared infection, so common with burns. "I will post your letter this afternoon."

"Thank you, miss," he whispered, tears flooding his eyes. She turned away to spare him embarrassment.

When she had finished her duties, she stepped into the small surgeon's office where her father was working on his weekly medical report. "Do you need me further, Papa?"

Ezra Kellogg looked up, his blue eyes gentle behind his spectacles. "You're a godsend, daughter, but we'll manage for the rest of the day."

Lily studied his pale face and stooped shoulders. There was an air of resignation or…a lack of vigor…something that had diminished him. It was as if when his wife's life drained away, his spirit had ebbed, as well. She and Rose did what they could to lighten his heart, but, in truth, all of them sorely missed Mathilda. Only after her death had Lily realized the extent to which her mother had been the family's anchor.

Not quite six years before, a similar shadow had passed over the family and forever changed them. During the war she, Rose and her mother had prayed unceasingly for the safety of her father and brother, David. Lily's chest tightened, as if a claw gripped her heart. David. So amiable and strong. It had been natural to idolize the big brother whose hearty laugh had charmed them all. In her innocence, she had thought him invincible. Until that awful news. The telegram from the War Department had stated in cold, impersonal terms that their beloved David had been killed in the Battle of Lookout Mountain.

She remembered the sickening feeling she'd experienced with the realization that he had been dead for many days before they received word. Days when he had still lived in her imagination—eating, laughing, singing and… fighting. That blow had been especially cruel since they had no efficient way to communicate with Ezra. Their father's return following the war, though a cause for celebration, was a somber occasion, the four of them grieving for the son and brother who would never again grace their family circle. Recalling past family dinners where there was always one empty place at the table, she was reminded of last night's meal.

"Papa, we missed you at the Hurlburts' dinner."

"I hope you and Rose enjoyed it."

"We did. The new captain dined with us."

"What did you make of him?"

"He seemed pleasant enough."

Her father rose to his feet and laid a hand on her shoulder. "I worry about you girls being in this place. There are good men here, but others…" He grimaced. "Others you shouldn't even have to see, much less come into contact with."

"Captain Montgomery is no cause for alarm."

He kissed her forehead. "I probably shouldn't have brought you here with me, but we had been so long apart during the conflict that I—" his voice cracked "—needed you."

"And we needed you, *do* need you." She patted his arm. "Never blame yourself for our circumstances. Rose and I are fine, and, after all, we are a military family. Women do their duty, too, you know." Then, to emphasize her point, she saluted airily and took her leave.

As Lily made her customary way from the hospital to the cemetery, the breeze carried a tantalizing hint of spring. Full sun warmed her back as she stood before her mother's grave, pondering the exchange she'd had with her father. Finally she spoke. "Mama, we miss you so. Papa is lost without you." She closed her eyes, picturing her parents embracing. "How he must have loved you. And you? How sad to die in a harsh place like this so far from the home you loved."

Turning to leave, she glanced in the direction where yesterday she'd seen the new cavalry troops arrive, led by Caleb Montgomery. He had none of the arrogance of George Custer, who had been stationed at Fort Larned a few months ago, nor the affected dandyism of some of the others. Montgomery seemed…was *solid* the word for which she searched? Yes, that, but more. *Dependable? Trustworthy?*

She chided herself for attempting to pigeonhole the dashing captain. His essence would not be captured, even as she ruefully admitted thoughts of him had captured her, despite her best efforts to will them away.

Although it had been a week since his arrival at Fort Larned, Caleb had slept poorly, troubled by disturbing dreams. Awake before reveille, he dressed quickly and stepped onto the front porch to watch the sunrise. Smoke rose from the mess hall kitchen, and in the distance a horse whinnied. After a few minutes, he made out the form of the bugler, who sounded notes that brought the fort from quiet to bustling activity. Lantern light flared in the barracks, and he heard the raucous shouts of prompt risers rousing the slugabeds.

From inside, the lieutenant with whom he shared quarters grunted and coughed. Will Creekmore, a fellow from Wisconsin, began every day with prayer. While Caleb found the practice laudable, he wondered how it had served the man on the battlefield. He himself had struggled to find God in the chaos of armed conflict, finally latching onto the instinct for sacrifice, even love, that he observed in the way men in extremity cared for their brothers in arms. He had concluded that just as evil existed and tempted men to war, so was mercy present in the myriad selfless acts he'd witnessed. That thought was all that made his duties bearable. Yet his uneasy truce with God had suffered a significant setback at the Washita River.

He would go to his grave with the horrors of November 27, 1868. On that wintry dawn, he had led his troop to a rendezvous point above the Washita River where they waited in hushed darkness for Lt. Col. George Custer's command to attack the camp of Chief Black Kettle and roughly two-hundred-fifty vulnerable Cheyenne. A survivor of the infamous 1864 Sand Creek Massacre, Black Kettle had negotiated for peace, but had been unable to control younger, more belligerent warriors, engaging in raids against white settlers.

Swallowing sourly with the memory, Caleb saw it once again in his mind's eye. Their orders were to take woman and children hostage, but to kill anyone who fired on them and destroy the enemy's horses. When the first rays of the sun illumined the horizon, the command came, bugles blew and the cavalry charged down on the sleeping village. It took only one shot from a single hapless Cheyenne to incite a frenzy of fighting. Screaming women clutching their children ran for the river, old people fell in their tracks, and bodies littered the snow.

In his nightmares he would forever see the little girl holding a cornhusk doll, a bullet hole through her chest and the lifeless body of a woman cradling beneath her a piteously mewling infant.

He had experienced horrific combat in the War between the States; however, that cause was justified and didn't involve women and children on the battlefield. But the engagement on the Washita? That was different. It was a massacre. To his eternal shame, he had been unable to prevent it. No wonder he had lost his zest for soldiering. It was even difficult to believe himself worthy as a man.

The orange ball of the sun brought light into his dark thoughts. "God," he whispered, "help me to understand. Why? Why?" Scraping a hand across his beard, he paused as if waiting for an answer, and then went back into his quarters to shave.

After breakfast, Major Hurlburt gathered the officers for a briefing. Spring wagon trains setting out for Santa Fe would soon be passing their way along with the usual supply wagons. Roving bands of Kiowas, Pawnees and Arapahos, angered by the white man's usurpation of their tribal lands and hungry after a long winter of deprivation, were on the prowl. Scouts had already located Kiowas camped along the Pawnee Fork. Caleb and his sergeant were ordered to accompany a seasoned troop the following day to deal with the situation and familiarize themselves with the immediate territory.

That evening, keyed up in anticipation of action, Caleb sought the quiet of the post library. Before the war, he had entertained thoughts of studying at university, but now that was a distant dream. However, he reckoned the lack of formal education needn't keep him from learning.

In a somber mood, he pulled a volume of Tennyson's poems from the shelves. The book fell open to "The Charge of the Light Brigade," and Caleb was transported instantly to the suicidal attack in the Crimean War. "Into the valley of Death / Rode the six hundred." He looked up from the page, grimacing at the image of men riding to certain doom. Did mankind ever learn? Such atrocities were no different from what his own army had inflicted on the peace-seeking Indians massacred at Sand Creek and the shameful Battle of the Washita.

He closed the book, rubbing his eyes, gritty with the need for sleep. Crimea. Unwittingly, Florence Nightingale came to mind, her lantern bringing hope to the wounded and dying there. How incongruous that the lovely Lily Kellogg could also be engaged in such grisly hospital work. Yet her name had surfaced again and again in the conversations of men at Fort Larned. Although she brooked no nonsense, they said, she had a fearless and compassionate heart, and sometimes their healing had depended as much on that as on any medicines or procedures.

As if he had conjured her, the door opened and Lily entered, her attention fixed on the stack of books she carried. When she saw him, she uttered a startled "Oh" and dropped her armload on the floor. He hastened to her side, where they both knelt to gather the volumes.

"I didn't mean to alarm you," he assured her.

At that same moment she was saying, "I wasn't looking where I was going."

In the lantern light, her hair cast a golden glow, and he found himself at a loss for words, finally managing, "Do you come here often?"

"It's my favorite place," she murmured.

He assisted her to her feet and then gathered the books and laid them on a shelf. "Mine, too. No matter the post to which I'm assigned."

Looking over his shoulder, she noted his book, abandoned on the chair. "What were you reading when I disturbed you?"

"First of all, you didn't disturb me. Besides, Tennyson's 'The Charge of the Light Brigade' is rather gloomy. In truth, I was daydreaming rather than reading."

She crossed the room, picked up the poetry collection

and skimmed it. "I do so admire his work. 'Flower in the Crannied Wall' is one of my favorites." She closed her eyes and recited, "'Little flower—but *if* I could understand / What you are, root and all, and all in all, / I should know what God and man is.'"

"A big *if*. Can we ever know about God and man? Would we even want to? Man has a habit of mucking up things."

She smiled, a glint of humor in her eyes. "Not only 'man.' In rare instances, 'woman' can also create problems."

Rather than going to the unhappy place where a woman had created a problem for him, he chose to respond to her lightheartedness. "In *rare instances?* My dear miss, have you forgotten Eve?"

She laughed, a delightfully musical sound. "I fear, sir, that any discussion of serpents and apples might take an unpleasant turn."

"Perhaps, instead, we should both pledge to reread Milton's *Paradise Lost* and compare our reactions later."

"He is a marvelous poet, isn't he? Such descriptions of the Garden of Eden. Why, I myself might have bitten into the forbidden fruit."

He had a sudden image of her rosy lips grazing a red-ripe apple. He mentally erased the charming picture. "Did you come for a particular title?"

She moved to the bookshelf, where she hesitated. "No, I'm browsing." She laughed again. "That's not exactly true. I've read nearly everything here."

"Then I shall look forward to hearing your recommendations." He was pleasantly surprised. From his brief exposure to her at the Hurlburts', he hadn't figured her for a bookworm. Discussing literature with her would provide at least one antidote for the boredom that was part of military life.

"I favor Mr. Dickens and the Romantic poets," she said.

"My, quite a divergence of taste."

"And why not? Fiction, poetry, biography, essays—we don't have sufficient time to read everything, but I try."

He inclined his head in an abbreviated bow. "Permit me, then, to take my leave so you may find the hidden gem that you have not read."

She bestowed a smile that banished any thought of the Crimea. "Good night, Captain."

"Good night, Miss Kellogg." Then as an afterthought, he added, "I shall look forward to sharing our opinions concerning *Paradise Lost.*"

"As shall I," she said.

Walking toward the officers' quarters, Caleb pondered the *if* in Tennyson's poem. To understand God and man. He longed to understand God, to find answers to his questions. As for "man," they were a mixed lot. As he had to admit women were, too. Even on short acquaintance it was clear that Lily bore no resemblance to Rebecca, the faithless woman who had broken his heart.

"In like a lion, out like a lamb," Rose announced on the last day of March as she and Lily made their way to the sutler's to buy provisions and collect the mail.

The day was warm, and wagon wheels and horses' hooves had churned the ground into dust that clung to their boots and the hems of their dresses.

"We'd best enjoy days like this," Lily observed. "Remember last summer? I swear equatorial Africa couldn't be any hotter. In mid-July, we will look back on this weather with gratitude."

Rose linked her arm with Lily's. "Enjoy the day, this day. God's day."

Lily squeezed Rose's hand. Their mother had often uttered those very words when her impatient daughters peppered her with questions: "When is Papa coming home from the war?" "How long until my birthday?" And more recently, "How are you feeling this morning, Mama?"

When they entered the store, enlisted men buying tobacco and assorted medicinal items made way for them. Several tipped their caps, a few ventured mumbled hellos and one insolent corporal winked leeringly. Jake Lavery, the proprietor, beamed as they approached. "Ladies, what can I do for you?

After placing their grocery order, Lily ushered her sister to a corner where yard goods and sewing notions were displayed. Thus removed from the prying eyes of men, the sisters studied some newly arrived bolts of cloth.

Rose stroked a brown calico covered with sprigs of tiny yellow flowers. "I rather fancy this for my summer dress."

Each summer and winter, their father provided them with money to make one serviceable gown apiece. Lily always had difficulty making up her mind, and today was no exception. She draped a navy blue muslin across her shoulders.

Rose shook her head. "Too drab. Try the gingham. It reminds me of the ocean. That is, if I'd ever seen it."

Lily unrolled a couple of yards and carrying the bolt to the small mirror on the wall, held the gingham to her face. The color did something magical for her eyes, tinting the usual blue with a hint of sea-green. She turned to Rose. "I like it."

"That was easy. I do, too. Have we need of patterns?"

Lily shook her head. "I have some ideas about adapting ones we already have."

"I trust you. You're the expert seamstress."

Mr. Lavery's wife measured and cut the material, then wrapped it in brown paper and tied it with string. "Come show me when you've finished the gowns." A wistful expression crossed her leathery face. Observing the woman's worn gray dress, Lily ached for her. Frippery was hard to come by on the prairie where simplicity and practicality were both necessary and valued.

Lily tucked their purchases in the mesh bag they had brought with them. Their last stop was the mail counter. "Kellogg. Anything for us?" Rose inquired of the red-bearded postal agent, recently arrived at the fort.

"I know who you are," the man said, as if offended that they would identify themselves to someone with such a brilliant memory. "You're those girls the men are always talking about."

Rose bristled. "I hardly think so."

The man leaned on the counter and folded his gnarled hands, peering at them with beady eyes. "Bet on it, miss. It's just as well your papa don't hear some of what they say."

Lily drew herself up to her full height. "Sir, our mail, if you please."

He grinned wolfishly, then took his time moving to the mail slots.

"I declare," Lily whispered to her sister. "The nerve."

Rose took the letters from the man, uttered a huffy "thank you" and led Lily out of the place.

"That was demeaning," Lily said when they were out of earshot.

"Yes, but, Lily, I imagine the men do talk of us...*you*. Think about it. They're far from home, missing their wives and sweethearts. And some of them are so young. Bachelors." She trudged on deep in thought, then added, "Don't you see how they look at you?"

"Me?" Lily blushed.

"Oh, there's some that might settle for me, but you're the beauty."

"Hush, Rose. Don't you go tempting fate with that talk. 'Pride goeth before a fall,' and I don't want to be prideful."

"You can't pretend you don't notice their interest. For example, that new captain couldn't keep his eyes off you at the Hurlburts' dinner." She stopped in her tracks and studied her sister. "You could do a lot worse," she said gently.

"I'm not husband hunting." Lily grinned coquettishly. "At least not until St. Louis, if that time ever comes."

"St. Louis. A den of iniquity, if you ask me."

"I didn't."

With a shrug, Rose held up the mail. "I suppose then that you'll be wanting to look over the letter that came today from Aunt Lavinia."

"Oh, do let's hurry." So eager was Lily to read the letter, she didn't notice how Rose lagged behind. Nor did she see the concern in her sister's eyes.

At home, scanning Aunt Lavinia's letter before sharing it with Rose, Lily sighed in disappointment. There was no invitation for either of them. Just a description of Lavinia's new Easter bonnet, the menu of a sumptuous dinner at the home of a local politician and a recipe for an elegant presentation of tenderloin of pork, as if they often had such a cut of meat available.

Bent over her crocheting, Rose looked up as Lily read the final paragraph.

"I shudder to think of you girls subjected to the cold winds and extreme weather of the prairie. Not to

mention living in a forsaken army post, surrounded by who knows what sort of individuals. For the life of me, I cannot understand why Ezra took you to such a place. Would that your mother had persuaded him to abandon his army career. Well, water over the dam. I pray for your safety and hope conditions will permit us once again to meet. Perhaps after the miasma that is summer here along the Mississippi.
Your devoted aunt,
Lavinia"

Lily put the letter aside and sought composure by going to the sewing cabinet to locate the pattern for Rose's new dress. Only now in light of Lavinia's vague promise could she admit how much she had counted on deliverance from this wilderness outpost. She tried to take each day as it came, but the fierce, unpredictable spring winds tried her soul and increased her longing to escape. At times she wanted to scream from sheer frustration.

Rose had said something, but lost in her thoughts, Lily had to ask her to repeat it.

"Dear sister, patience." Rose wasn't trying to irritate her, and, yes, patience was needed, but right now the advice rankled.

"What's the matter with me, Rose?"

Her sister set aside her crocheting. "You really do want to leave. It's more than a dream, isn't it?"

Lily sank back into her chair. "I'm so restless. Every day is like every other day. Rose, there's a whole world out there, and I want to be part of it. If only I were a man, I could choose my lot and go wherever my fancy took me."

"I would miss you."

Chastened, Lily hung her head. "And I you." She had

thoughtlessly hurt her sister. The tug to home and to Rose and Papa was strong, but so was the pull of the exciting world beyond the prairie. Why couldn't she lay aside these dreams that only grew more compelling with each passing day?

"Are you very disappointed? Had you thought Aunt Lavinia's invitation would come this soon?"

Lily looked helplessly at her sister, unable to confess the degree to which she had counted on Aunt Lavinia to save her. "Mama wouldn't like me to act like this. She would say everything happens in God's time, not mine."

Rose nodded as if her suspicions were confirmed. "Then leave it to God." She began crocheting again. "Meanwhile, I so love having you here for company. And take heart. Aunt Lavinia didn't rule out a visit later in the year."

Lily unfolded the pattern, but, disappointed by the letter and consumed by guilt over how her departure would affect Rose, she couldn't concentrate on dressmaking.

Several nights later, Caleb stretched out by the campfire, wearily resting his head on his saddle. This morning the cavalry had caught up with a band of Kiowas secluded in a small grove of trees. The soldiers had mounted a charge. Outmanned, the Indians had fired a few warning shots and then, to Caleb's relief, had fled on horseback. Since the Washita, he had no stomach for engagement.

He understood there was no stopping the westward migration of his own people, but at the same time he grudgingly admired the Indians, both those who came in peace and those risking their lives for their tribal lands and honor. Perhaps the Indians weren't that different from the emancipated slaves with whom he had fought in the war. Rarely had he been in battle with more dedicated or able fighters. Yet so many of his fellows treated these so-called "buffalo soldiers" as inferiors and made known their prejudice both with their abusive words and their fists.

Gazing up at the infinity of stars, Caleb wondered what God thought of the arrogant human beings He had created, so anxious to lord it over their fellow creatures whom they deemed ignorant or savage. Were the Indians and the former slaves that much different from himself? He suspected all any man wanted was dignity. Yet he knew firsthand that any one of them was capable of barbarity.

Tired of his gloomy thoughts, he withdrew a worn letter from his pocket. Slowly he unfolded it and squinted to make out the words, although he had already practically memorized them.

Dear brother,
Sister Sophie, Pa and I are continuing to purchase additional acreage near Cottonwood Falls for the Montgomery cattle operation. As I've told you, grazing land is lush and water is plentiful. The other settlers are welcoming and enthusiastic for the prospects in this sparsely populated part of southeastern Kansas.

Thank you for the monies you have sent us. Your share of the ranch will be waiting for you when you muster out. We are all thankful that time is fast approaching. We are adding to the herd, so with hard work, this fall when we go to market, pray God we will see the realization of our hopes.

We likewise pray for your safety as we await the day of our reunion.
Your affectionate brother,
Seth

Their ranch—a dream come true. Joining his father and brother in the exciting enterprise would finally anchor him in one place. His place. A place where money could be made. Where a family could grow and prosper. A peaceful place.

Once before he had thought to establish a home. To live in harmony with a woman he loved. To plan a future together. That dream, interrupted by the outbreak of war, had sustained him through long marches and frenzied battles. Until Rebecca's letter, creased and soiled from its long journey, made its way to him in the winter of 1864. It was painful, even now, to recall her flowery words, made no less harsh by their embellishment.

It is with profound and heartfelt regret that I rue causing you any disappointment or loss of marital expectations. It has been my greatest endeavor to pass these uncertain days in the hope of your deliverance by a beneficent providence. But we are all, in the end, human beings—human beings with a need for love and companionship. So I beg your understanding and forgiveness for informing you that on Saturday last your friend Abner and I published the banns for our upcoming marriage.

Rebecca had, with a single blow, severed their relationship, one he had entered into wholeheartedly and purposefully. Beyond that, Abner's betrayal of their boyhood friendship had cut deep. Caleb closed his eyes, the lullaby of coyotes baying on a distant hill doing little to induce sleep. The Garden of Eden. The tempted Eve. Caleb snorted under his breath. Rebecca had certainly succumbed to temptation and, in the process, taught him a bitter lesson concerning trust.

And what of Miss Lily Kellogg, the first woman since Rebecca to interest him? Was she made of sterner, truer stuff? Did he dare acknowledge how appealing he found her? Even for an intrepid cavalryman that was a daunting thought. One he should not entertain, not when his hands were tainted with the blood of innocents.

Chapter Three

Caleb joined his fellow officers Saturday night at the tavern just a short walk from the fort. It was a rough frontier establishment, crudely built and redolent of sweat and beer. Loud, harsh voices assaulted his ears. A bar covered one wall, and in the back were several tables of serious card players. Two women, no longer young, their faces caked in makeup, sashayed among the men. Caleb didn't drink liquor, but neither did he want to appear standoffish. Through the years, he had learned a great deal about those under his command by observing their off-duty activities. Yet such places made him uncomfortable.

"Cap!" Maloney, a cavalryman who had been with him during several engagements, waved him over. Maloney was always good for a few stories. Caleb settled into a chair at the man's table and didn't have long to wait for the opening line. "Did you hear the one abut the general who saw a ghost?"

While the storyteller waxed eloquent, Caleb studied the crowd. Some gambled, some ogled the ladies, others, their eyes glazed over, threw back whiskey, undoubtedly searching for oblivion. He, too, sometimes longed for oblivion, but had long ago made the decision not to drink or gamble. He'd seen firsthand what such indulgences could cost a man—in some instances, not only his dignity but his soul.

When Maloney's story came to its hilarious conclusion, Caleb rose and headed toward the door. Passing by a table of enlisted men, he overheard the tail end of a conversation and recognized Corporal Adams as the speaker.

"…and that one's ripe for the pickin' and I might just be the one to harvest her."

"In a pig's eye," his fellow cackled. "She's too good for the likes of you, Miss Lily is."

"They's all the same beneath that flouncin' and finery. You just wait. I've got my eye on her. Some dark night—"

Caleb jerked the man to his feet. "You'll do no such thing, Adams, or I'll have you on report so fast it will seem like a cyclone hit you." It took all of Caleb's will to refrain from hitting the man in his obscene mouth.

Sniveling, Adams looked up at him through bleary eyes, his mouth stained with chewing tobacco. "'Twas just talk."

"You make sure of that or you'll deal with me." Caleb thrust the man back in his seat and glared at him to be sure he understood.

"Mighty protective, aren't you?" the corporal mumbled.

"What was that?"

"Nothin'." Then he added, "Sir," as if that would vindicate him.

"Change the subject, then," Caleb said before striding out into the night, fists clenched at his side. This wasn't the first man Caleb had heard talking about Lily, but most were respectful. Adams was a sneak, and Caleb hoped he was all talk, but based on his history with the corporal, he wasn't so sure.

Walking back to his quarters, he wondered if he would

have reacted so strongly had it been just any woman under discussion. He hoped so. But the mere suggestion of such a creature touching Lily Kellogg made his blood boil.

The much-anticipated spring band concert was a break from the monotony of life at the fort. This particular evening featured two fiddlers, a banjo player and a wizened harmonica player. Benches had been set up in the commissary, and the officers' wives and daughters had prepared cookies and tea for a social following the musicale.

Major and Mrs. Hurlburt sat in the front row. Effie gestured to Ezra to bring Rose and Lily and join them. There was a stir of anticipation as the musicians took their places. The band performed old folk tunes as well as more recent camp songs. Early on, some of the enlisted men began clapping in time to the beat, and for an hour, all thoughts of danger and homesickness were suspended.

Lily was aware of the bachelor officers sitting in the row behind her, their buttons brightly polished, their gloved hands resting on their knees. Since the arrival of Aunt Lavinia's letter a couple of weeks ago, Lily had been pondering her future. Was it unrealistic to consider another world—one of sophistication, intelligent discourse and high fashion? Rose had urged her to encourage Captain Montgomery, yet it would be hypocritical to lead him on. Attractive as he was, her favorable impressions of the man were surely skewed by the limited world of Fort Larned.

At the conclusion of the concert, the musicians bowed to enthusiastic applause and then asked the audience to join them in singing "Aura Lee." Behind her, Lily heard a rich baritone voice and discovered when she stood to leave that the singer who had pierced her heart was Captain Montgomery.

Effie shoved her way between Rose and Lily and grabbed the captain by the arm. "Rose and I are helping serve the tea, but perhaps you could get some refreshments for this young lady." She nodded at Lily.

"My pleasure," the captain said, following the major's wife to the food table to comply with her request. Before Rose moved off to join Effie, she poked Lily in the ribs and whispered, "It won't hurt you to flirt a bit." When Lily glared at her, Rose affected wide-eyed innocence and added, "Consider it a rehearsal for your assault on St. Louis beaux."

Juggling two cups and a plate of cookies, Captain Montgomery returned to Lily. Most of the crowd had gone outside to eat, but he set the refreshments on a bench. "Shall we stay here?"

She looked around, flustered to see how few concert-goers remained. "This is fine," she said, sinking onto the bench.

He handed her a cup, then made a toasting gesture with his own. "To you," he said quietly.

"Whatever for?"

He smiled. "For gracing this place with beauty and gentleness. Most of us have lived with men for far too long. You are a breath of fresh air."

The compliment both flattered and disturbed her. "Sir, I think you give me too much credit. I would suggest it is easy to say such things when, by your own admission, you have been long deprived of feminine companionship."

"Do you think me so devoid of discernment that I am drawn to just any woman?"

Drawn? He was drawn? How to answer such a question? "Forgive me, Captain. Of course, you must know your own mind."

"As I believe you must know yours. From what the men

tell me, you are a fair, but demanding taskmistress—is there such a word?—among your patients."

"A hospital is not the place for indecisiveness or the encouragement of malingerers."

"Although one might not blame them for preferring your company to that of a drill sergeant."

"I assure you there are times in that environment when I bear a closer resemblance to a drill sergeant than a docile maid."

"From what I've seen of you, *docile* isn't a word that comes readily to mind."

She couldn't help herself. She chuckled. "What word *does* come to mind?"

He leaned back as if to study her. "Perhaps *curious.* Or maybe *determined.*"

"And what led you to such conclusions?"

"Your interest in medicine, your passion for that which interests you, whether it is nursing or literature. I suspect there is more going on in that head of yours than meets the eye."

"You, sir, are a keen observer. I shall have to watch my *p's* and *q's.*"

He set down his cup. "Would it be presumptuous to ask you to call me by my Christian name?"

Lily was flustered. This conversation was moving beyond her powers to control it. "You have me at a disadvantage, Captain. Are we to become friends, then?"

"That is my intent, especially as we are both book lovers."

"Then, as friends—" she leaned forward by way of emphasis "—in informal situations, I will call you Caleb."

"Good." He hesitated as if hearing his name echo. "Would you object to saying it again?"

She looked at him quizzically, then softly repeated, "Caleb."

"Thank you. It has been many months since I have heard my name uttered by a lovely woman. And, then, only by my sister, Sophie."

Unaccountably, Lily felt her eyes moisten. She had never considered how a soldier might miss simple feminine interactions or long for a soft, endearing voice. Casting about for a safer topic, she said, "Tell me about your sister."

He stood. "Perhaps we could take a turn around the parade ground while I relate some Sophie stories." He held out his hand to assist her to rise.

Tucking her arm through his, she was startled by a sensation very like happiness. Surely, she told herself, it was the beauty of the spring night rather than her companion that provoked such an emotion.

On their walk, she discovered that he was a gifted raconteur. His mother had died giving birth to Sophie, and he obviously doted on his younger sister, a tomboy of the first magnitude. His tales of her cutting off her long hair when she was ten in order to look more like a boy and wading into the river to noodle for catfish were both humorous and poignant. He painted a vivid picture of his sister's flyaway curly red hair and ended by saying, "Sophie possesses a mind of her own, but she has a generous heart."

"I think I'd like her," Lily said, full of admiration for the independent young woman who dared to live beyond the conventional.

Caleb faced her. "She would like you." He clasped her hand between his own. "*I* like you."

"Captain—"

"Caleb, please."

"Caleb, I don't know what to say."

He snugged her hand beneath his arm and started walking slowly toward her home. "You don't need to say anything."

She decided silence was the best course lest she offer any more encouragement than, inadvertently, she may have already given. As they walked, an awkwardness seemed to develop where earlier there had been camaraderie. She could ask him about the mother he had lost, but they were nearing the hospital. Perhaps another time. *Did she want another time?*

At her door, he gently disengaged his arm and faced her. "Miss Lily, I pray I have not overstepped my bounds."

Again, she was at a loss for words. "It's late, Captain. It's best to say good-night." When his eyes clouded, she took pity on him. "Until we meet again, Caleb." She liked saying his strong, masculine name.

"Good night, Miss Lily." As if remembering his manners, he added stiffly, "Thank you for a pleasant evening."

Inside the house, she leaned against the closed door, bewildered. He had shown signs of his interest in her, but in the past few minutes had seemed to retreat into formality. She had enjoyed his company more than she cared to admit. That concerned her. She would need to steel herself and not let her fickle emotions sidetrack her plans.

When Lily entered the bedroom she shared with Rose, her sister was just finishing plaiting her long reddish-blond hair. The light from the candle on the bedside table cast an intimate glow. Lily loosened her buttons, plucked her nightgown from its hook and prepared for bed. Rose watched her, a smug smile playing about her lips. "Well?" she finally said. "How did you find your Captain Montgomery?"

"He's not mine," Lily said decisively, taking the pins

out of her hair and beginning her ritual one-hundred brush strokes. Knowing that those three words would not satisfy her sister, she went on. "Like many of our officers, he is lonely. I provided a temporary diversion, no doubt."

Rose hooted. "Are you blind? The way he looked at you was special."

"He can look all he wants, but I will not encourage him. He would only be a distraction in my life."

"The life that's taking you to St. Louis?"

Lily set down her brush and put her hands on Rose's shoulders. "I'm sorry it's difficult for you to understand, but I have to be true to myself."

Rose reached up and clasped Lily's hands. "I know. Papa and I have realized for some time that this place is too confining for your spirit." She bowed her head, whispering so quietly Lily had to bend closer to hear her. "But it is so hard to let you go." Rose looked straight into Lily's eyes. "I suppose I had hoped that if you married an army officer, our paths would cross now and again. And of the lot, Captain Montgomery seems a good man—a man who would cherish you or whomever else he chose."

"It is a fine thing to be cherished. Pray that I may find such a suitor in the city."

"I cannot honor your request. I will pray for you, of course, but for your well-being, happiness and the fulfillment of God's purpose for you, wherever you may be."

Lily embraced her sister, so good and true. Then she blew out the candle, and they curled into the depths of the feather bed they had shared since childhood. Soon she could hear her sister's gentle exhalations, but sleep eluded Lily. She lay awake for some time, not thinking so much about St. Louis as remembering the name *Caleb* and how he had needed to hear it spoken.

She turned on her side and shortly before falling asleep whispered to the shadows, "Dear God, why can't life be simple?"

When Caleb entered his quarters, Will Creekmore was sitting at the desk writing a letter by lantern light. "Did you enjoy the concert?"

Caleb stripped off his gloves and jacket and tossed them on a chair. "It was a welcome morale boost. Routine drills get mighty boring for the men."

"And for us."

Caleb noticed a daguerreotype sitting on the desk. He pointed to it. "Your family?"

The lieutenant picked it up and gazed at it fondly. "No. Fannie, my sweetheart back in Wisconsin." He hesitated and then added, "She's been waiting a long time. I'm asking her to come here. To be married. But it's far from her home. I don't know if…" He sighed. "All I can do is ask, though I do hate to inflict such a long journey on her."

"It's a lonely life out here. For your sake, I hope she says yes."

"Speaking of the ladies, how was your evening with Miss Kellogg? I couldn't help noticing how you favored her."

In the confusion of his feelings, Caleb didn't want to discuss Lily, but neither did he want to be rude. "She is a delightful young woman."

His fellow officer speared him with a look. "Whose company you enjoy."

Caleb shrugged helplessly, wishing he had done a better job of resisting Miss Kellogg's charms.

Will stood and clapped a hand on Caleb's shoulder. "Heaven help us, then. We can fight the rebel and the savage, but one look from a pretty woman and we're goners."

He gathered up his ink, pen and paper. "I'm turning in. Good night, Montgomery."

"Good night. Leave the lantern. I want to read for a while."

After the man departed, Caleb picked up the book he'd left on the shelf and settled in a chair. But the book remained unopened, forgotten in the swirl of his thoughts. Lily Kellogg was a puzzlement. At the same time she had seemed interested in their conversation, he'd sensed a reserve on her part, as if she was unwilling to commit fully to their dialogue. Perhaps he had been too forward and she was merely being proper. Given his lack of recent experience with women, he was at a loss. He fingered the leather-bound volume in his lap. If only there were a treatise to teach him how to read women. How to court them without the fumbling awkwardness he had felt when he left Lily at her doorstep.

Courtship? Where had that idiotic notion come from? But even as the idea formed, the specter of Rebecca rose in his mind, and his spirit curled in on itself. He was too near his goal of joining his family in the cattle business to be waylaid by a woman.

He closed his eyes, picturing the verdant hills of the Montgomery Ranch, the beauty of the blooming redbuds his brother had described and the panorama of orange-pink sunsets stretching across the horizon. It was there he would ultimately build a home and father children. Someday he would have a wife. But why, lately, did the "someday" wife of his imagination look like Lily? Could she—or any woman—endure his nightmares? Accept his role in the Washita battle, especially when he couldn't?

The unseasonably warm April afternoon was made even more unpleasant by wild winds rattling windows and blowing dust high into the air. Lily moved among the beds of men laid low by spring fevers, following her father as he stopped to recommend treatment or offer encouragement. After their rounds, Lily prepared medications and folded clean laundry.

She consciously tried to appear busy to avoid the unpleasant stares of one of the enlisted men recently assigned to hospital duty rotation. He had a weasellike appearance and followed instructions to the bare minimum a chore might require. It seemed every time she moved around the ward, he was lurking nearby with the same insolent look on his face. She was probably overreacting, but something about Corporal Adams made her distinctly uncomfortable. She shuddered before resuming her work.

Late that afternoon her father asked her to go to the post office to check on a package he was expecting, a medical book about the treatment of snake and insect bites. She welcomed her escape.

However, when she stepped outside, strong winds buffeted her, whipping her skirt around her legs. She tightened the sash on her bonnet and struggled toward the sutler's. Once there, she checked with the officious postal agent. "Have you a parcel for the surgeon?"

"Nasty day, what?" he said, his eyes roaming over her in an unseemly manner.

"Indeed."

He waited another beat before withdrawing a package from under the counter. "Wouldn't do to get it wet. Best hasten home, missy. Clouds are comin'."

"I'll hurry." She grabbed the package and turned to leave, stunned to see Corporal Adams slouched against the door, hands in his pockets. When she tried to slip past him, he fell in beside her. "Doc sent me to help you."

She eyed him with suspicion. Her father had never before sent anyone in such a situation. "I'm fine, thank you, Corporal."

Despite her dismissal, he followed her outside. Suddenly the fierce winds died, and a humid, pea-green canopy fell over the fort. Looking to the west, Lily saw thunderhead upon thunderhead mounting to the heavens and rolling toward them. She picked up her pace, leaning protectively over the package as the first pellets of rain fell. Then before she had gone more than a few yards, the sky went black, a gust of wind hit her and the heavens opened up.

"Here, miss." Adams seized her by the arm and pulled her into a darkened storehouse. "We'll be right cozy in here." His eyes glinted dangerously, and his grip on her arm hurt.

She struggled against him. "I'm going home."

The soldier moved closer. "You'll get wet. Now don't be a spoilsport. Besides, ole Adams just wants to have a bit o' fun."

He grabbed her around the waist, and she smelled his foul breath on her face. She could hardly breathe. "Get your hands off me!"

In the dim light, his mocking look said it all. He had no intention of letting her go. Fear such as she had never known buckled her knees. It was then that he pulled her to him, pinching her cheeks between his callused fingers. "You ain't goin' anywhere, missy."

Outside the wind roared among the buildings, zinging with power. In some corner of her brain, Lily registered the torrents drumming against the roof.

Adams's tone changed to sinister cajoling. "Now calm yourself, and give us a kiss."

Drawing on all her strength, Lily reared back, raised

her arms and hit him over the head with the book, then raced into the storm, praying she could outrun him.

Blinded by the rain and slowed by her soaked dress, she sprinted toward the headquarters building, visible in the lightning flashes that briefly illumined the parade ground. Behind her, she heard the corporal's howled oaths, but as she neared headquarters, he fell back and gave up the chase.

Breathless, she kept on running until she had nearly reached the wooden boardwalk outside headquarters. Then, somehow, she felt herself being lifted into strong arms and held in a protective embrace. When she looked up and saw Caleb, so great was her relief that she was racked with trembling. "Shh," he murmured in her ear. "You're safe now." Then he stared out over her head. "Was that Adams I saw?"

Bile filled her throat and all she could do was nod.

Caleb's voice was steely. "He won't be bothering you any more. I'll see to that."

Weak as a kitten, Lily laid her head on Caleb's broad shoulder, drawing from him warmth and security and reminding herself over and over, "I am safe."

Afterward she had no idea how long she had remained sheltered in the comfort of his arms. All she knew was that she had found peace in the storm.

Chapter Four

Scarcely daring to breathe, Caleb held Lily, moved by both her trembling and her floral-scented hair brushing his chin. Conflicting emotions tore through him—the unexpected joy of the embrace set against his rage at Corporal Adams. He itched to get at the man. First, though, he needed to see Lily safely to her family. Reluctantly, he stepped away. "I'm sorry, Miss Kellogg. This man should never have accosted you. I assure you he will be punished."

She straightened to her full height, adjusted her collar, then smoothed flyaway tresses back from her face. "I will count on that, Captain."

"Are you steady enough for me to escort you home?"

"I think so. It was all so sudden…and shocking."

"I'm glad I could be of assistance." He was aware of the forced formality of their conversation. Had she been offended by his embrace? Yet she had lingered there contentedly as she recovered from her panic.

"Please give me a moment," she said, turning away from him as if to study the storm, now diminishing in strength. She held herself purposefully, like a shattered vessel that had been glued back together. She seemed to be composing herself by sheer effort of will. "All's well that ends well," she finally said.

His pent-up anger threatened to explode. It hadn't ended well. That cad Adams had terrified her.

With a deep sigh, Lily faced him. "When we see my sister and father, I would ask you not to dramatize the situation. Rose doesn't need undue worry. As for Papa, he already suffers guilt for bringing us here with him. I fear he might never forgive himself."

"Eventually the facts must be told and Adams held accountable. But I will permit you the telling of the tale."

"Thank you, Captain."

"Caleb?" he asked hopefully.

For the first time in their conversation, she mustered a half smile. "Caleb. You were more than a friend today. You were my rescuer."

"I'm thankful I was here to help."

They stood a foot apart, their gazes locked, until a clap of thunder caused them to start. Caleb took Lily's arm and they dashed through raindrops to the Kellogg home.

Rose must've seen them coming. She flung open the door and hugged her sister. "We've been worried about you. Were you caught in the storm?"

Ezra Kellogg stood behind Rose, his eyebrows knit with concern. Never taking his eyes off Lily, he acknowledged Caleb with a curt "Captain."

Caleb squeezed Lily's arm gently before relinquishing his grasp. "Your daughter had a bit of a fright—"

"But I'm quite fine now, thanks to Captain Montgomery."

"Please come in, Captain." Rose took Lily's damp cloak and stood aside. "We all need a cup of tea. Lily, sit down and collect yourself and then do tell us what has happened."

Ezra directed Caleb to a chair by the fire and settled Lily on a small sofa. While Rose brought in the tea, Ezra wrapped Lily in a wool afghan, then sat down beside her, pulling her close. She rested her head on his shoulder. "Now," he said, "what's this all about?"

When Lily didn't respond, Ezra turned to Caleb. "You, sir. We're awaiting an explanation."

"Papa, there is little to explain." Lily raised her head and looked at them one by one. "I had started home when the storm broke. When it raged all about me, I sought temporary refuge in a storeroom and then made a dash for headquarters. There Captain Montgomery was kind enough to ease my fears."

Caleb sent her a questioning glance. She couldn't let it go at that. "Lily?" he said by way of encouragement, then inwardly reproached himself for taking the liberty of using her first name in this setting.

She glared at him, defying him to correct her version of events. While he hoped the matter of Adams could be taken care of discreetly, Ezra Kellogg deserved a fuller answer. Caleb suspected in a more intimate setting with her sister, Lily would confide the truth, but perhaps the incident was still too raw for her to discuss with her father.

Ezra turned to Lily. "Daughter, I recommend you take a tonic when you finish your tea. Then after supper it would be best for you to retire for the evening. You have had a trying experience, but rest should restore you." He leaned over to kiss her forehead. "You are safe now, for which I thank God."

She touched her father's cheek. "And Captain Montgomery."

"Ah, yes."

Rose stepped forward and gathered Lily, afghan and all, and led her from the room.

After the women had departed, Caleb stood and prepared to leave. The surgeon crossed to him and laid a hand on his shoulder. "Sir, might I have a word with you in private?" Ezra Kellogg was no fool. The look on his face revealed his suspicion that Lily had withheld information. "Follow me."

The surgeon ushered Caleb to his office in the hospital, closed the door behind him and leaned against his desk, arms folded across his chest. "There is more to the story, am I correct, Captain?"

"Yes, sir." Although Caleb felt uncomfortable telling the part of the tale that Lily had chosen to omit, her father needed to know.

Ezra gestured to the wooden chair against the wall. "I'm listening."

Caleb lowered himself into the seat, then fixed his eyes on the doctor. "One of our enlisted men attempted to assault Lily."

Ezra raked his fingers through his graying hair. "I've been afraid of something like this."

"Fortunately Lily was able to escape his grasp and run away from him before anything more serious happened. When I first saw her from headquarters, she was running lickety-split across the parade ground, pursued by the cad, who fell back when I stepped outside. I did what I could to calm her and assure her she was safe."

Ezra spoke in a steely tone. "Do we know the identity of this scoundrel?"

"I do. Corporal Adams. I will be ordering him held in the stockade as soon as I leave here."

Ezra rounded his desk and slumped into the chair, burying his face in his hands. "I should never have brought my family here. I knew what rough-and-tumble places military forts are. I permitted my own needs and desires to override my common sense."

"With all due respect, sir, I think you're being too hard on yourself. Most of the men are good souls who respect women."

As if he hadn't heard, Ezra said, "I'll never forgive myself. What have I done to my daughter?"

Caleb realized he needed to get the man's attention. "Sir, listen to me. This was not your fault. It was the result of one man's actions, a man who needs to be drummed out of the army in disgrace." He paused to gather his thoughts. "Lily begged me not to tell you about this. I think she was afraid you'd react just as you have. In no way does she regard any of this as your fault. Furthermore, she seemed to recover well. She is brave and resilient. She will worry about you if she thinks she has been a cause of your increased concern."

"Have you ever had a child, Captain?"

"No."

"Then you cannot know how strong is a father's instinct to protect his children. It is a grave responsibility, which I have failed."

"Even the best father cannot foresee and prevent all circumstances. Let Lily guide you. She loves you very much and wanted only to spare you pain."

Ezra scraped his hands across his face, then looked at Caleb. "I fear I have forgotten myself. My daughter called you her rescuer, and for that I am most grateful. I know that for every scoundrel and hooligan, there are fine, conscientious men like you, Captain." He stood then and offered his hand across the desk. "Thank you, sir. I am in your debt for your service to Lily."

Caleb grasped the man's hand and said, "Rest assured

justice will be done in this matter, sooner than later. I will attend to it directly."

"I would expect no less."

Exiting the hospital, Caleb strode across the parade ground to the enlisted men's barracks. Inside, some men were playing cards or writing letters, but in the back corner a tight group clustered around a dice game, Adams among them, the visor of his cap pulled low as if to make himself invisible. The minute the duty sergeant saw Caleb, he shouted, "Attention!" The men rose to their feet, braced for what might follow and saluted.

Caleb let his eyes rove over the assembly, before closing in on Corporal Adams. Then he called him out. "Adams, front and center. You are summarily ordered to the stockade, pending investigation of a charge of assault."

No one looked at the culprit as he slunk through the stony silence toward Caleb, his shifty eyes darting about as if soliciting sympathy. Caleb waited until the man stood in front of him. "Do you understand the charge?"

"I didn't do nothin'," Corporal Adams whined.

"That is for your superior officers to determine. Thank your lucky stars it isn't solely up to me. Consider yourself officially on report. Come along."

Caleb saluted the sergeant and, accompanied by the unrepentant corporal, strode from the room, holding on to his temper by only the shortest tether.

In the days that followed, Lily tried to forget the afternoon of the storm. She couldn't bear to think what might have happened had she not escaped the leering corporal, nor did she want to remember how protected she had felt in Caleb's arms. It had been bewildering to go from the clutches of one man to the welcome embrace of another. Rather than dwell on either sensation, she threw herself into her work at the hospital, even though her father had expressed reservations. "Are you sure this isn't too much for you?"

From Ezra's obvious concern, Lily suspected that Caleb had told her father exactly what had happened. The captain had sought her out the day after the attack to assure her that Corporal Adams was locked in the stockade awaiting a hearing.

Even so, Lily was now more cautious as she moved among the men, no longer innocent concerning the occasional one who eyed her just a trifle too long or smirked when he thought she wasn't looking. But mostly the soldiers were embarrassingly solicitous of her. Whatever hopes she had entertained of keeping the affair quiet had been disappointed. A military hearing could hardly be kept secret, but thankfully justice had been swift. Adams would remain under guard pending transfer to Fort Riley.

Rose had been tender with her the night of the incident, finally coaxing the story out of her. Lily had confessed to the fear that had clotted her throat when the corporal dragged her into the storeroom and laid his hands on her. Even now the rasp of his coarse fingers on her skin and the smell of his sour tobacco breath lingered in her memory. Rose had wiped away her tears and rocked her in an embrace. "There, there," she had said. "Try to concentrate instead on your good fortune that Captain Montgomery saw Adams and protected you."

Every day since, warm spring winds howled and dust flew in the air and choked the throat. Restlessness unlike any Lily had ever known surged within her. No place— not the hospital, the library or the cemetery—brought her peace. Even thinking about St. Louis made her dejected— it seemed a distant goal. She felt as if the flame of her soul had been snuffed out.

Near the end of April a few wagon trains appeared. Camped near the fort to avail themselves of both protection and the opportunity to restock provisions, the settlers brought with them stories of previous hardships as well as their idealized hopes for the future. The women, in particular, gazed fondly at the fort, perhaps wishing they could stay rather than launch into the dangerous, unknown sea of prairie grass.

Lily had seen Caleb going about his duties, and once or twice they'd been together in the library. However, others were present so no further literary discussions had ensued. Lily fretted in a limbo of frustration.

Late one night a few days later, she was awakened by frantic knocking on their door, followed by her father's commanding voice. "Take her into the hospital and I will get my daughters to assist."

Closing the door, he called to them. "Girls, are you awake? Come quickly to the hospital to assist with a delivery. Bring plenty of towels."

Rose, dressed first, fetched clean towels. Lily slipped into a shift, and both donned clean white aprons before extinguishing the candles and hurrying next door.

Behind the curtain drawn around one bed came the sound of a woman bawling in pain. Lily moved to the head of the bed where the woman lay, her skin ashen, her cracked lips caked with the salt of her tears. Rose had gone to boil water, and her father stood at his patient's side palpating her abdomen, his face grave. "She has been in labor since yesterday evening," he said quietly. "I fear both she and the child are in distress. Daughter, can you determine how the baby is presenting?"

Lily dipped her hands in hot water, scrubbed them with soap and moved to the foot of the bed. What she saw upon examination was not reassuring. When her father raised his eyebrows in question, Lily shook her head in the negative.

As another contraction racked the whimpering woman, the surgeon made his decision. "I fear mother will not last long. We must take the infant."

While he went to inform the father, Lily and Rose prepared the instruments and changed the bed linens. The woman watched them with large, sad eyes. "Save my baby," she whispered. Then she added in the howl of a wounded animal, "I told Jacob I never wanted to come west." Her tone hardened. "Never."

Lily knew that many women died in childbirth on the trail. That, along with cholera and typhus, posed an enormous threat, not to mention possible attacks by hostile Indians. Yet so many of these wives had no choice; they were tied to their husbands and lacked alternatives. Lily vowed under her breath that she would never submit to such grim realities. If only she could wait in God's time for deliverance from this wilderness.

Ezra reentered the room, and after that, all extraneous thoughts fled in the intensity of the procedure. Her father's deft movements were swift, and soon he had extracted a tiny, wrinkled infant who, with Rose's ministrations, finally managed a feeble cry. While Rose cleaned and swaddled the baby, Lily and her father worked frantically to stem the woman's bleeding and close the incision. Lily sutured while her father listened to the mother's heartbeat and took her pulse. "Thready" was all he said. A knowing glance passed between the two. They had done what they could, but the mother's life hung in precarious balance.

Lily's nimble fingers tied the last knot and she stood back, flexing her hands. Ezra seemed preoccupied. "We've done all we can," he finally said. "I'll fetch her husband."

In her father's absence, Lily gave the woman a drink

of water and gently wiped her feverish face with a cool cloth. The woman's eyes fluttered briefly. "My baby?"

"A boy."

The woman's features relaxed and she closed her eyes, her breath now coming in irregular rasps.

After a few moments, Ezra led the father into the room, followed by Rose carrying the newborn. The father rushed to his wife's side. "Good news, Patience. We have a son."

Rose placed the baby in his mother's arms. She opened her eyes and gazed at the child, her limp fingers caressing his face, his hair, his tiny hands. A tear traced its way down her sunken cheek. "Beautiful," she murmured.

Lily turned away.

The husband knelt at his wife's side, cradling her and his son. His body language conveyed knowledge of the end, but his words spoke denial. "My love, our boy will grow into a fine young man." He kissed her forehead.

Once more the mother examined the baby. As her son studied her in return, his little hand curled around her finger. "Alas." The word came with an effort. "I shall not see that day, Jacob."

His expression wild with questions, the husband looked around the room, seeking reassurance. In honesty, neither Lily, nor Rose nor Ezra could offer any. Then a strangled "No!" rose from his chest. When he looked back down at the bed, the baby kicked weakly against the lifeless body of his mother.

Lily bowed her head, struck, as always, by the random quality of death, whether it claimed her brother, her mother or this hapless woman. *God, in Your mercy, bless this dear soul, her motherless baby and her grieving husband.* She bit her lip and then added, *And help me to accept what is so difficult to understand.*

After Ezra led the father away, Lily washed and prepared the corpse while Rose went in search of a wet nurse among the women of the wagon train. This poor soul! One more poignant example of the risks women took in the isolated country they traversed.

When Lily finally left the hospital, the eastern sky was streaked with pale light. Too disturbed to go home, she instead sought refuge in the cemetery. Better than anyone, her mother would understand her tears of helplessness.

As she crossed the parade ground near the officers' quarters, she noticed a man sitting in the shadows of the porch. Caleb. She couldn't think about him right now. Yet standing beside her mother's grave a few moments later, he was the person she thought of.

He, too, was a son whose mother had died in childbirth. How had that loss affected the young boy and influenced the man he had become?

Tonight's was the first birth she'd attended that didn't have a happy outcome, and she could not have foreseen how deeply it would affect her. She wept for the mother and father and for their baby. She wept for herself. And she wept for the motherless eight-year-old Caleb.

Caleb stood at the edge of the cemetery, not daring to interrupt what seemed to be a sacred moment. In recent days, he had rarely spoken to Lily privately. When she had emerged so early from the hospital and walked toward the cemetery, lost in her thoughts, some impulse that she not be alone seized him and he'd followed her at a distance. Yet drawn to her as he was, he hesitated, trapped in self-doubt.

He watched as she touched the headstone, much as one might dip fingers into holy water, and then, head down, walked toward him. Fearful of startling her, he spoke softly. "Miss Kellogg?"

She looked up and upon recognizing him, halted. In her piteous glance he read both exhaustion and sorrow. "Captain?"

He hastened to answer her unasked question. "I saw you walking across the parade ground at this unusually early hour. You looked sad, and I wanted to be of assistance…comfort…" He struggled to find the right note. "It is not my intent to intrude, but…"

She laid a hand on his shoulder. "No harm. You are right, I am overwhelmed with grief, frustration—and questions."

Confused by her answer, he tucked her hand in both of his. "Pray what has happened to cause you such distress?"

She shook her head as if dispersing cobwebs. "I shall not burden you with my concerns."

"Let us walk together." He took her elbow and they started slowly toward the hospital. "You could never burden me. If you want to speak of whatever has happened, I will gladly listen."

Then, more to herself than in dialogue with him, she told of the senseless death of the settler's wife despite efforts to save her. She bit her lip in the effort, he guessed, to keep from crying when she told him about the precious little boy, now motherless. As if coming out of reverie into the harsh light of reality, she vented. "I can't bear thinking about the travails of women, subject to the whims or ambitions of their husbands, who risk their lives and the lives of their children, for what? For some distant paradise gained only by crossing vast miles of unknown land where death waits at every turn of the trail?" She stopped again, sweeping one arm in a gesture encompassing the empty horizon. "Who leads them? God or ruthless ambition?"

Caleb knew he should be shocked by her outburst, which went beyond the accepted standards for polite conversation. Instead, he was moved by her passion and grateful that she could speak so openly.

"Last night had to be a wrenching ordeal. I have known that same kind of powerlessness to stop the inevitable." His jaw worked as he recalled his inability to alter the unconscionable massacre at the Washita, over in a matter of minutes but horrific for its victims. "Sometimes there are no answers to the question 'Why?'"

"God may know, but at times like this, that is little comfort." She cocked her head to one side, studying him intently. "Tell me about your mother. How did you go on without her?"

He rarely spoke about that time before his mother died when she filled the house with laughter and song. About her cinnamon rolls which had spoiled him forever from savoring any others. About the way she cuddled him and his brother at bedtime and made Bible stories come to life.

He must've gone to another place, because Lily's voice returned him to the present. "Forgive me, Caleb. That is an overly personal question."

"Not between friends," he said, swallowing hard. They resumed strolling. "As a little boy, I thought I was the luckiest child in the world to have a mother who looked like a princess. Ours was a happy family. My older brother, Seth, and I never tired of her songs and stories. But she also didn't put up with too much mischief from us. As hard as I try, though, there are some things I can never remember. But I always knew she loved me." He was silent for several minutes. "After she died, Father, Seth and I had difficulty speaking of her. It was too painful. Besides, boys don't cry. It was easier to let baby Sophie divert us."

"Your mother would be proud of the man you've become."

"I hope so." Yet even in that breath, guilt washed over

him. His mother, who had revered each living creature God had put on the earth, would havc been appalled by what happened with Black Kettle and his band and, no doubt, ashamed of her son's role. And even though it was a necessary cause, could she have countenanced his behavior in the heat of battle in the War between the States when his very survival depended upon killing the enemy? He sighed as he thought about the dubious acts he had committed when following orders. Perhaps it was best that he would never know what his mother might have thought of his soldiering, nor was he eager for Lily's opinion.

The two of them were approaching the hospital when she said, "Thank you for your concern on my account and for sharing memories of your mother. Death is hard, but perhaps it shapes us in ways known only to God. We must believe something good ultimately comes from such experiences."

He prayed it could be so, but nightmares and insomnia argued to the contrary. "Your outlook is more sanguine than mine."

She looked up at him. "It would appear we are both searching for answers."

To lighten the dark mood, he said, "Perhaps we should turn to the poets. John Donne would say, 'Death, be not proud.'"

She smiled sadly. "Indeed."

They had reached her door. "Thank you for coming to my side this morning," she said, her eyes glistening with unshed tears, the blue-gray cast to the skin beneath her eyes an indication of her exhaustion.

He gave a short bow. "Miss Kellogg, we seem to have traveled some similar roads. It is a comfort to know I am not alone."

Now the smile relaxed and her eyes deepened into pools

of blue. "Lily. My name is Lily. Your friendship is most welcome."

He exhaled in relief. "Lily." The name was melodic on his tongue. "Until we meet once more."

He waited until she was safely inside and then ambled toward his quarters. The sun was full now on the horizon, and morning activity buzzed all around him. But he was ignorant of it, lost in the memories of his mother, the horrors of battle and of the one person who might either understand it all or condemn him. Lily.

Chapter Five

On an afternoon in late April, Rose, Lily and two lieutenants' wives, Carrie Smythe and Virginia Brown, gathered around Effie Hurlburt's dining room table to sew bandages for the hospital. Talk ranged from the gardens they planned to variations on bean recipes. Effie, ever cheerful, laughed when they complained of the upcoming heat of summer. "You cannot stop the seasons in their turn. Just as the cold winds blew in January, so July will become an oven. Best not to let either overwhelm your spirit."

Lily acknowledged Effie's sound advice even as she felt weighed down by the prospects of boiling temperatures. "I wish I shared your optimistic nature," she said.

"Bother. It's all in what you decide—life is either a pleasure and an opportunity or a dismal ordeal to be endured."

Carrie shrugged. "You are undoubtedly right, but there are days it is hard to keep positive."

"I think what Mrs. Hurlburt is trying to say," Rose interjected, "is that it serves no purpose to let conditions we can't control alter our natures."

Lily lowered her eyes to her sewing. Was her sister criticizing her desire to escape the frontier? In fairness, each single day was bearable, made sweeter by proximity to her family. But taken in total, day after day of this existence with no end in sight ravaged her soul. Boredom was the greatest enemy. Perhaps she should be grateful for her work at the hospital, the occasional conversations with people like Effie and Caleb and the solace of a good book.

Effie's warm voice intruded into her thoughts. "What we need is to create diversions to occupy us and help pass the time."

"What do you have in mind?" Virginia inquired.

Effie laid down her sewing. "Now that the weather is better, the men are starting to play baseball again. Perhaps we could organize a pie supper after a few Saturday games. Not just pies, but cakes, too."

Rose warmed to the idea. "The men enjoy home-cooked food. It would occupy us and please them. Sometimes we forget that they are far from home, just as we are."

"Excellent point, Rose." Effie looked around the table. "What else?"

A thought occurred to Lily. "We could organize a monthly reading—poetry, biographies, travel books. I've seen several of the men in the library, so I'm confident we could engage their participation."

"I like that idea," Carrie said. "Some of the troops cannot read well, if at all, so they might enjoy listening to others."

"You see?" Effie beamed in satisfaction. "We can be the authors of our own entertainment."

She rose from the table, gesturing to the rest to remain seated. "I shall fetch the pound cake and tea from the kitchen. Then we can celebrate our brilliant ideas."

After she left the room, Rose began folding the completed bandages for laundering. "We are blessed to have such an accommodating commander's wife."

"I've been told some are cold and condescending," Carrie ventured.

"True enough," Virginia confirmed. "At our last post, I lived in fear of an invitation to the commander's home."

Lily nodded. "Our mother always said to count our blessings. And surely Effie Hurlburt is one."

As they were eating the delicious cake, talk turned to marriage and the balance between supporting one's soldier husband in his duties and, at the same time, attending to a marriage.

"I confess impatience with my husband when he is away on a mission," Carrie said, "or even when he is right here, drilling, but still unavailable to me."

"We're always at the whim of the regiment," Virginia complained. "Sometimes I feel as if I have no influence on our lives whatsoever."

Lily was surprised. Usually the junior officers' wives were more circumspect with a commander's wife, but Effie seemed not to mind. Lily thought of her as a mentor and protector of the women stationed at the fort, and they certainly needed one.

"Marriage is a challenge, especially in military life," Effie agreed.

Overcome by sudden curiosity, Lily laid down her fork. "What is your secret? How do you and the major make it all work?"

Effie brushed a crumb from her lips. "There is no mysterious formula. Commitment to one another and to overcoming any challenges is foremost. Honesty is the other."

"What exactly do you mean—*honesty?*" Lily asked.

"My husband and I promised at the beginning that there would be no secrets between us. Regardless of the subject and its pleasantness or unpleasantness, we would share our thoughts and feelings."

"Not all men are good at that," Carrie mumbled.

"No, they are bred to be brave and to withhold their emotions. This is especially true of soldiers. But—" she grinned conspiratorially "—they can be trained. The point is not to overreact when they say something you might prefer not to hear or which is initially painful to you. With practice, husbands can become more comfortable with confidences."

"What you call 'training' could be difficult," Rose said.

"I'm not denying that, but consider the results. I'm happy, and I believe the major is, as well."

A morsel of cake lodged in Lily's throat. She longed for the kind of relationship Effie described, but she had already experienced one man's reluctance to confide. Caleb had finally—and only briefly—talked about his mother, but had never said a word about his war experiences, which surely formed a large part of his identity. Lily admired the bond Effie had with her husband, one characterized by freedom and openness. Was such a thing possible? Not for most people, she imagined. Subservience was the more accepted practice for wives.

She wondered whether her parents had shared everything. For instance, could her mother have expressed her reluctance to leave Iowa? Or had both husband and wife held back, fearful of offense or hurt?

As if realizing the conversation had grown overly intimate, Effie changed the subject. "Now then. The first baseball game is this coming Saturday. Let's talk about the desserts we will prepare."

Rose agreed to make three raisin pies while Lily volunteered a chiffon cake. She wished a pie supper or a series of readings would change her attitude about being here, but she doubted it. When she returned home today, she would write a letter reminding Aunt Lavinia of her hopes for a St. Louis visit.

"Caleb!" Buried in darkness, Caleb heard a voice, felt himself being roughly shaken. "Wake up, man!"

Indians screaming war whoops hounded him from all sides, bullets hailed down upon him and the earth trembled with the reverberations of cannon fire. Moaning, he clawed his way to consciousness. Will Creekmore stood over him, his face illuminated by the moonlight filtering through the window of the officers' barracks. "Montgomery, can you wake up?"

Caleb tried to focus, then sat gingerly on the edge of the bed, groggy and disoriented. "The dream," he croaked.

"Again?"

All Caleb could do was nod in disgust and humiliation. The ghosts of combat refused to relinquish him. He had come to dread sleep because of the horrific night visitors. He wiped beads of sweat from his brow even as he shivered in the cool night air. Mustering strength, he stood and clapped Will on the back. "Sorry to have disturbed you."

Will smiled ruefully. "You're not alone. We all have our battle scars."

That was true, and Caleb understood each man's struggle was personal. "Go back to bed, friend." He drew on his trousers. "I'll be fine. I just want to clear my head."

He stepped out on the front porch, needing to purge from his body and soul the terrors that sat upon him like lead weights. Would this torment ever abate? Could anything or anyone cleanse his poisonous memories? He leaned on the railing, gazing over the encampment. Others were sleeping, most, peacefully, he surmised. But on nights such as this, sleep was a luxury he could not afford to indulge, not when it might invite again such troubled dreams.

He looked up at the sky, brilliant with moonglow and starlight. If there was a God, was He up there? Amid the countless stars, why would He concern himself with one tortured cavalryman? And yet… "His eye is on the sparrow…"

He reminded himself of the good in the world. His family. His loyal troops, some risking their lives to carry wounded mates to safety. Lily—a lovely young woman acquainted with grief. He must not, however, come to depend upon her to be the light in his darkness. Rather he should spare her his demons.

Such wisdom, though, was at odds with his instincts toward friendship. What could friendship hurt? Her frequent visits to her mother's grave confirmed that a military outpost could be a lonely place for a woman, too. As he remained on the porch, surrounded by night sounds, gradually an image of Lily replaced that of his nightmares. He fixed on it, grateful for his clearing mind and slowing respiration.

He didn't know how long he stood there, but finally he went back inside, lighted the lantern and tried to lose himself in Charles Dickens's *David Copperfield.* Unable to concentrate, he set the book aside and picked up a piece of paper and a pen. He held the pen in the air, gathering his thoughts. Finally he dipped it in the ink and began writing. With each succeeding stroke, he felt his torment subside.

May 1 dawned with the cheery songs of birds and the tantalizing aroma of hotcakes. Lily patted the empty space on the mattress beside her. Rose was already up and cooking. Cocooning herself in the covers, Lily lay listening to the avian reveille, soon joined by the bugle version. She found something predictably reassuring about military schedules, which, like clocks, remained constant.

She had posted her letter to Aunt Lavinia and hoped she had been subtle but effective in saying how much she anticipated reuniting with her aunt and being introduced to the wonders of St. Louis. She knew such a trip would be expensive and that her father could not afford the entire cost. Months ago, Lavinia had offered to underwrite the expense. Had she forgotten? Or was the delay merely about timing? Lily appreciated that summer was not the season to go, but if she was to travel in the fall, plans had to be made.

She sighed, then reluctantly left the warmth of the bed and moved to the pitcher and basin on the nightstand to make her morning ablutions. She chose her rose-colored dress, which seemed a fitting way to greet the new month.

Her father was already sitting at the kitchen table, a cup of coffee cradled in his hands. Rose bustled at the stove, pouring more batter into the sizzling iron skillet. "Good morning, everyone," Lily said.

Her father smiled. "Top of the morning, daughter."

"I didn't mean to dawdle, but it was so cozy." She moved to Rose's side. "How can I help?"

"Put the butter and honey on the table and I'll bring the hotcakes."

When they were all seated, Ezra said grace. Lily had just picked up her first forkful of food when she thought she heard a light tap on the door. Rose, too, cocked her head toward the sound. "Did you hear that?" Lily asked.

Her father looked up. "What?"

"Perhaps a knock," Rose said. "I'll go."

When she didn't return right away, Ezra called, "Was anyone there?"

"Not exactly," Rose said, a hint of laughter in her voice.

When she came back into the kitchen, she concealed something behind her back. Ezra regarded her expectantly. "You look like the cat that ate the canary."

"A surprise was left on our doorstep." Then she produced a small bouquet of wildflowers wrapped in a newspaper secured with twine. "Happy May Day, Lily." Rose beamed, handing the bouquet to her sister and winking at her father.

A blush rose to Lily's cheeks as she studied the flowers. Nestled among the wild violets, primroses and sprigs of fern was an envelope inscribed with her name.

"It would seem you have an admirer," her father said. "I remember well the times I left a May Day bouquet at your mother's door when I was courting."

Lily set the bouquet on the table and pulled a note from the envelope. Scanning it for a signature, she murmured, "Not an admirer, Papa. A friend."

Then engrossed in the message, she failed to see a knowing look pass between her father and sister.

In strong masculine handwriting, the words blurred in her vision as she recalled her last conversation with Caleb at her mother's grave.

If when thy thoughts to gloom do fly
And sorrow seeks thy soul to cloy,
Mayhap these blooms may still thy sigh
And serve as harbingers of joy.
A friend

"Well?" her father studied her inquiringly.

Rose, as usual in sympathy with her sister, deflected his question. "I think, Papa, that such a gift is not meant to be immediately shared." She picked up the platter and handed it to Ezra. "Have another hotcake."

Lily, overcome with confusing emotions, silently blessed her sister for her tact. And blessed Caleb, whose poetic bent and sensitivity to her mother's loss belied a soldier's stoicism.

The Saturday of the baseball game was especially hot for May. By late morning, the flag hung motionless from the pole and open windows did little to cool interiors. Lily pulled her cake from the oven, lamenting the slightly burned top. Rose's pies were perfect, so, as usual, Lily's baking paled by comparison. No matter. The soldiers would not be picky.

By one o'clock Rose and Lily were at the makeshift ball field where, under Effie Hurlburt's direction, some enlisted men were assembling trestle tables for the baked goods and others were erecting plank benches along the baselines for the spectators.

As soon as all the desserts were laid out on the tables, Effie covered them with cheesecloth to protect them from dust and insects. Most of the ladies wore summer-weight dresses and sported sunbonnets for protection. Lily's blue-and-white-sprigged muslin was last year's dress, but showed off her tiny waist and fair complexion. When everything was done to Effie's satisfaction, she herded the women to the benches set aside for them. Only then did the nonplayers fill in, jostling for position. Lieutenant Creekmore's troop was opposing Captain Montgomery's, and there was much good-natured joshing and more than a few wagers placed.

When the teams ran onto the field, the crowd clapped and hooted. Major Hurlburt, the umpire, stepped up to the team captains and appeared to be reminding them of the rules. Before the game began, the players stripped off their jackets and rolled up their sleeves. Lily noticed that

Benjamin, her former concussion patient, was playing in the outfield while Caleb took the pitcher's position. Although she couldn't follow all the fine points of the game, she understood that Caleb's skill was frustrating those attempting to strike the ball. Just as she was feeling sorry for Caleb's opponent, he connected with the ball and sent it soaring into the outfield beyond any of the players to the great delight of that team's boosters.

When it was Caleb's team's turn at bat, Rose poked her in the ribs. "I imagine you're partial to this nine."

Had Rose noticed her eyes following Caleb's every move? "You should be, too, sister. We know Captain Montgomery better than we know Lieutenant Creekmore."

Despite Lily's determination not to play favorites, she couldn't help noticing Caleb's broad shoulders and muscled forearms. Before he pitched again, he came over to the nearby water bucket and ladled out a drink. She lowered her gaze lest he discover her staring at him. He was one fine-looking man.

As the game wore on and the high jinks in the stands grew louder and more partisan, Lily reflected that events like this benefitted morale. From the beginning, the score seesawed. Finally in the last inning, Caleb's team eked out the winning run. Amid whooping and huzzahing, the teams left the field, many heading out to wash up before the pie supper.

Lily and Rose hurried to the dessert tables to slice cakes and pies and set out plates and cutlery. Major Hurlburt, his face red from the exertion of umpiring, approached them. "Mighty nice of you women to provide such a treat," he said with an approving smile.

As the men reassembled, the major made a short speech. "A fine sporting event, gentlemen. Played fair and square. To the victor belong the spoils. Captain Montgomery, lead your team to the desserts."

Caleb, his thumbs hooked in his suspenders, grinned. "We'll try to leave some food for the others." Amid good-natured catcalls from the opposing team, the men descended on the dessert tables.

Carrie and Virginia dispensed lemonade while Rose and Lily helped Effie dish up servings of pie and cake.

Caleb eyed the selections. "Which one is yours?" he asked Lily.

"Oh, don't try mine," she said. "You'd prefer Rose's pie."

As other men moved past him, he looked her in the eye. "Why wouldn't I want yours?"

"Let's just say I'm a better nurse than I am a cook."

"I'll be the judge of that." He studied the table. "Which one?"

Reluctantly she pointed out the less-than-perfect chiffon cake.

"Cut me a big slice."

She had no choice but to serve him what he wanted, but she added a sliver of raisin pie to his plate. "I'll be sitting over there." He nodded in the direction of the first base bench. "Would you do me the honor of joining me when you're finished here?"

Heads bobbed up all around and curious stares settled on the two of them. She felt trapped. "You may be finished with your food before I have completed my duty."

His quirked eyebrow told her he knew she was procrastinating. "I'll wait," he said, moving off to the field.

Lily bent over the food, avoiding anyone's gaze. It was one thing to take a companionable stroll from the cemetery or to be escorted home from a band concert. This meeting would be all too public. Already she felt the pressure of the I-told-you-so looks passing among the troops.

Rose sidled up to her. "You can't be rude," she murmured.

Lily wasn't worried about rudeness, more about the erroneous perception she felt growing all around her. "We're just friends," she said to her sister. "Don't go thinking anything else."

Rose smiled innocently. "Of course you are."

One of the sergeants in Caleb's troop insisted on carrying her lemonade and cake to the bench. "Here, ma'am," he said, setting them down. "Take good care of this little lady, Captain."

"My pleasure, Sergeant." Caleb shoved his empty plate aside and turned to Lily. "Now what was the matter with that cake? As you can see, I had no trouble disposing of it."

Lily held up her dish. "This is Effie Hurlburt's perfect apple cake, so much better than my burned one."

"Burned? I didn't notice."

"You're just being polite," she said, spearing a piece of Effie's dessert.

"When you know me better, you'll find I don't say much of anything I don't mean. Your cake was delicious."

Lily feared they were not talking merely about cake. She continued eating while he stretched out his legs. The informality of his attire and the sight of his hair, tousled from the ball game, made him seem unfamiliar, more… she couldn't find the word. *Manly?*

"It was thoughtful of you ladies to feed us. The men were really looking forward to today." Then he turned toward her. "So was I."

"Speaking of thoughtful—" she hung her head, overcome with sudden shyness "—thank you for the May Day bouquet and poem. The sentiments were timely and so well expressed." She gazed up at him, sensing that he, too, was suddenly bashful. "I'm in awe of your poetic powers, sir."

His rich, hazel eyes swept her face. "If my words in any way could be described as poetic, it is because I had a most insistent and lovely muse."

Again feeling put on the spot, she took a hasty sip of the lemonade, willing herself not to blush. She desperately needed to change the subject. "I understand from my father that there is trouble brewing with the Indians."

His lips thinned and his expression grew more serious. "It's the time of year. The winter has been harsh, so when the wagon trains start through here in earnest, the Indians seize upon that opportunity both to protect their lands and to replenish their supplies. We will be setting out at the end of next week."

"Will you be gone long?"

"It depends on how widespread the threat is and how successful we are in quelling disturbances."

Despite her vow not to make this encounter personal, she felt a frisson of alarm on his behalf. "Please, be safe."

"I will do my duty, but I assure you I will also exercise care for my men and for myself."

"I will pray for all of you."

"That can do no harm."

She eyed him speculatively. "Do you doubt the efficacy of prayer?"

"I cannot say. At times I have felt abandoned by God, but at other times only His grace has saved me." He stared up at the clouds, now gathering on the horizon. "You could say I'm still searching for answers to such questions."

"Perhaps we are not supposed to know the mind of The Eternal."

He picked up her hand. "We're getting mighty serious here." He glanced again at the sky. "It's cooling a bit. Would you favor me with a walk down to the river?"

She should say no, but the hopeful look in his eyes was compelling. Besides, the day was too glorious to go home. "That would be just the thing after indulging in dessert."

They picked up their plates and returned them to the table where the other women had succeeded in clearing nearly everything away.

"Rose, Effie, I'm so sorry. I should've been helping."

Effie waved her on. "Nonsense, we were all enjoying seeing you and the captain together."

Lily's heart sank. Why must a simple conversation be taken for more than it was. She wished now that she hadn't agreed to the walk.

Caleb moved to thread her arm through his. He nodded to Rose and Effie. "Ladies, may I borrow Miss Lily for a stroll?"

"Enjoy yourselves," Effie said, nudging Rose in the ribs.

Lily was caught. On the one hand she couldn't wait to move away from the women and their approving glances. On the other, she wondered why she had ever agreed to the walk.

By now, most of the men had dispersed to their barracks or the taverns beyond the fort. As Lily and Caleb moved into the shade of the trees bordering the river, it felt as if they were entering a private bower. She stooped to finger a tiny white flower. "It's a joy to see blooms again after such a long winter."

"In the same way after months of cold weather, it's great for the men to let off steam with events like this afternoon's game."

"Baseball seems a fine, though complicated, game."

"Perhaps one day I can give you a tutorial on the rules."

"Perhaps," she repeated, not wanting to commit to any further meetings. Yet, in the same breath, she knew she didn't want this day to end.

They came to a place where a fallen log formed a kind of bench. "Shall we sit?" he asked.

She gathered her skirts and sank onto the log, which presented a peaceful view of the stream, overhung with leafy branches.

He joined her. "Sitting here, it's hard to believe that the world can be in such turmoil."

"All the more reason, as my mother was wont to say, to live in the day, this day."

His voice grew husky. "I am pleased to be living this one with you."

She looked up. The need in his eyes rendered her breathless. Several seconds passed before she could look away. "I treasure our friendship," she said softly.

For the second time that afternoon, he took her hand in his. "As do I. Perhaps this is a way God has blessed us."

She was suddenly curious. "What is it that causes us to be friends?"

He ran his thumb over the top of her hand before replying. "You provide a sympathetic ear. We have both experienced loss. We share an interest in literature. We have profound questions about the nature of God."

Everything he said was true. "I, too, feel as if there are few subjects we cannot discuss."

He did not relinquish her hand. They sat in companionable silence, listening to birds chirping and watching a squirrel jump from branch to branch in a nearby oak tree. She relaxed into the sheer pleasure of the moment.

Finally she pulled away, leaning back on her hands to study the blue sky, crisscrossed with trails of cloud. "Do you ever miss home?"

"I've been in the army so long, home seems like a distant memory."

"We've talked about your mother and sister, but I've never known where you grew up." It suddenly seemed important to fill in the gaps of her knowledge about Caleb.

"I was born in Jefferson City, Missouri. We lived on a small farm just outside of town along the river. My grandfather owned a grist mill. After he died my father took it over, but he was never really happy being confined at the mill. Like him, we kids loved the farm and the freedom to roam. Summertime was the best. We could be gone from dawn until dusk." He picked up a small twig and twirled it between his palms. "That all seems a long time ago in another time and place. My family relocated to southeastern Kansas a couple of years ago."

"The war changed a great deal for all of us." There was no need to elaborate. How could one ever gauge its impact on individual lives? "Papa couldn't return to Iowa as a doctor. Another man had already taken his place. He'd been so long away that continuing in the military seemed the best alternative."

"But it uprooted you."

"I didn't want to leave. But as my mother said, 'Sometimes you have do what you'd rather not.'"

Caleb laid aside the twig. "She supported your father, then?"

"Always, at least outwardly." Now that she thought about it, Lily had even greater appreciation for her mother's sacrifice—and for her love of her husband. "Wives often have little choice, I suppose." All the more reason Lily intended to chart her own course.

The drowsy hum of bees and the slow-moving current lulled them both into silence. After an interval, Caleb turned to look at her and said, "I'm growing quite fond of you, Lily Kellogg. If ever I doubted womanhood, you and Sophie have set me straight."

Lily smiled. "That's quite a compliment. I know I'm in good company when you mention your sister."

The lightening of the mood led to a resumption of their stroll. They started back along the riverbank and then moved into the sunlit grassland. On a small hillock slightly off the path, Lily spotted a delicate purple blossom she'd never seen before. With a delighted "Oh," she scampered on ahead and knelt in the grass. She had just reached out to cup the petals in her hand, when she froze, her heart catapulting in her chest.

At her feet, concealed in the grass near a hole, was a nest of copperheads. One of the larger snakes slithered directly toward her. Paralyzed with fear, she screamed hysterically, "Moses, Moses!"

Chapter Six

Moses? Caleb couldn't fathom why Lily had called out that name, but no matter. He reacted instantly to her urgent cry, running to her and pulling her back from the nest of vipers. She trembled in his arms and her eyes had a distant, glazed expression.

"Oh, oh," she repeated tremulously. He picked her up, cradling her against his chest and carried her quickly toward the fort.

As they neared the cemetery, she asked him to stop. He headed for a stone bench under a huge sycamore tree and then gently set her down, still encircling her with his arm. Waiting patiently for her to stop shaking, he murmured an occasional "There, there."

He picked up her hands, noticing how icy they seemed to his warm flesh. Finally, she sighed deeply and relaxed a bit.

"Thank you, Caleb. I'm sorry." Her eyes glistened with unshed tears. "I'm terrified of snakes."

"You've had a bad experience in the past?"

She nodded, then stood up and paced in front of him, as if that effort could dispel her fears.

"And Moses? Was he part of that experience?"

She stopped in front of him, wringing her hands in the effort to calm herself. "Without him, I doubt I'd be here."

Caleb waited, knowing he could not rush her story.

Lily glanced around as if assuring herself of their privacy, then settled back on the bench. She began quietly, but in the telling of the tale, her voice grew gradually louder.

"Last summer a troop of buffalo soldiers was stationed here."

"I have fought with them," Caleb said, remembering the valiant emancipated slaves who had found a home in the army. "Committed soldiers and generally fine human beings."

"Alas, not everyone here thought so. Some of the white soldiers treated them shamefully. They were good hospital workers and were more orderly than most of the men."

That had been Caleb's experience, as well. He nodded, encouraging her to go on with her tale.

"One August day, I went out on the prairie behind the officers' quarters to collect sunflowers, growing wild there, for a bouquet to put on the table for my father's birthday." She hesitated as if not wanting to face her memory. "Moses, along with a few other buffalo soldiers, was in a nearby field, hoeing weeds. I had gathered an armful of sunflowers when I heard an unmistakable, spine-tingling sound."

"Rattles?"

She shivered. "Yes. I froze. Tears ran down my cheeks, and I clutched the flowers as if they would somehow protect me. Then I spotted the snake, coiled not six feet from me. So great was my terror that it seemed as if all sound but that of the rattling had vanished.

"Then as if from a great distance, I heard myself screaming. Moses raced past me, his hoe raised over his shoulder, and then with one mighty swing, he chopped the snake in half. I could neither look away from the severed reptile's gyrating body, nor could I move.

"Before I could scream again, Moses came to my side, not daring, of course, to touch me. 'Whoa, easy, missy,' he said in a deep, gentle voice. 'You be all right. Mister Rattler gone to his maker. Moses saw to that. You can be breathing again. He won't hurt you no more.'"

Caleb silently thanked God for Moses. "No wonder you were so frightened today."

"If it hadn't been for Moses…" She shuddered. "From then on, we had a special bond. I would slip him pastries and help him write letters home. I was sad when he left Fort Larned, but proud of him. He had made corporal. I still correspond with him occasionally."

"I hold the buffalo soldiers in highest regard and, along with you, regret the abuse and harsh treatment they often receive. They, too, are God's creatures with the same needs and hopes as the rest of us."

She looked up at him as if with newfound interest. "Except to my family, I've never dared speak of my friendship—that's the only accurate word—with Moses, nor my gratitude to him. He not only saved my life, but taught me a great deal about tolerance."

"Then perhaps your scare with the snake served God's purpose."

For the first time in many minutes, she smiled. "Perhaps, sir. But I still do…not…like…snakes." She drew out each word by way of emphasis. "And there won't always be a Moses or a Caleb to rescue me."

He recognized the truth of her words. They sat quietly for a time, resting. It was as if the effort to tell the story had exhausted her. Finally he said, "Are you ready for home?"

Nodding, she stood, then faced him. "I'm not usually such a frail flower. Thank you for saving me for the second time."

In her eyes he read such vulnerability and affection that without stopping to think, he drew her into his arms and laid her head against his chest. "I will do everything in my power to keep you safe," he murmured.

She remained in his arms while time seemed to stand still, then drew a deep breath and stood back, searching his face as if seeking some impenetrable answer. "You do me great honor, Captain."

With a racing heart, he sought to regain a semblance of normalcy. The woman had a dangerous way of making him forget caution. "Caleb?"

She ran a hand up and down his sleeve, as if appreciating their customary name game. "Oh, yes," she agreed. "Caleb."

Then she took his arm and together they walked toward her home.

On the way, they passed the barren ground and charred timbers standing in mute testimony to the fire that had destroyed the buffalo soldiers' stable the previous January. A fire, she told him, believed to have been set by some bigoted person objecting to the buffalo soldiers' presence at the fort.

As they skirted the scene, Caleb heard Lily whisper the poet's words he had often muttered himself, "'Man's inhumanity to man.'"

Caleb walked slowly across the parade ground toward his quarters, thinking about Lily. He didn't often find someone with whom he could share his views about emancipation. Many of his comrades from the North had shared his revulsion over the concept of slavery, but others were openly hostile about giving freedmen the right to vote. As for the buffalo soldiers, Caleb had found most of them to be decent fellows. One sergeant with whom he had fought had been a house slave in Virginia whose master had treated him so humanely that the soldier was at least as literate as Caleb himself. Reaching the porch, Caleb reflected how interesting it was that Lily's experiences with the buffalo soldiers mirrored his own.

When he entered his quarters, Will was seated at the table, writing a letter. He looked up and grinned at Caleb. "Out sparking, were you?"

"Sparking?"

"That is surely what it looked like to me. Sitting with that pretty Miss Lily fawning over her dessert and then taking a bit of a stroll. Reminds me of how I courted Fannie."

Caleb was still trying to understand. "Sparking? Courting? Is that what you think I was doing?"

"The signs are all there, Cap'n."

Caleb collapsed onto a wooden bench. "We're just friends."

"Are you convinced that's all?"

"Friendship. That's all I've ever intended."

Will laid down the pen and faced him. "That, my friend, is how it always starts, at least if the relationship has any future. Think about Fannie and me. If she says yes to my proposal, and I pray she will, then I'll be marrying not only my sweetheart, but my best friend."

"Marrying? Why, that's the furthest thing from my mind."

Will shot him a knowing look and before turning back to his letter, he simply said, "We'll see. But if I was a wagering man…" He let the sentence die.

Suddenly feeling confined by the four walls of the

room, Caleb headed for the door, grateful for the cooler evening air. He stood on the porch, his thoughts aboil, Will's words flustering him. Courting? Was that what others thought he was doing? Worse yet, could that be Lily's interpretation of his behavior, even though they both kept emphasizing friendship as the basis for their relationship?

If he was brutally honest, Caleb had to admit to flights of fancy where he'd imagined himself in the future with a wife like Lily. But that was a long ways down the road. Not now. Not here.

He shut his eyes against unwelcome memories of Rebecca. He had courted her once. He had loved her and, more fool he, had believed his affection was returned. He grunted in disgust. Not only was she faithless, but she had betrayed him with a man he had considered his friend. Will Creekmore's insinuations about Lily had struck fear in his heart. No man walks twice into the same trap.

He sank down on the top step of the porch, his elbows on his knees, hands dangling. Had he given Lily a false impression? Truth be told, he had come close to kissing her on a couple of occasions and had enjoyed holding her in his arms, but any fellow would be likewise tempted. He tried replaying their encounters in his mind. Surely he'd never been less than gentlemanly.

The problem was, he would now have to be more guarded around her, lest he mislead her. Anyway, how could he possibly fall in love when his future was uncertain and his past was a cautionary lesson? Beyond that, how could he inflict his nightmares on Lily or any woman? What kind of a man could expect a wife to share his demons? Or exorcise them?

For a moment, he wished he was like Will Creekmore, so sure of his love and confident about his future. Caleb assumed he would one day find a suitable mate, but the timing was all wrong now. In some ways it was a pity because it would be difficult to ever find someone as intelligent and compassionate as Lily.

Following the snake scare, Lily had experienced even greater difficulty abiding life on the prairie with all its hidden dangers. Despite the lack of an enclosed note, the latest package from Aunt Lavinia, containing new issues of *Peterson's Magazine* and programmes from concerts, had only whetted her desire to escape. Her sole refuges were the hospital, where work kept dissatisfaction at bay, and the library, where she could lose herself in a book.

With Effie Hurlburt's help, she was recruiting a group to offer a poetry reading during the first week in June. One of the Scots in the cavalry had volunteered to read Robert Burns's "To a Mouse," and Colonel Hurlburt had agreed to render Longfellow's "The Wreck of the Hesperus." Lily hoped Caleb would consent to read from *Paradise Lost,* but his troop was still out on a foray to root out small bands of Pawnees intent on preying upon the wagon trains.

One afternoon she and Effie found themselves alone in the quiet of the library as they searched for possible poems to include in the reading. Effie pulled out a slim volume including Elizabeth Barrett Browning's sonnet "How Do I Love Thee?" and handed the book to Lily. "This is a moving poem. Amid all the rough-and-tumble of the men's lives, they need an occasional sentimental touch. This might even bring a tear to the eye."

Lily scanned the familiar poem cataloging the forms of true love. For an unknown reason, she found herself profoundly moved. Such a love as that described by the poetess was rare.

"Well?" Effie asked. "Would you be willing to read it?"

"Me?"

"Yes. The words lend themselves to a gentle female voice. I know you could do it justice."

"You have more experience of love than I."

"Experience? Yes. But there is nothing like the first tender beginnings of a romance."

"I know nothing of that, either."

Effie responded with an affectionate smile. "Are you so sure, my dear? The way you and Captain Montgomery look at one another is enough to remind me of those heady first days with Hurly."

Lily was appalled. How could Effie jump to such a conclusion? "I don't mean to be rude, but you are mistaken if you think there is aught but friendship between the captain and me." She felt a compelling need to set the record straight. "In fact, I plan within a matter of months to be on my way to St. Louis to visit my aunt Lavinia. It is there I hope to establish my future."

If she had thought to sidetrack Effie, she was mistaken. "Be that as it may, Lily, I know a love match when I see one." Effie turned and replaced the book of poetry on the shelf. "Time will tell," she murmured.

Later that evening when a serious case of malaria required her presence in the hospital, Lily welcomed the distraction. As the patients fell asleep one by one, she found herself sitting quietly through the early hours of the morning with only her thoughts for company. Surely Effie was wrong. Caleb had always made it clear that theirs was a friendship, nothing more. Surely it was her *friend* she was missing while his troop was out in the field, because she had to admit, she often wondered about Caleb and prayed for his safety and that of his men. Any friend would do likewise.

Love was something altogether different. As Elizabeth

Barrett Browning had put it, "I love thee to the depth and breadth and height / My soul can reach…" Could a person ever achieve that degree of affection with another? Why Effie would think her capable of such feeling for Caleb, she couldn't imagine.

Irritated by that line of thinking, Lily rose from her chair and walked slowly through the ward, checking on the men. She could not explain why she was terrified of snakes, but able to deal calmly with unpleasant illnesses and ugly wounds, even finding in her nursing a kind of fulfillment. Perhaps the answer lay in the fact that she felt useful and skillful.

She settled back in her chair and was nodding off when she felt a gentle touch on her shoulder. She opened her eyes to find her father looking at her with concern. "Are you all right, daughter?"

"I'm finc, Papa. The men have been quite peaceful."

"Why don't you slip on home and get some rest now that I'm here?"

She stood and kissed him on the cheek. "Thank you." She paused and then went on. "And thank you for giving me this training and the opportunity to be of use."

"Lily, you are a highly qualified nurse, and I am proud of your dedication and skill."

Later as Lily slipped into bed beside Rose, she glowed. That was high praise from her father. Just before falling asleep she mused that it had been a strange day. First Effie's misconceptions about her relationship with Captain Montgomery, the thoughts about love the poem had raised for her and now her father's rare and heartfelt compliment. Yet a niggling concern persisted. How would she use her skills in St. Louis? She doubted the crowd Lavinia moved among thought it fitting for a young woman to minister to the needs of the ailing or maimed.

Her eyes were heavy, but she managed brief prayers. The last word on her lips before she fell asleep was *Caleb.*

The ride had been long and hot. Columns of dust billowed behind the hooves of their many horses. Early on in the mission, Caleb had felt reinvigorated. Action was welcome after weeks of routine drilling, but the constant glare of the sun and the wind cutting across their faces had made parts of their trek unrelieved misery. Maddeningly, the marauding Indians had been canny in their efforts to elude the troops. Even when the army scouts located them, often by the time the column of riders arrived at the rendezvous point, the enemy had vanished into the endless rolling prairie. The high point, thus far, had been searching for and finding a five-year-old boy who had wandered away from his wagon train encampment.

Despite the heat and the lack of success in fighting the Indians, it was a comfort to be back in the saddle, performing familiar functions and sleeping under the stars. The final night's bivouac was a scant ten miles from Fort Larned. After making a routine sweep among his men, most of whom were already asleep, he bedded down shortly before midnight.

He had barely closed his eyes when he was awakened by a sentry. "Horse thieves," he muttered. Caleb struggled into his boots, grabbed his rifle and took off at a lope toward the perimeter where the horses were tethered.

The sentry whispered hoarsely, "Indians. They're hiding among the horses."

Caleb whistled for Bucephalus, then fired a warning shot in the air. Several more troops staggered toward them. "Rout them out before they steal our horses."

Led by Caleb, several of the men plunged into the mass of horseflesh. With only a sliver of a moon for light, it was difficult to distinguish between horses and Indians, especially when they were adept at straddling an animal, clinging to the mane and dropping over the side so as to be undetectable.

Caleb leaped on Bucephalus, clutched his mane with one hand and prodded him forward. In the distance he could barely make out a group of eight horses slowly detaching from the herd. He galloped after them as they began moving more swiftly toward a nearby hill. To his right he noticed one of his cavalrymen. "Follow me!" he shouted. They charged into the open prairie fifty yards or so from the group of stolen horses. The Indians, slowed by the horses they were leading, tried to escape. By then a few more mounted cavalrymen had joined the hunt. When they narrowed the gap, Caleb yelled, "Spare the horses, but fire on the riders."

In the ensuing fray, three cavalry horses broke loose and galloped off, but five still remained in enemy hands. Every time Caleb thought he had a clear aim, the Indians changed direction. Finally he drew a bead on the leader. With one shot, he succeeded in bringing him down. Almost simultaneously, other deafening shots rang out, felling two more thieves. One pinto tore for the hills, its rider bent low.

The remaining horses were rounded up by morning. Thankfully, no cavalry mounts had been lost. The three dead Indians would either teach their fellows a lesson or incite them to retribution. Yet Caleb took no satisfaction in killing. This was a war without rules and little way to distinguish peaceable Indians from their more hostile numbers.

After burying the dead and packing their gear, the troop made its way toward the fort. Even considering the excitement and danger of the night, Caleb, instead of feeling spent, was energized. They had foiled the horse thieves and were headed home at last. The steady rhythm of horses' hooves and the creak-crack of saddle leather provided accompaniment for the mental exercise of preparing his report for the colonel. Before he knew it, they had crested the rise just beyond the fort. Something clenched within him, and he knew, despite Will Creekmore's remarks about courting, he had been counting the hours until he would see Lily again. As they trotted into the fort, it was all he could do to keep his eyes forward instead of sweeping the scene for her slight figure.

After securing the horses and checking in at headquarters, he and Will headed for their home and the welcome bath that awaited them. Will unpacked quickly, bathed first and then strode toward the sutler's to collect their mail.

Caleb had just finished shaving when Will burst through the door with a loud huzzah, waving a letter over his head. "She's coming! My Fannie's coming!" He danced a jig before stopping in his tracks, a large smile wreathing his face. "Cap'n," he said in a wondering tone, "my Fannie is going to marry me."

"You're a lucky man, Will."

"A blessed man," the lieutenant corrected him. "Blessed beyond all measure." He stared at the letter before slowly folding it and stowing it in his pocket. As if speaking only to himself, he said, "I am half a man without my Fannie."

Caleb turned away, lest he reveal too much of himself. Thanks to Rebecca, he knew that feeling of being half a man. Yet he, too, had a restless urge to complete himself, to know the kind of love Will celebrated.

That evening after supper, he sat rocking on the porch with Will, who smoked a cigar, its pungent aroma perfuming the night air. Mourning doves cooed in the distance. From the enlisted men's barracks came the sound of singing, the rich harmonies a plaintive reminder of so many nights around campfires.

Suddenly, his breath quickened. Lily came out of the library and stood for a moment, a small book clutched in her hand, scanning the officers' quarters. She must have seen him then, for she raised her hand in greeting.

He nodded, incapable of speech even if it had been called for.

Then she picked up her skirt and walked toward her home.

Caleb leaned back in the rocker, the sounds and the smells of the fort a comfort to him amid his questions. Had Lily been looking for him as he had been looking for her? And why, despite the need to exercise reason, had the sight of her filled him with such spontaneous joy?

Chapter Seven

Not for the first time Caleb wondered why he had agreed to take part in the poetry reading. It was one thing to find personal enjoyment in the genre, but quite another to expose himself to possible ridicule by his men. At least his selection—Milton's description of Satan's fall from Heaven—had teeth in it. He stood at the back of the commissary, listening to the others rehearse. Major Hurlburt did a fine Longfellow, but the wife of a junior officer massacred her assigned Shakespearean sonnet.

Effie Hurlburt, self-appointed director of the production, positioned the readers on the makeshift stage, then hurried to the back of the room to be certain each could be heard.

Caleb was surprised by Lily's absence. With her love of poetry, she, of all people, should be involved. As if anticipating his unvoiced question, Effie returned to the front and reviewed the program. "You will begin, Sergeant." She nodded at a barrel-chested man with oratorical skill who had selected "No More Words," a Civil War poem. "Then we will follow in the order by which we practiced, ending with Miss Kellogg's reading. Alas, duties at the hospital prevented her from joining us for rehearsal, but

I assure you she will provide a fitting conclusion for our evening's entertainment." She paused, eyeing them in the manner of a strict schoolmarm. "Now then, are there any questions?"

"Do you think anyone will come?" asked a jittery company clerk.

"If I have anything to say about it." Effie glanced smugly at the major. "And if I have to pull rank, I will." She smiled encouragingly at the clerk. "Listen to me, son. This is fine entertainment. Afterward, the others will all wish they could so commandingly declaim poetry."

Caleb mentally rolled his eyes. It would take more than that to impress some of the more jaded fellows, but even poetry trumped boredom.

As the group dispersed, Effie Hurlburt approached him. "Captain, would you kindly help me hang streamers from the walls? A bit of bunting will add a festive air to the proceedings."

As they went about their work, Effie chattered about the weather and offered tidbits of fort gossip. Caleb couldn't help wondering why she had selected him, rather than an enlisted man for this duty, but the answer soon came. When they finished, she turned to him. "For your labors, you deserve a reward. Escort me home for tea cakes and a spot of lemonade." From the brisk way she began walking toward her house, he had little choice but to follow.

At her door, she led him in and urged him to sit in what was clearly the major's armchair. When Caleb raised his eyebrows in question, she anticipated his concern. "You stay right there. Hurly's in his office working on a dispatch, so we won't be disturbed. Now, if you'll excuse me, I will see to our refreshments." She bustled from the room, leaving him to study the lacy antimacassars on the sofa and the Chinese vase on the fringed scarf atop the piano. It was almost as if Mrs. Hurlburt had lured him to her parlor for some purpose.

"Here we are." She set a tray on a nearby table. After she had served him his lemonade, she took her own drink and sat on the sofa facing him. Without preliminary, she said, "I understand you will be leaving the army late this summer."

"Yes, ma'am."

"It's just the two of us, dear. You don't need to 'ma'am' me. I'm Effie. Besides, we're just two friends having a cozy tête-à-tête." She paused to sip from her lemonade. "What are your plans after you muster out?"

He told her about working with his father and brother on the ranch.

"Then you should not be too far from here."

"About one hundred-fifty miles as the crow flies."

"Do you plan to marry and start a family?"

"Eventually, but that's down the road a long ways."

"Why?"

Her bluntness set him back. "I'm not ready yet. I need to get settled."

"Forgive an old woman's candor, but I think you're fooling yourself."

A trickle of perspiration worked its way down the small of his back. This was more inquisition than polite chat. "I'm sorry, but I don't understand."

"It's simple. Why are you waiting when golden opportunity is knocking at your door? You'll be hard-pressed to find the likes of Lily Kellogg again."

The light dawned. Just as he'd originally deduced, Effie Hurlburt delighted in matchmaking. "I do not dispute that she is a fine young woman. I value our friendship, but a friendship it must remain."

"Poppycock!" Effie pursed her lips. "I do not understand why you are deluding yourself when you are so clearly in love with Lily."

He couldn't have been more shocked if she'd suddenly turned into a lioness. He sputtered, searching for a response. "With all due respect, wouldn't I know that better than you?"

"Not at all. You young people can be oblivious to what's right under your nose." She fixed her eyes on him. "Are you going to sit there and tell me you've never thought of Lily as a potential wife?"

There was no satisfactory answer to that question. "No matter, because she would never regard me in that light."

Ellie's tinkling laughter unnerved him. "Are you daft, boy? She is crazy about you. She just hasn't admitted it to herself yet." She stifled a giggle. "And you? You big galoot. Whatever nonsense you tell yourself, you are in love with Lily Kellogg as all the world can clearly see."

In love? He couldn't be. He wouldn't be. Not after Rebecca's betrayal. "You mock me, ma'am."

"On the contrary, I'm trying to knock some sense into that thick head of yours. If you let Lily Kellogg get away, you'll regret it the rest of your life." She sat back, leaving the idea suspended in the silence. Then in a gentler tone, she said, "Now then, young man. Something is holding you back. What is it?"

He swallowed against the bitterness rising in his chest. "Love? It's not all poetry and moonlight." He bit off the words threatening to pour out of him. He'd already said too much.

"I see." Effie's expression softened. "So you've been hurt." She nodded in apparent sympathy, gazing at him with such affection that he felt embarrassed. "I understand you don't want to put yourself in that position again. And, yes, love involves risk. But are you convinced you want to let the woman who hurt you control your destiny?"

He looked at her quizzically. "What do you mean?"

"As long as you fail to act when love presents itself, you permit what she did to you to determine how you respond to new women in your life. Women like Lily. Tell me this. Was it Lily who hurt you? Lily who rejected you? No, so why do you make her the scapegoat for your past disappointments?"

Dumbfounded, he could scarcely take it all in. Effie Hurlburt had spared nothing in trying to open his eyes. "I hardly know what to say."

"No need to say anything. You could, of course, call me a romantic meddler, but I'd prefer you think of me simply as one holding up a mirror to what is already in your heart."

Desperate to avoid her penetrating gaze, he rose to his feet. "I appreciate your interest, but if you will excuse me, I really must take my leave." As she stood to usher him out, he relented and took her hand. "I have no mother, but if she were still alive, I know she would like you."

"That's a fine compliment, Captain." She squeezed his hand. "I'd like to think that she would say to you exactly what I've just said."

Over the next hours, he vacillated between irritation at Effie Hurlburt's interference and an attempt to probe the nature of his feelings for Lily. Could it be that others were seeing what he could not? Certainly Will Creekmore had come to the conclusion he was courting. Every time Caleb saw Lily it was as if his heart outpaced his brain. He was a soldier. Discipline was his stock-in-trade. Where Lily was concerned, though, he'd failed at governing himself. Even admitting his affection for her, could she ever accept a man flawed by the violence of battle? Yes, he had some serious thinking to do. He must face his reservations and come to a conclusion. Either court Lily or break off their friendship. While he would hate to end the latter, perhaps that was best. She could go her way, and he could leave the fort with a clear conscience and no encumbrances.

Once he'd decided that courting was out of the question, he spent the next day filled with relief. He'd made a decision. Now he merely had to act upon it.

That good intention prevailed only until the poetry reading. About half the troops turned out and were generally more attentive than he'd predicted. Some relished the poetry while others listened in bored stupefaction. Caleb had been well received, but he attributed that more to Milton's magnificent words than his own elocution.

As soon as the readers had presented their offerings, they took their seats in the audience. After a dull rendition of "The Destruction of Sennacherib," Lily came to the center of the stage for the finale. Lantern light cast an aura around her, creating a halo of her hair. She wore a misty sea-green dress, which made her resemble the beautiful lily for which she was named. Quiet settled over the audience. Then she began.

"How do I love thee? Let me count the ways.
I love thee to the depth and breadth and height
My soul can reach, when feeling out of sight
For the ends of Being and ideal Grace.
I love thee to the level of every day's
Most quiet need, by sun and candle-light."

Caleb clenched his hands. He was unmanned by her words. By her. Then in a voice that spoke to his soul, she continued.

"I love thee freely, as men strive for Right;
I love thee purely, as they turn from Praise.
I love thee with the passion put to use
In my old griefs, and with my childhood's faith.
I love thee with a love I seemed to lose
With my lost saints—I love thee with the breath,
Smiles, tears, of all my life!—and, if God choose,
I shall but love thee better after death."

Caleb heard neither the hushed silence when she finished, nor the thunderous applause which followed. Stunned, he choked back the sobs threatening to tear from his throat. Pain. Promise. Where did one end and the other begin? He had no answer. All he knew was that, come what may, for good or for ill, he was desperately in love with Lily Kellogg.

After the poetry reading, Lily was surrounded by well-wishers, eager to comment on her emotional delivery of Elizabeth Barrett Browning's sonnet. She caught a glimpse of Caleb across the room and hoped to find him later to congratulate him on his masterful reading of Milton. Given the fiery nature of the lines he read, she doubted even the most insensitive of his fellows would ever mock him.

"Miss Kellogg?" She'd noticed the private, barely out of his teens, waiting to speak with her and yielding his place to officers and their wives. Finally, the others had dispersed and he approached. "You don't know me, but I'm Private Sydney Long. I, well..." He ducked his head. "I wanted to tell you how moved I was by your poem."

"Private—may I call you Sydney?—I'm grateful for the compliment." The lad looked up, and she was astonished to see tears pooling in his eyes. "Dear me, are you all right?"

He pulled a handkerchief from his coat, turned aside and blew his nose. "I'm sorry, it's just that—"

"So you have a sweetheart, Sydney? Is that it?"

"*Had,* miss. *Had.* She died of the diphtheria."

"Mercy, I'm so sorry. Is there anything I can do for you?"

"You already did it, ma'am." Then, in a mournful tone, he recited, "'and, if God choose, / I shall but love thee better after death.'"

When he finished, Lily touched him gently on the shoulder. "Your young woman was lucky to have you, even for so short a time."

When the private moved toward the door, Lily studied the nearly empty room. She caught a glimpse of Caleb in the company of Lieutenant Creekmore. She considered hurrying after him to compliment him, but she didn't want to make a spectacle of herself or give rise to rumors. Just before Caleb left, he turned in her direction, but without raising a hand in greeting or otherwise acknowledging her. On his face was the strangest look—serious, yet detached, and more puzzled than welcoming. Almost as if he were a man she didn't know.

Thinking about it that night and most of the next day, she felt a prickly sense of uncertainty. Theirs had been an open and pleasant friendship, but that impression had been sorely compromised by his distancing stance at the reading. Had she done something wrong? Had something changed? And why did she permit such questions to plague her throughout the day?

Arriving home from her work at the hospital, the distraction of a letter from Aunt Lavinia pushed all thought of Caleb to the back of her mind.

Rose handed her the envelope, then stood wadding her

apron in her hands. "Open it, Lily, or I shall die of curiosity."

"I'm almost afraid. What if she thinks I've been presumptuous to write her and practically invite myself? Maybe I've offended her."

Rose, ever practical, harrumphed. "Quit stalling. No amount of fretting will change by one whit what's in that letter."

With a silent plea heavenward, Lily slit the envelope and extracted the letter, written on heavy stationery embossed with Lavinia's monogram.

My dearest niece,

I received your recent letter and am gratified by your interest in our fair city and your eagerness to visit Mr. Dupree and me. My understanding is that it is only you and, alas, not also your sister, Rose, who entertains the notion of traveling to St. Louis for what I hope can be an extended stay.

At this time, it is impossible for me to offer you firm plans for your trip. For a month this summer we will be traveling to New York City where Mr. Dupree has business and then on to stay with friends in Newport, Rhode Island, a welcome respite from a Missouri summer.

When we return from that trip, I shall have my husband's secretary investigate suitable means of transportation and establish a travel schedule for you. I regret the uncertainty of my response, but you may tentatively plan to leave Fort Larned sometime in August. It will be my pleasure to attend to the financial arrangements for your trip. We may anticipate September for your possible arrival, which will thankfully give us sufficient time to work with the dressmaker to sew you up a new wardrobe more suitable to the demands of the social events you will attend.

A shiver went down Lily's spine. Now that her dream was on the verge of being realized, she was overcome with trepidation. The fantasy of lovely gowns and sophisticated soirees had always been blessedly in the future; the genuine possibility now seemed daunting. What did she know of high society? Of ball gowns and coiffures? Caught up in the moment, she had nearly forgotten Rose, rooted to the spot, her face pale, her freckles prominent. "I can't believe it," Lily whispered. "It may actually happen."

"I want to be happy for you, I really do." Sniffling, Rose reached in her apron pocket and withdrew a handkerchief.

Lily wrapped her sister in her arms, and they clung to one another for several moments. Then Lily patted Rose's back. "Nothing has been decided," she said. "I won't count on anything until I have the tickets in my hand. We will simply wait to see what God has in store for me."

"Yes, that is best." Rose stifled a half giggle, half sob. "I am not about to question the Almighty, even though His ways can be mysterious."

A new thought struck Lily. "What shall we tell Father?" She worried about leaving him, especially since he'd already lost David and her mother.

"The truth. If and when it happens, your departure will trouble him sorely, even as he will understand it's the right course for you. Perhaps the longer he has to anticipate your leaving, the less painful will be the actual fact of it."

"Or will it just give him more time to fret?"

"There is no easy answer, Lily, but honesty is best."

Later as Lily sat darning her father's socks, she pondered the question of honesty. Of course, she wanted the adventure she'd always longed for, but leaving her father and sister was painful to contemplate. She had always blithely assumed they would flourish without her, but Private Sydney Long's loss had reminded her that nothing could be taken for granted or wished away.

Keyed up, Caleb repeatedly tapped the toe of his boot against the fence post. In the corral, horses milled, snorting and pawing as if sensing the onset of action. Behind him, men checked saddles and harnesses, while in the armory, weapons were being cleaned and oiled and ammunition stacked for transport. The anticipation of their upcoming mission coupled with the need for careful preparation set his nerves on heightened alert. This would be no ordinary foray into the prairie. Instead, they would be marching over fifty miles to engage a massing force of hostile Indians intent on protecting their tribal lands.

Although a small contingent would remain at the fort for protection, most of the troops would be leaving at sunrise the next day. Caleb wished he could share in the elation and bravado of his men, itching for a fight. Instead, he was experiencing nightmarish reservations about the looming engagement with a motivated and desperate band of Indians.

He shut his eyes against the remembered stench of the horses and smell of blood. He prayed this would be his final assault before leaving the army. August couldn't come soon enough. He had done his duty—and would do it the upcoming days—but his soldier's heart had deserted him. He knew that spelled trouble. He could ill afford to become overly careful or protective. A leader carries the charge to his men—skilled and fearless, an example of courage under fire.

He turned away from the corral. When had cynicism replaced idealism? Sadly, he knew, almost to the minute. On a winter's day at the Washita River. Determined to rid his mind of such grim phantoms, he walked briskly toward the officers' briefing with Major Hurlburt, resolving to focus on business.

Passing by the hospital, he flushed. All his best intentions of bravery in battle were one thing. Confronting his feelings for Lily was something else, strangely akin to cowardice. Effie Hurlburt had shot an arrow squarely into his heart. Listening to Lily read Elizabeth Barrett Browning's sonnet had opened the wound. How was it possible for him to be in love? How could he again expose himself to rejection? But with the swiftness of an eagle came his next thought. How could he leave Lily? Or imagine a life without her?

He had deliberately avoided her over the past week, knowing that until he could master his feelings, it would be unwise to see her, even as he longed to do that very thing.

Nearing headquarters, he paused, glancing up at the flag atop the pole. He had sworn loyalty to his country. How could he deny his feelings for either country or Lily and still regard himself as honorable? In that moment, he made up his mind. When he returned from this mission, he would declare his love for her. After he spoke with her, he would know one way or the other—either she returned his feelings or she didn't.

All day the atmosphere at the fort had been bustling, the troops purposeful as they made preparations for their departure the next morning. In the hospital, Lily heard much grousing among the men confined there. "I can't believe I'm missing this" and "My fellows need me, and here I am, laid up with a bum leg." Privately she was appalled by their appetite for warfare, but she supposed battle was part of their culture.

In the late afternoon, a young corporal suffering from a serious case of poison ivy tugged at her sleeve. "Miss, please, talk to the doctor."

"Pray tell, what for?"

"I can go with my men. I know I can." The urgency of his plea was a tribute to his sense of duty.

"Corporal, Dr. Kellogg has told you how dangerous it would be for you to leave and risk further infection."

"But it's cowardly to remain here."

"Never. The cowardice would lie in your possibly endangering others during the mission. The honorable course is for you to remain here, heal and be fit for the next call to duty."

He covered his eyes with his forearm. "You're right, but 'tis hard to be a slacker."

"No one will accuse you of that. If they do, they will have to deal with my displeasure."

He uncovered his eyes and managed a wan grin. "None of them boys would want to face the wrath of Miss Lily."

"Very well, then. Lie still and get some rest."

As she finished her duties and headed toward the cemetery, she felt a sense of accomplishment. She was not only a nurse, but, at times, a kind of counselor. She was often touched by the confidences her patients shared with her and, as with the corporal, their disappointments. Although she never forgot the specter of the terrible day of the storm and the leering Adams, thankfully now removed to Fort Riley, by and large she found the men to be both forthcoming and, ironically, vulnerable.

The late sun sent shafts of light sparkling through the leafy trees. After the high temperatures of the day, the shade gave at least an illusion of cool. Lily sank down on the grass beside her mother's grave and removed her bonnet. Not for the first time it occurred to her that if she went to St. Louis, she would leave not only her father and sister, but this sacred place where she communed with her mother's spirit. Only here did she feel a peace which often eluded her at the fort.

Engrossed in her thoughts, she only belatedly became aware of a figure standing several feet behind her. Looking around, she saw Caleb. He stood silent, erect, his expression unfathomable.

"I thought I would find you here," he said, extending a hand to help her to her feet.

"'Tis my custom," she said, avoiding his eyes. She had been halfway irritated with him ever since he so obviously ignored her at the poetry reading for reasons she could not imagine. Why had he bothered to approach her now?

"I know." Silence hung awkwardly between them.

"Well?" She clasped her hands in front of her and waited for some explanation of his presence.

"I ride out tomorrow."

"I wish you and your men a safe journey." Their conversation was perfunctory and stilted, and she chafed under the clumsiness of this meeting.

"Before leaving, I wanted to apologize for failing to compliment you on your poetry reading."

"I, likewise, would have complimented you, but, alas, you made a hurried retreat before I could do so." She cringed at the sarcasm in her tone.

"There was a reason for that."

"Ours is not to wonder why," she said.

He moved closer, staring at her so intently, she had to avert her eyes. "I was avoiding you."

Surprised, she looked up. "Whatever for? I thought we were friends."

"And so we are." He lifted a hand and gently caressed her hair.

Dwarfed by his broad shoulders and the sudden warmth in his voice, she felt herself grow breathless in response.

She struggled for the words that would still her racing heart. "I am glad of it," she finally said.

He tilted her chin, so that she was helpless to avoid his honey-brown eyes, swimming with affection. "Friends we are, but, Lily, is there a possibility we could be more than friends?"

Thunderstruck, she stared at him, trying to fathom the implications of his words. More than friends? Yes, she admired him. And, yes, in her bed in the dark hours of the night, she had admitted to an attraction to him. But... more than friends?

He gently cupped her face in his hands, preventing her from looking away, or even breathing. "Please, Lily. While I'm gone, say you'll think about us."

Us? Rioting emotions rendered her incapable of speech.

"Will you?" he asked in a low, insistent voice.

She would say anything to subdue the tingling she felt in every nerve. "Yes."

"Thank you, dear Lily," he murmured, just before leaning forward and kissing her.

Nothing had prepared her for the riot of emotions sweeping through her, for the undeniable need she had to feel his lips on hers or for her new, topsy-turvy sense of self.

He stepped back and held her hands in his. "We will talk when I return. I have much to tell you." He paused, then added with a rueful shake of his head, "And much to confess." He leaned down and picked up her bonnet, holding it tenderly against his chest before handing it to her. "I will miss you, Lily."

She couldn't help herself. The words popped out, uncensored. "And I you."

Then he was gone, leaving her standing in the twilight of the cemetery, warmth suffusing her body. What had she just promised? Whatever it was, it was profound. She turned and faced her mother's headstone. *Oh, Mama. What is happening to me?*

Chapter Eight

Along with the other women, Lily waited in the dawn watching the cavalrymen assemble on the parade ground, their postures erect, their eyes fixed on Major Hurlburt, mounted on a white steed. Other than the occasional nicker of a horse, it was eerily quiet. Rose stood on one side of her and Effie on the other. Walking his steed back and forth in front of his troops, the major began to speak.

"Duty calls us to restore order and peace to Kansas and the Indian Territory. We cannot afford to let the native peoples pose additional threats to the settlers moving through the frontier. Obey your officers, fight with valor and bring honor to these United States of America. Let us go with God and return safely." Then with a flourish, he wheeled his horse and led them from the fort.

Beside her, Effie drew a ragged breath, belying the usual calm she projected as the commander's wife. Stifling a sigh, Lily wondered into what dangers the men were advancing. They made a grand sight trotting in formation. The sound of hoofbeats and the clouds of dust made talking difficult, a relief to Lily. What words were there for such an expedition? She supposed that any being uttered were in the form of prayer.

What irony lay in the major's words to "go with God." Was it presumed God was partisan and would protect the soldiers while the enemy was killed? She wondered to whom the Indians prayed. She suspected both sides were capable of bloodlust and both of humanity.

From the first massing of the troops to the now diminishing line crossing the prairie, she had focused on Caleb, sitting erect in the saddle, his jaw set with purpose. Even after Rose and Effie wandered off, Lily remained, an arm around a post, watching as Caleb became nothing more than a speck on the horizon.

Tossing and turning in the night, she had examined and reexamined her encounter with Caleb in the cemetery. She had imagined the many different ways their conversation might have played out. She could have reacted angrily to his admission he had been ignoring her. She might have brushed his hand away when he touched her hair. And most certainly she could have rejected the surprising kiss. And what had ever possessed her to agree to "think about" something beyond friendship? Yet even in this recital of possible alternatives, she could never bring herself to renounce her final statement to him, because it was true. She would, indeed, miss him.

Yet she was disturbed by what he might tell her when he returned. He had used the word *confess*. He must carry some burden unknown to her. She had already observed that he was tight-lipped about his past, especially his war experiences. Most soldiers had their individual stories. Some shared their adventures with gusto; others remained steadfastly silent. She suspected Caleb was in the latter group. She wondered how a "confession" might change him and the nature of their relationship.

When the last of the horses disappeared over a hill,

she glanced around the fort—too empty, too quiet, the life seemingly having gone out of it with the departure of the soldiers.

She walked slowly toward the house, caught up in the one memory she couldn't dismiss, no matter how she rationalized it. The kiss. Surprisingly sweet, it had aroused emotions in her with which she had no experience. Why, she had practically swooned at the delicious sensation of his lips warm and soft on hers. If she was honest, as Rose reminded her they always should be, she was attracted to Caleb in ways it was no longer possible for her to deny. Perhaps their *friendship* was a mere code word for feelings they both had been fighting—feelings they would need to confront when he returned.

Lost in thought, she didn't see Effie standing on her front porch. "Lily, could you spare me a minute? I am in need of a friend."

Grateful for the intrusion upon her disturbing thoughts, Lily climbed the steps to the porch. "Happily. I am not yet due at the hospital."

"Sit with me, then," Effie said, gesturing to the wooden rockers. "I find the void after Hurly leaves difficult to bear."

A flash of empathy stirred Lily. "The fort has lost vibrancy, that's for certain."

"It never changes, this leave-taking. You would think I might have grown accustomed to it by now." Effie rocked awhile in silence before going on. "Hurly and I are a true love match, and I simply cannot contemplate a life without him."

"We must continue, as always, to pray for the safety of our men."

"And to busy ourselves so that the time will seem to elapse more quickly."

"Is that ever really possible?"

The older woman smiled at the absurdity of it. "Never."

"Effie, thank you for setting such an example for us. We would all be blessed by a relationship like the one you and the major share."

Effie eyed her shrewdly. "Do you think such a match is possible for you?"

"Perhaps. When I meet the right man."

"And when might that be?"

"I am hoping to meet someone when I go to St. Louis to visit my aunt."

"Ah, I see." Effie slowed her rocking. "The perfectly handsome, sophisticated, successful man-about-town. Am I correct?"

For reasons Lily couldn't grasp, the image Effie had created sounded downright distasteful. She felt her cheeks redden. "Something like that."

"Posh. Why hold out for a fantasy man when you have a flesh-and-blood man right here who loves you with all his heart?"

Caught off guard, Lily could only stammer. "Ef-effie? You're quite mistaken."

The older woman hooted. "Oh, child, I know you're doing your best to discourage Caleb Montgomery and stifle your feelings, but mark my words. God has brought you two together for a purpose. You can fight it if you want, but in the end, you'll remember this conversation and allow as how Effie Hurlburt knew a thing or two about love."

"It is true I am fond of the captain, but—"

"Stop right there. No *but*'s. For now, being fond of him will do."

Lily had the distinct impression that based on some innate, superior knowledge, Effie was inwardly laughing at her—that she knew Lily's feelings went beyond fondness. How she had stumbled into this awkward conversation she had no idea, but she knew she needed an escape. She consulted the watch suspended from a chain around her neck. "Dear me, I must fly to the hospital." She rose then, and as she prepared to leave, laid a hand on Effie's shoulder. "We will all help you pass the time until the men are safely home. I know the major will make haste to return to you."

Effie smiled. "Thank you, dear. May that day come in God's good time."

Walking toward the hospital, Lily was struck by the message she continued to receive from so many sides—everything in God's good time. That included her upcoming conversation with Caleb.

That night Lily was awakened by a ferocious wind howling around the house and rattling the panes of window glass. In the intermittent flashes of lightning, she could see clouds of airborne dust swirling through the air. A clap of thunder seemed to split the house in two. Somehow Rose continued sleeping, oblivious to the maelstrom outside.

Lily stepped out of bed and pulled her robe over her gown before tiptoeing downstairs. She didn't like storms, especially since she'd arrived here and heard troubling stories about cyclones and the damage they could inflict. Despite telling herself she was safe, she trembled with fear each time the wind battered the walls. Entering the kitchen, she was surprised to find her father sitting at the table in the dark, a blanket pulled about him. "Papa, you couldn't sleep, either?"

"No, but then I've always enjoyed watching storms."

She knew there was more to it. Perhaps at times like this, his thoughts, like hers, turned to Mathilda's and David's absence. She sought to divert him. "And maybe you're standing watch over two young ladies and a few men in a hospital?"

In the illumination of lightning, she saw a grin crease his face. "That, too."

Just being in his company, she noticed that her shivering had ceased and the knots in her stomach had eased. They sat in companionable silence until her father spoke. "Lily, perhaps we should talk about Captain Montgomery."

She gripped the edge of the table. "Papa, whatever do you mean?"

"He has taken quite an interest in you."

"What is the harm? We are friends."

Ezra sighed. "These are the times when I wish your mother was still alive. I am hopeless at delicate conversations." He paused, as if marshaling his thoughts. "While there has been no unseemly talk, many of us have noticed that he seeks you out and enjoys your company. I have no doubt that thus far, your relationship with him has been within the bounds of propriety. But—"

Out of the blue came the image of Caleb's kiss and the forbidden thoughts it gave rise to. Lily hoped the dim light masked her blush.

"—it is a father's duty to caution that you must not encourage a man's attentions unless you have deep feelings for him."

"Papa, you know I cannot undertake a romantic relationship. You know Mother's dream and mine has been that I might one day go to St. Louis."

"Does *he* know that?"

She shrugged. "No, but it is of no consequence."

"My dear, I fear you are misreading the captain's intentions."

Was she? What exactly had Caleb meant about moving beyond mere friendship? So confused had she been by their conversation and the memorable kiss that she had avoided full consideration of his remarks. How naive she must appear. "Help me understand, Papa."

"The captain will one day be leaving the army. If he is like most, he will want to settle down, establish a home… marry. Has it occurred to you he may think of you in that regard? If so, you have the potential to hurt him. I would hate to see that happen for you or to such a good man."

She stiffened her back. "I am going to St. Louis. I will make that clear to him when he returns."

"You are decided, then?" When she nodded her head, he continued. "I confess I have entertained the hope that you might give up that dream and stay with Rose and me. Or perhaps marry an army man."

She knew he was referring to Caleb. But marriage? In a flash of insight, she realized she had not been forthcoming with Caleb. She vowed she would tell him of her St. Louis visit as soon as he returned. It would not do for him to think she was toying with his affections. Above all, she did not want to inflict any further pain upon him.

"Lily?" Her father succeeded in regaining her attention. "Regardless of what I think or want, you must follow your heart, both in matters of love and in self-fulfillment. Much as I would like, I can no longer protect you from the world nor be the arbiter of your behavior and decisions. Your mother and I always wanted the very best for you, but I see now it has to be *your* best, not ours."

Never had Lily loved him more than in that moment. She rounded the table, came up behind him and put her arms around his shoulders, resting her chin on his head.

"Thank you, Papa. I will search for happiness, and when I find it, I will thank you."

A comfortable silence fell, punctuated only by the sound of raindrops on the roof.

Storms alternating with hot humid days had made conditions during the march challenging. Once the cavalry reached the area from which they would launch their attack, the rains disappeared, leaving only the unrelieved misery of sun and high temperatures. Caleb did his best to circulate among the encamped men and keep them motivated, but as time dragged on, the weather, bugs and winds took their toll. Mealy rations and the long wait did nothing to improve conditions. Lurking in all their minds was the upcoming task of subduing the Indian uprising. The veterans knew full well with what ferocity the tribes could fight and how fearlessly the warriors faced death.

Now with the attack set for the next day, the men grew increasingly quiet and restive. By midmorning Caleb felt perspiration dampen his undershirt. He ran a brush through his gritty hair and buttoned his jacket before heading out to Major Hurlburt's command tent for a briefing.

Along the way, he passed by a slightly built private sitting against a tree, scribbling on a piece of paper. "Sir?" The fellow stood up, then looked about as if fearing detection. "Would you deliver this message to Miss Lily? Well, you know—" he cleared his throat "—if something happens to me."

Caleb wondered how the young man was acquainted with Lily, but set that thought aside as he observed the fear in the private's eyes. He took the proffered note, then stepped closer so as not to be overheard. "Son, have you been in battle before?"

The soldier hung his head. "Just once, but that time

the Indians ran away. I, uh, I don't think that'll happen this time."

"Nor do I." Caleb had seen it before—the terrifying projections made by raw soldiers. Any reasonable man would admit to some fear, but paralyzing fright ill-suited a soldier in the thick of an attack. "You will see action tomorrow, but remember that you will be surrounded by battle-hardened, well-trained comrades. We live as a unit and we fight as a unit. They will do their part, and you will do yours." He clapped a hand on the youth's shoulder and looked deep into his eyes. "Rely on your training and instinct. We're counting on you, son."

"Yes, sir. Thank you, sir."

Caleb pocketed the note, then turned away, concerned for the untested soldier about to come under fire. From naive, idealistic boys playing fifes and drums to grown men deserting their fellows in the thick of an engagement, warfare took the measure of a man and cruelly destroyed illusions. He groaned inwardly. Only time would tell whether his talk with the private had stirred his fighting blood.

Inside the command tent, the officers huddled around a field map. Studying the terrain, they ultimately decided on a three-prong approach. Lieutenant Smythe would march on ahead to outflank the enemy from the west, Will Creekmore would lead his men on the east flank and Caleb, the most experienced of the officers, would direct the frontal charge from the south. The plan was to force the enemy back against a line of sand hills. While many of the Indians would be armed with lances and bows and arrows, a significant number also possessed rifles. The cavalry would set out at 3:00 a.m. to be in place for a sunrise attack.

Caleb spent the rest of the afternoon and early evening

speaking with his men, checking their preparations and offering encouragement. After the sun set, he retreated to his tent, lit a lantern and pulled out the small, leather-bound volume of Tennyson's poems he always carried with him. However, between his nerves and the discomfort of his scratchy uniform, he couldn't concentrate. His thoughts were elsewhere. Could he acquit himself with honor one last time on the battlefield, even though he had come to believe that his tolerance for warfare had run its course?

Sitting there, watching darkness blot out light, he closed his eyes and tried to picture the lush green grass of spring in the Flint Hills where the Montgomery Ranch's healthy herd grazed. There under vast blue skies, he could build something permanent and productive. Tomorrow, by contrast, would be characterized by bloodshed. He closed his eyes, formulating a prayer. *Dear God, deliver us from danger, protect us from our own worst selves and make us always aware of Your ultimate goodness.* The words seemed inadequate, but he knew that somehow God understood the yearnings of his heart.

One battle. One day. Then they would return to Fort Larned. He would return to Lily. Until then he would hold her in his heart in the full and surprising knowledge of his love for her. He drew in a sharp breath with the realization that not for a long time had he personally had so much cause to desire his own deliverance in armed conflict.

Lily awoke with a start, her damp gown wrapped around her legs, her heart racing. Not one breeze filtered through the open window to cool her feverish skin. Beside her Rose gently snored. Lily tried to get her bearings. What had so abruptly awakened her? She heard nothing unusual. Creeping to the window, she scanned the quiet, nearly deserted fort. All appeared normal. Stars twinkled in the sky and the sliver of a moon rested on the horizon.

Yet she was in a panic. Something was terribly wrong. Had a nightmare thus upset her? Snippets of a dream slowly came to her. Screams. Tortured screams. Suffocating dust. Then she remembered being part of a long line of mounted soldiers galloping off a cliff. "Into the valley of death." Tennyson's lines swirled alongside chaotic visions. No matter how she tried to orient herself to reality—to her bedroom and the quiet army post outside the house—she felt only the presence of doom.

How long had the cavalrymen been gone? She counted the days. Nearly two weeks. A long time. A sense of dread came over her. Were the men of Fort Larned in danger?

Under the cover of darkness, the mounted troops slowly advanced toward their attack position. Caleb could only imagine their thoughts. Anticipation was almost the worst part of battle. As they waited with drawn breaths astride quivering horses, each moment seeming at once an eternity and a flash, and they longed for action even as they prayed never to hear the order to advance.

Unbidden memories washed over Caleb—the adrenaline rush of the first charge, the cacophony of gunfire mingled with the screams of the wounded and dying, and the slippery earth, sodden with sweat and blood. He hated it. That realization took him by surprise. Never before had he so openly admitted his reservations about being a soldier. He squared himself in the saddle and stroked Bucephalus's neck. Pray God, he would use that hatred to fuel his courage.

Then came the strident bugle summons. Following Caleb's lead, his troop raced toward the Indian encampment, flags flying and weapons drawn. Then all rational thought was overwhelmed by a rain of gunfire and a long line of mounted braves charging toward them with frenzied battle cries. Caleb found himself surrounded in a sea of clashing forces, lances and arrows too often finding victims among his men. An Indian with startling war paint raced toward him, shrieking like a banshee. Only at the last minute did Caleb succeed in shooting him through the chest. The man fell from his horse as if in slow motion. Behind Caleb, another brave raised his rifle, and he avoided that shot only by ducking low over his mount's head. Wheeling around, he dropped his assailant. Out of the corner of his eye, he noticed several soldiers whose horses had gone down, leaving them relatively defenseless. He spurred to their side, handed his pistol to one and then rallied others to form a defensive position behind the horseless soldiers.

All up and down the line pandemonium raged. Several of his men lay on their backs, arrows still quivering from their chests. In the thick of it, Caleb could not tell whether Smythe and Creekmore had yet attacked from the flanks. He devoutly hoped so, or his men would become victims rather than victors.

The sun crested over the battlefield, illuminating downed bodies and soldiers locked in hand-to-hand combat with their nearly naked foe. Caleb could hardly take in the shattering violence of it all. What in God's name were they doing? With angry tears, he turned away from the sight, bent on going to the rear to urge his men forward to reinforce their fellows.

Kicking Bucephalus, he bellowed into the din. "Rally, boys, rally!" Reaching the reinforcements, he had just turned to urge them forward when the sky exploded in a blinding flash of color. His vision blurred and nausea clogged his throat. Sounds, as if wrapped in cotton batting, echoed far, far away. Why couldn't he hold on to the reins? Caleb's last conscious thought was how awkward and unsoldierly it was to slip from a horse and end up facedown in buffalo grass.

Chapter Nine

After supper a few nights following her nightmare, Lily sat on the porch with Rose, both of them fanning themselves. A pall had fallen over the fort. Even the usual racket of the cicadas sounded listless. No lively harmonica music issued from the barracks, and dogs lay motionless on doorsteps, panting. The sinking sun was a molten stone and nary a wisp of cloud adorned the sky.

Lily rested her head against the back of her rocker. In a strange way, her body felt as if she were constantly holding her breath. Indeed, the entire fort seemed to be suspended in time, waiting for something, anything, to happen.

"Remember last March when we talked about dreading summer?" Rose fanned herself more vigorously. "This is what we meant."

"Memory can't compare with the real thing." Given the heat, Lily was grateful that because of the cavalry's absence, they had few patients in the hospital. She had perfunctorily gone through the motions of reviewing the inventory, changing sheets and linens, and restocking the medicine chest. Yet even those duties failed to fill the time dragging by interminably.

"Do you suppose it's this hot in St. Louis?" Rose asked.

"Lavinia's letters suggest that summer is even worse there with the humidity from the river."

"Malaria." Rose sniffed in disapproval. "The newspapers are full of stories of how widespread the disease is in low-lying places."

"Are you trying to tell me something?"

Rose's expression softened. "I don't intend to borrow trouble, but I want you to be safe when you leave us."

"*If* I leave you." Lily gestured with an arm at the expanse of the fort. "Besides, there are plenty of dangers and diseases right here, and working in the hospital, I've already encountered most." She went through a mental catalog: typhus, diphtheria, snake bite, influenza and, even here, the occasional case of malaria. She winced against the memory of the ordeal of the woman who died in childbirth.

Rose grudgingly agreed. "I suppose."

Lily sensed that Rose had something she wanted to say. "You're a good sister to worry about me."

"I try not to, but I do. With our dear brother gone, I worry even more about you. How you will make the trip to St. Louis, what ruffians you might encounter and even how you'll be received by the elegant people you will meet there. It seems such a strange world to me."

Lily wouldn't admit that her sister had just voiced some of her own concerns. "A different society, assuredly, but one I long to experience."

The two sat rocking, praying for the hint of a breeze to relieve the oven of the porch. Lily finally spoke. "We talk a great deal about my dreams, but, Rose, what about yours? What is it you want in life?"

"Oh, Lily, I'm a simple soul. For now, I'm content keeping house for Papa. I confess I've thought about marriage and a family someday, but I'm no beauty and most fellows look for that."

Lily interrupted. "But you have so much to offer."

"Even if that were true, most men don't view me as a potential mate."

"It will be a very special one, indeed, who recognizes your inner beauty as I do."

"I try not to dwell on the future," Rose said with a sad smile. "What will be, will be, according to God's plan."

Lily sat forward with a sense of urgency. "Promise me you won't compromise. You deserve a good man who will cherish you as Papa and I do."

"Just as you deserve such a one, sister." Rose rocked for a few moments before adding, "One like Captain Montgomery."

Lily sank back in her chair. First Effie, then her father and now Rose. Was the entire fort conspiring to engage in matchmaking? And was this pressure coming from a genuine sense that Caleb was right for her or a desire to keep her from going to St. Louis?

"You, too? Why is everyone pushing Caleb at me?"

"Now don't get touchy. Maybe we see something you don't want to acknowledge."

Lily felt suddenly suffocated, not just by the heat but by others' expectations. She couldn't deny the attraction she felt to the handsome captain who shared her love of literature or the sense of safety and comfort she felt in his arms, but she had advanced too far with her dream of the city to jeopardize it for a summer fling.

Hearing footsteps, the two women simultaneously looked up. Their father, his shoulders drooping, approached from the direction of the cemetery. Lily knew he sometimes went there to seek peace just as she did.

Lily stood. "Papa, come rest a spell with us."

He raised his hand in greeting as he approached. "Gladly." He mounted the porch, pulled a vacant rocker nearer to them and sat down. "It's the calm before the storm," he said.

Rose examined the horizon. "I don't see any clouds."

"Not that kind of storm, child. The kind humans make." He folded his hands in his lap, but his thumbs circled each other in a nervous dance. "This is the period of inertia followed by the loosening of hell."

"What do you mean?" Lily asked.

"The war. Field hospitals. We would experience an unearthly calm before an attack followed immediately by the chaos of bodies upon bodies piling up around us." He seemed to choke back both his words and his memories. "I have that same sense tonight."

Despite the heat, Lily shivered. "About our troops?"

"Maybe it's just an old man's premonition."

Rose leaned toward him. "About what exactly?"

Ezra sighed forlornly. His words fell like stones into a deep well. "About the fact that Lily and I are soon to get very busy." He clutched Lily's hand. "My dear, I fear you have not yet seen battle wounds on the scale I am anticipating."

Early the next morning Lily was awakened by the bugle's alarm followed by the sound of a galloping horse. Hurrying to the bedroom window, she saw one of the scouts dismount and run toward the house. Her father must've heard him, too, for he stepped out on the porch before the soldier could knock. Through the open window she heard the man's breathless words.

"Prepare the hospital, Doctor. I regret to report that we have several casualties." He paused to catch his breath and then added with awful finality, "And deaths."

* * *

During the next few hours while the ambulance wagons were en route to the fort, Ezra Kellogg corralled the enlisted hospital aides, reviewed procedures, and exhorted them to stay calm and follow his orders. Meanwhile, Lily rounded up some of the women to serve as a soothing presence and assist with follow-up care. Rose busied herself at the stove preparing tisanes and broths. Lily prayed she could remain professional and bring her experience to bear for the benefit of the wounded. About the dying…she couldn't even contemplate. Nor could she let her mind assume the worst about those she knew. About Caleb. Sadly, there was no mistaking the cause of the hammer blows emanating from the carpentry shop. Coffins.

Just as the first wagon rolled into the fort, Ezra took Lily aside. Putting his arm around her as if to steady her, he said in a low voice, "Daughter, you are going to see things I had always hoped to spare you, but I need you today. The wounded need you. No one else has your skills." He pulled her closer and uttered a brief prayer that they might be instruments of God's healing. Then the first wagon arrived at the hospital, and from that point on, the groans of the wounded and Ezra's barked orders filled the room along with the odors of alcohol, sweat and blood.

After the litters were unloaded from the wagon, Ezra moved swiftly from man to man assessing injuries. One he immediately sent to the operating table; another, already feverish, was taken by Effie and a stunned private to be stripped and bathed in cool water. A terrified-looking Carrie Smythe administered chloroform just before Ezra amputated the first soldier's left leg. Out of the corner of her eye, Lily watched Carrie nearly swoon before collecting herself, but Lily had no time to intervene. She was too busy cleansing the dirty head wound of a dazed sergeant.

From him, she moved on to a lad whose makeshift bandage was coming loose.

Time lost all meaning as the hospital crew worked frantically to patch up those with minor wounds and deal with the pressing needs of the more grievously wounded. Lily wiped perspiration from her moist brow, willing perseverance in these difficult conditions. Two more ambulance wagons discharged soldiers in all stages of distress. Some had suffered arrow wounds; others, gunshot wounds. A few, as a result of losing their mounts in the thick of the conflict, had broken bones, including Lieutenant Creekmore. Aside from the calm orders of the surgeon, the grinding of his saw and the swish of skirts as the women moved from cot to cot, the only sounds were piteous groans and cries of "Mother" or "Help me."

Dear God, yes, help them and grant them relief from pain. Lily hoped her prayers and those of others would suffice, since unfortunately the fort had been without an assigned chaplain for some months.

Although she recognized several of the wounded, Lily was relieved that so far Caleb appeared to have been spared. That comfort deserted her when patients were unloaded from a late-arriving fourth wagon. She saw him immediately, his eyes closed, his face ashen, his breath coming in faint wheezes. Her legs started to go out from under her, and she had to grab the arm of a nearby soldier to keep from falling. The man shook his head regretfully. "We tried to get Cap out first, but he came to just long enough to order us to remove the others first."

Recovering herself, Lily ran to her father, who had just finished a second amputation. "Papa, come quickly. I fear Captain Montgomery is mortally wounded."

As her father examined the field-dressed shoulder wound which had stained Caleb's jacket a deep red, Lily steeled herself by concentrating her anger at an enemy who had inflicted harm on so fine a man and by praying, *Save him. Save him.*

Ezra beckoned both Lily and Caleb's litter bearers to follow him to the operating table, recently vacated by the amputee. "Lily, I need you to be strong. His only chance depends upon whether I can extract the bullet lodged so close to his heart. If I am successful, I will need you to bathe the wound and suture it closed."

Once more, Lily fought off light-headedness. "Yes, Papa." Her hands shook so that she could hardly imagine how she would be able to thread the needle, much less close the wound. Caleb lay so still, his arms resting at his sides. She picked up his nearer hand, cold to the touch, and held it in her own. She felt the calluses on his palm, saw embedded dirt beneath his fingernails and, to her relief, felt a pulse under her index finger. Her thoughts and emotions whirled. *Focus,* she reminded herself. *You've done this before.* An orderly bared Caleb's shoulder, revealing an ugly-looking open wound. Carrie, her eyes the size of small pancakes, poured chloroform onto a cloth, and Ezra reached for his instrument.

In that moment, a miraculous calm enveloped Lily, and her whole world reduced to the supine body on the table and the function she was to perform. Ezra's face screwed up with concentration. When his initial efforts to probe for the bullet were unsuccessful, his eyes met Lily's from across the table. "I don't know, daughter."

"Please, Papa. Try once more."

Ezra bent to his task and then, by changing his angle, found the bullet. "Aah," he breathed, pulling it from the wound.

Without conscious thought, Lily cleansed the wound and then carefully sutured it shut, thanking God that sewing was her talent. Throughout the procedure, Caleb's respiration remained shallow. She dared not ask her father about his chances. It was enough that Caleb had survived thus far.

The orderlies moved him to a cot near the window where several of his men already lay. Lily was shocked to see that night had fallen. Yet with that realization, she began to feel the wretched ache in the small of her back, the crick in her neck and the fog of exhaustion threatening her. The hospital was quieter now, and she saw the figures of men and women sitting beside the patients, cooling their faces with damp cloths or murmuring encouragement.

She gathered up Caleb's undershirt and jacket, holding them in her arms as a kind of perverse good luck charm. When her father nodded to her in dismissal, she couldn't leave. Instead, she sat on the chair beside Caleb, studying his pale face and willing his recovery. Sleep was necessary as a restorative, but how she wished just once he would open his eyes and whisper her name.

She began to fold his garments. In one pocket she felt a bulge and, inserting her fingers, came into contact with an envelope. Slowly she drew it out and stared at the name on the front—hers. Was it something Caleb had written? Curious, she slit the flap and pulled out a single sheet of paper. The signature took her by surprise. *Sydney Long.*

In the dim light she barely made out the scrawled words.

My dear Miss Lily,
I asked Cap'n Montgomery to give this to you in case I don't make it back. I'm a'scared of this battle, but not of dying. If I pass on, I'll dwell in eternity with my sweetheart, and you know I been a'grieving her sorely. The Almighty knows better than us'ns

what we need. So if I'm supposed to be with my beloved now, please write my parents and tell them I've made my peace.

Your friend,

Sydney Long

Tears obscured the sad message. She dabbed at them, then reread the letter. Glancing down at Caleb, then around the room, she felt her heart break. What could possibly be the purpose of the human carnage she saw around her? Where was God in this?

She knew what she had to do next, whether she wanted to or not. Adjusting the sheet around Caleb's shoulders and placing a hand on his warm forehead in blessing, she stood, left instructions with an orderly and walked out of the hospital, across the parade ground toward the carpenter shop.

There, driven into a post by a nail, was a scrawled list she had hoped never to read. Steeling herself, she approached the post. In the dim light of a flickering lantern, she read the names of the five men killed in action. The fourth was *Long, Sydney, Pvt.*

Returning home, Lily saw through her tears the figures of Major and Mrs. Hurlburt sharing an embrace on their front porch. Relieved for Effie, Lily fell into her bed, not pausing to remove her clothes in case she was suddenly called to the hospital. She needed to sleep, but every time she closed her eyes, images of wounded soldiers, looking strangely like David and Caleb, jolted her awake. She was used to dealing with illnesses and the occasional accidental wound, but nothing had prepared her for the numbers and severity of battlefield injuries. Most would survive if they could avoid infection. But Caleb? She stuffed a fist in her mouth to avoid waking Rose with her outcry. Beyond the threat of infection was the specter of pneumonia. He would need constant monitoring.

She pictured him as she had seen him that day at the ball field—young, vigorous, even playful—and at the cemetery where he had listened and calmed her fears. The memory of a sweet baritone singing "Aura Lee" filled her ears. She rolled over, away from her sister, lest Rose awaken and see her crying. *Is there a possibility we could be more than friends?* Caleb had asked before leaving on this mission. He had expected an answer when he returned, an answer now deferred by his precarious state and one for which she had, as yet, no clear response.

There was no question they were drawn to one another. On her part, could their bond be simply a result of gratitude for his twice saving her or of the ennui of post life? She wiped her tears with the edge of the sheet. All such issues were moot, pending the outcome of his injury. At heart, though, he was special to her.

She lay on her side, knees pulled up to her chest, listening to her sister's soft breathing. In the dark, she began whispering the Twenty-third Psalm. "'The Lord is my shepherd, I shall not want… Yea, though I walk through the valley of the shadow of death, I will fear no evil; for Thou art with me…'" Her heavy eyes fluttered closed and she felt herself drifting away to oblivion. "'…and I will dwell in the house of the Lord forever.'"

Something was fighting her. Fists pummeled her; she struggled but could not escape. Burrowing under a blanket, she resisted, but voices kept calling her. "Hurry!" "Come now!" Surfacing from a distant dream world, she realized no one was pummeling at all, just gently shaking her. Opening her eyes, she beheld Rose standing over her. "Wake up, Lily. Papa needs you in the hospital."

Groggy, Lily sprang from the bed. How long had she been asleep? Rubbing her eyes, she observed the faintest cracks of light seeping through the window. Dawn. She buttoned up the collar of her dress and tried to shake out the creases. Stepping to the mirror, she repaired her hair, all the while filled with alarm. "Tell Papa I'll be there momentarily," she told Rose, who was already hurrying down the stairs.

By the time she arrived at the hospital, some of the patients were stirring and occasional moans betrayed their discomfort. She scanned the room and quickly spotted her father bent over Caleb's cot. With a thudding heart, she hurried toward him. During the night, someone had put an extra pillow beneath his shoulders, so that he was semireclined. Even at a distance, she could see from his flushed face that he was feverish. His hair was matted with sweat, and as she approached, he flung one arm off the cot. "Papa?"

Her father looked up, and in his bloodshot eyes she read both exhaustion and deep sorrow. "The captain is delirious and needs to be kept still. He is fighting infection. You will need to bathe his face and chest with cool water and stay with him lest he begin thrashing about." He glanced around the room. "We have sufficient help for the others." He nodded at a young enlisted man carrying a basin toward them. "Private Nathan will assist you and fetch anything you need."

"The baby!"

Both Lily and her father started at Caleb's sudden harsh cry.

"Get the baby. The baby!" The word *baby* reverberated from the rafters.

Shaking his head, Ezra rose to his feet and handed Lily

the damp cloth he'd been using. Lily's throat was paralyzed with fear. "Papa?"

He stood a moment or two without speaking, then pulled her into his arms. "It's in God's hands now." With a heavy sigh, he released her. "Do what you can for him, Lily."

Lily crumpled into the bedside chair, knowing that no base Corporal Adams or vicious serpent had ever filled her with the terror now consuming her being.

Colors. Firebursts. Reds. Yellows. Flashes of white. Then blankets of black. He kicked his horse, spurring him on, but no matter how vigorously he urged the steed, the beast refused to move. *Help her! Help her, I say.* Dropping the reins, he leaned over, stretching out his arms for the doll. *The doll. I'll save it, little girl.* Then suddenly he was grasping not a doll, but a dry shuck of corn. Where was the little girl? The doll?

A mewling sound like that of a trapped kitten. Where? *The baby! Help the baby!*

A heavy weight crushed his lungs. A savagely painted warrior straddled his chest mouthing words he could neither hear nor understand. Flailing. Flailing. He could fight him off, couldn't he? Couldn't he? Then came the thunderous roar—a cannon blast throwing up blue-clad bodies and great clumps of earth. *Charge!*

Then he was thrashing in cold water, fighting the current, futilely grabbing at tree branches traveling past him in a green haze.

Breathing. Too hard. He couldn't find the word. The one he needed. The one that would make the difference. The cold river water filled his mouth, slithered down his windpipe and clogged his lungs. The word, the word.

Help!

* * *

Every half hour throughout the day, Lily sent Private Nathan to fetch more cool well water. As she bathed Caleb and smoothed his damp hair back from his feverish forehead, she hummed softly. Hymns. The familiar tunes eased her body and brought a kind of suspended peace to her soul. She couldn't explain it, but here in the midst of life and death, surrounded by those victimized by man's inhumanity to man, instead of the baffled anger at God she had often experienced, she found hope in the tender care being lavished upon the fallen.

Even Caleb's frenzied outbursts seemed God's way of helping him exorcise demons she could only guess at. Someday perhaps he would tell her about whatever baby had taken root in his heart and what doll had been so important to him. He repeated the word *Charge!* at intervals throughout the day, shuddering in the aftermath of his order.

When he tossed about, Private Nathan would help her massage his limbs while she crooned lullabies she hoped were among those his mother had sung to him. Even when he slept, he slept fitfully, lashing out at her with his hands. Periodically her father came to check on Caleb, but he offered no encouragement beyond saying, "Keep doing what you're doing."

Toward nightfall, Lily stood and took in the scene. So focused had she been on Caleb that she was surprised to see that several of the men had apparently undergone treatment and returned to their barracks. The two amputees were receiving special care from Effie and Rose. Lily was numb with fatigue, but she would not leave her post. Sometimes she thought Caleb's fever was breaking, but then it would rage and he would become agitated again.

More than anything, one pathetic word, repeated again and again, glued her to the spot. *Help!*

Just after seven, Lily overheard her father speaking with someone at the door. When she glanced around, her jaw dropped. A young woman, barely five feet tall, wearing a simple gray dress and bonnet, was saying clearly, "I am here to see Lieutenant Creekmore." Lily didn't recognize the dark-haired stranger, but couldn't mistake the determination in her voice.

When Ezra pointed toward the nearby bed where Will Creekmore lay, the woman uttered a hurried "Thank God" and made a beeline for his cot. She was only halfway across the room when Will, one arm in a sling, struggled to his feet, swaying with pain. "Oh, Fannie, is it you? Tell me it's you!"

The woman called Fannie arrived at Will's side just in time to hold him up in an embrace that seemed to have no end. "Will, my darling Will." At long last, she pulled back and helped him sit. Even from across the way, Lily could hear the man's sobs of relief. Fannie knelt in front of him, wiping his tears with her handkerchief. "Beloved Will."

He cradled her face in his hands. "I can't believe it's you. That you're not a dream."

"I'm no dream. I'm your betrothed." She brushed back a stray lock of his hair. "If you'll still have me." Lily heard the smile in her voice.

"*Have you?* I can't wait." Will looked around the room then. "Hey, folks. We're going to have a wedding here!"

Scattered applause and muffled laughter greeted his announcement. Beaming at Fannie, Will then said, "Thanks be to God for you, Fannie Jackson. I love you with all my heart."

Moved by the affectionate reunion, Lily turned away, wondering what had induced a young woman to leave her home and family for life in an alien wilderness. She dipped the cloth in water, wrung it out and bathed Caleb's neck and shoulders. There was no accounting for Fannie's devotion.

Fuzzy. A face. Out there, just beyond his reach. Then a light. Behind the face. He lifted his arm, but watched it fall back down. Now he was walking on a path. In the forest. Toward the sun. From the trees, a doe studied him, her limpid eyes full of...what? Love? Then he heard a voice. An angel's voice. He walked faster toward the sound. It was a song he knew. *Mother?*

Warm light bathed him, soothed him.

"Caleb!"

His legs were tired, so tired. He sat down on the path.

"Caleb, don't you dare give up!"

Not his mother, he thought. Then the face was close to his. A woman. Not his mother. An angel?

"Caleb, I want you to squeeze my hand."

Then he felt soft fingers on his hand, the pressure of a palm. Squeeze? He tried.

"Again!"

As he gripped the hand, it felt like a lifeline tugging him back from the forest, back from the sunlight.

With great effort, he opened his eyes and looked into the face. The beautiful face of a woman. He knew her. Like a balloon his heart inflated with ecstasy. Her name. He needed to remember her name. Then the strange, raspy sound of his own voice filled his ears. *Lily?*

In response, another voice thundered. "Caleb, this is Ezra Kellogg. Keep fighting, lad. I think you're going to make it."

The pretty woman was there again, and something wet was falling from her eyes onto his skin.

Chapter Ten

Throughout the long night, Lily refused to leave Caleb's side except when Rose took her place. His fever had broken, but he was so weak that only by scant teaspoonfuls were they able to force him to sip water or broth. When he opened his eyes, Lily was unsure whether he recognized her. His only words—*angel* and *baby*—were uttered in a hoarse whisper. Rose had brought a small jar of bacon fat to rub on his dry, cracked lips, and every few hours Ezra appeared to change his dressing and examine the wound.

In the wee hours of the morning, Lily, exhausted, rested her weary head on his bed. She was instantly lost in the white gauze of sleep until she was roused by a gentle voice calling her name. With the greatest effort, she sat up, squinting dazedly at the woman standing by her side. Coming into awareness of her surroundings, Lily panicked. "Dear God, Caleb?"

"Your man is asleep. That will hasten his healing more than anything."

Your man? Lily shook her head, trying to reorient herself to the situation. Running a hand through her disheveled hair, she studied the diminutive young woman whose brown eyes were seas of calm.

"Let me introduce myself. I am Fannie Jackson, come to wed Will Creekmore."

Events of the previous night washed over Lily—Fannie's arrival, her romantic reunion with Will and Lily's admiration for the young woman's devotion to the lieutenant. Lily extended her hand. "Welcome to Fort Larned. I'm Lily Kellogg."

Fannie held Lily's hand in both of hers. "I know who you are. Will has told me wonderful things about you, and I am so eager to make your acquaintance. I shall be so in need of a friend here."

Lily reacted with both spontaneous affection and guilt. Even in these few minutes, it was obvious Fannie could, indeed, become a special friend; but if she went to St. Louis, she would disappoint Fannie by leaving Fort Larned.

She paused to gather the sheet around Caleb and adjust his pillow before continuing the conversation. "We are impressed that you would make such a long trip. Was it difficult?"

Fannie smiled. "It had its moments, but nothing could have kept me from coming. I concentrated on Will and God's plan for us to be together."

Lily envied Fannie her certainty. She had thought she knew her destiny: to go to St. Louis and live a cosmopolitan existence. Yet, so great had been her fear for Caleb's life that all thought of the city had been knocked out of her awareness until just this minute. How difficult it had suddenly become to distinguish her own plan from God's. "I envy you, Fannie."

"How so?"

"You seem so certain of your direction."

"God planted love in my heart, and I have never doubted His purpose for me."

"But how do you *know?*"

Fannie began massaging the coiled muscles in Lily's neck. "It just feels right in a way nothing else ever has."

It just feels right. How Lily wished she knew what might "feel right" for her. At this moment, though, questions were all she had. What if she never saw Caleb again? What if she never experienced life at Aunt Lavinia's? What if she was following her own stubborn will, rather than God's? In resignation, she bent her head and for several minutes gave in to the ministrations of Fannie's soothing hands.

Finally Fannie stopped, but not before wrapping Lily's shoulders in a warm embrace. "Why don't you go get some breakfast and take a nap?"

It dawned on Lily that she was ravenous. "Perhaps I will."

"Please do not fret. I will be tending to your man."

There it was again. *Your man.* Lily had neither the energy nor the will to correct her new friend. Ever since the kiss in the cemetery, she had avoided speculation concerning her relationship with Caleb. Was there any way at all by which he could be considered *her* man? If so, she was simply too tired to ponder the implications.

Rather than commenting further, Lily simply said, "Thank you."

"How're you doing, son?"

Caleb pried his eyes open and saw Major Hurlburt standing at his bedside. "I'll make it, sir."

"If determination plays a part in your recovery, I have no doubt of that."

Caleb felt disoriented. "How long have I been here?"

"Nearly a week."

Painfully, Caleb pulled up on one elbow and glanced around the hospital. "The others?"

The major settled in the bedside chair. "We took some casualties."

Caleb closed his eyes against a question he didn't want to ask. "How many?"

"Twelve wounded. Five dead."

He was glad the major hadn't minced words. The toll had been high. "Who?"

"There will be time enough for that, son. Right now, your duty is to get well."

Caleb wasn't sure he would ever be well again, not with the scars of so many comrades lost, not just in the recent battle, but in every conflict in which he'd participated. "I'll do my best." With sudden urgency, another question filled him with dread. "Bucephalus?"

"Your mount is safely home."

Caleb closed his eyes, limp with relief.

After a few moments, the major spoke again. "You've had mighty attentive nursing."

"Lily." Caleb looked away so his commander wouldn't see the emotions threatening to unman him. In the midst of his horrific memories, her name itself was a balm.

"Yes, Lily, but also Rose Kellogg and Fannie Jackson, Creekmore's fiancée."

Caleb racked his fuzzy brain for the information he knew he should be seeking. "The mission? Was it a success?"

The major rubbed a finger under his nose. "From a strategic point of view, yes, but those Indians fought to the death."

Exhausted, Caleb sank back on the pillow. He had so many questions, some that only God could answer. "Thank you for coming, sir," he managed weakly.

The major stood. "No problem, Captain. You work on getting better. I need men like you."

Caleb closed his eyes. The army might need men *like* him, but not *him*. He was leaving this all behind and for the promised "greener pastures" of the Flint Hills. A place of tranquility and peace where he could become a different man.

Eight days after the battle, a chaplain arrived from Fort Riley to conduct the service to honor the dead. The mood at the fort was subdued. It was almost as if the men had too much time to think…and remember. Effie Hurlburt assembled a makeshift choir for the event, and in her spare time after working at the hospital, Lily played the piano for their rehearsals. The entire fort gathered at the cemetery on a hot July morning. The soldiers stood in ranks and the women clustered together.

Lily listened to the singers. Every chorus of "Abide with Me" threatened to undo her, and the final, piteous notes of taps hushed even the birds. The service was more personal for her as a result of her own brother's death at Lookout Mountain and her brief, but poignant encounter with Sydney Long. The young soldier had already known tragedy, but for his life to be cut off so soon…unthinkable. Following the ceremony, she fulfilled the difficult task of writing his parents. She had delayed so that she could describe the service. Yet she knew that mere words, no matter how heartfelt or eloquent, would be of little comfort.

Caleb, still weak and chafing about the slow pace of his recovery, had wanted to attend the service, but Ezra Kellogg would not permit it. Lily knew Caleb felt it was his duty to be with his men to bid farewell to their comrades. "They were good soldiers," he had told her. "It was an honor to fight side by side. I just wish…" He had clamped his mouth shut, unable to continue.

Because the chaplain planned to stay at Fort Larned for several weeks, Will and Fannie took advantage of his presence to plan their wedding. Fannie was living temporarily with the Hurlburts, and she and Effie were thriving on making arrangements. Lily continued to be in awe of Fannie's equanimity. "Naturally, I miss my parents and sister," she confided one evening to Lily. "I would've liked them to be at my wedding, but it was more important that I be with Will."

The officers' wives had pitched in to purchase a rich, amber-colored material for a wedding dress. Lily had agreed to make the gown, and deep in a chest containing her mother's clothes, she had found some antique lace with which to trim the collar and cuffs. She was humbled and pleased when Fannie asked her to stand up with her and Will. If Caleb was sufficiently recovered, Will hoped he would serve as his best man. Ezra was pleased with how well Will's bones were mending, but the eager bridegroom had said whether his arm was healed or not, nothing would postpone the wedding.

Working on Fannie's gown was therapy for Lily. She could lose herself in darts and hems and briefly forget the sad events of recent days. Watching Fannie and Will was a tonic in itself. Their obvious love spread a kind of magic wherever they went and occasioned many a smile.

One evening as Lily was leaving the hospital, Caleb detained her. "I'd like to go outdoors."

"You are too weak to walk that far."

"Not by myself. But if you helped…?" He hoisted himself to his feet, pausing to get his legs under him. "If you put your arm around my waist, like so—" he guided her arm "—and I rested my hand on your shoulder, we could make it."

She staggered slightly when he shifted his weight onto her and wrapped his arm around her shoulder. Apprehensive, she braced for their first step. "I'm not sure this is a good idea."

Sounding more like the old Calcb than he had since his injury, he said, "To the contrary, it's a fine idea."

Was it her imagination or had he squeezed her shoulder? "We must proceed slowly," she said primly.

"Slow is good." They advanced toward the door. "I am so weary of confinement."

"You've been very ill. Healing takes time."

Just outside the door was a row of benches, and Caleb, supported by Lily, slowly eased himself onto a seat. His breath came in gasps. Even that small amount of exertion had cost him dearly. "Here." He patted the seat beside him. "Sit with me."

Lily could no more refuse than fly. Besides, if she didn't stay at his side, who would help him back to bed?

"'Healing takes time,'" he repeated, expelling a long sigh. "There will never be enough time."

The resignation in his voice caused Lily to study him carefully. His hands clenched his knees and his jaw was rigid. "Are you talking about your wound…or something more?"

"Oh, the injury will heal," he said dismissively, "but any man who has seen battle will tell you that though scars may form, there are some wounds that are with you until Gabriel's trumpet blows."

This was the moment for which she had waited, but would he risk confiding in her? What she said next would make all the difference. "Caleb, you would honor me with your trust. Perhaps you could begin by telling me about the baby."

"The baby?" His expression went blank, and Lily immediately regretted making an assumption.

"When you were delirious, there were two memories that recurred over and over in your speech. One was something about a little girl and a doll. The other was the word *baby*. You kept repeating it with great agitation."

"Washita."

"I beg your pardon?"

"The Battle of the Washita River. More even than my experiences in the War between the States, it haunts my dreams." He seemed to go into another world, one inaccessible to her.

After a few moments, she prompted him. "The baby?"

He shrugged. "I couldn't save it."

"I don't understand."

"It isn't a pretty story."

"If it affects you, I want to hear it." Lily sensed they were on the verge of passing into strange new territory.

Briefly he recounted the nature of the mission they were to undertake with Black Kettle and his encampment. "But something went horribly wrong. To this day, I don't understand what. One minute we were poised to disperse the Indians there, and in the next, we were thrust into horrific confusion. They fired on us, and our men began slaughtering them—men, women and children." He paused with a ragged hiccup. "I tried to stop them, but there was confusion on every side. I could not believe the evidence of my eyes and it plagues me still."

He paused, and Lily knew better than to interrupt the memories now spewing from a place deep within him. When he resumed the story, it was as if to leave out any detail would dishonor the victims.

"There was bloodshed all around, but two images seared themselves into my brain. The first is of a little girl, not more than seven I wager, who still clutched a sad little cornhusk doll with a blue dress. The poor child lay on her back, eyes vacant, shot through the chest."

With economy of motion, Lily laid her hand atop one of his, now busy kneading the fabric of his trousers.

"Nearby was a woman lying facedown, her long braid blood-soaked. She must've been shot protecting her baby. I could hear the baby crying, oh, so weakly, but when I attempted to dismount to save the child, I myself was attacked. By the time the gunfire ceased and I returned to the scene, the infant had suffocated." His tortured eyes sought hers. "I have killed men in battle, both in the recent war and now fighting Indians, but I never signed on to be part of a massacre. And that's what the Battle of the Washita was. As God is my witness, I never would have gunned down a woman or child. But I was there. I am guilty." He swiped a sleeve across his eyes. "I can't do this anymore, Lily," he said, his voice shaking.

Lily had no notion how to respond. She had wanted him to be more forthcoming, to share himself with her. Well, her wish had been fulfilled, but in no way had she been prepared for the anguish of his nightmarish memories. Healing? She realized she didn't know the first thing about this kind of wound.

"So there. Now you know what kind of man I am. Damaged."

Reaching up, she turned his ashen face toward her and gazed purposefully into his desolate eyes. "Here's what I know. You are a man who has seen what no one should ever have to witness, a man who grieves for innocent souls caught up in violence, a man who cares deeply about human life." She hesitated before adding, "A man who will always have my utmost respect."

"Those are fine words, but you may change your mind after you think about what I've told you. Until the end of my days, I will live with what I've done. That is not a burden to put upon another."

She wanted to say she would gladly accept that burden, yet how might such a sentiment be interpreted? Would she be committing to a deepening of their relationship? Her mind blocked further contemplation of that question. Now was not the time. Instead, she offered what solace she could. "Caleb, God has forgiven you. I have forgiven you. Can you forgive yourself?"

"I despair. Where was God that day? Where is He now?"

"God was present in your compassion, with the mother who so fiercely protected her child and with every man who ministered to another on that battlefield. In the same way, He is here holding our hands and healing our broken hearts." Lily had no idea where her answer had come from. Perhaps divine inspiration?

"I'd like to believe that." He straightened up and his voice grew stronger. "I will try to believe that."

"We can pray for such understanding." She studied his pale face and trembling hands. "I fear our conversation has tired you. Let me help you back to your bed."

On the return trip, his body hunched with exhaustion and pain, and she took the full brunt of his weight. He seemed too tired to utter a single word. She eased him onto his bed and poured him a drink of water.

Finally he spoke. "You must think me a coward."

She guided the cup to his mouth. "Quite the contrary. To have confessed what you just did is an ultimate form of bravery. It took courage to reveal yourself to another."

He swallowed, then waved the cup aside and fell back on the pillow. "I shouldn't have told you such a gruesome story. It is not fit for a woman's ears."

"Caleb, your trust in me is a gift."

"Trust. Yes, that must be it." He sighed again and closed his eyes.

Lily tiptoed from his side, knowing that after such an ordeal, he needed his sleep.

Caleb lay still, his eyes shut, listening to Lily's skirt brush the floor as she moved away. *Trust?* What had he been thinking? How had she wormed that story out of him? Lily was the woman he loved, yet he had undoubtedly shocked her. From boyhood, he had been taught to honor and protect women, to treat them with gentleness, but what had he done? Spit out the venom built up within him during his years in the army and revealed his own dark nature. The weird thing was that, despite his shame, he also felt so great a relief it was scary. Like when he was a child and held his emotions in check until, finally, at night he loosed tears upon his pillow.

His lungs ached now with the breath he held. He didn't know if he would ever breathe easily again until he next saw Lily. He didn't want her pity, nor would he welcome any attempts she might make to heal his past. He threw an arm over his face. What did he want? He knew. He'd spent much of his recuperation thinking about it. Especially after today, though, he had little prayer of receiving it. He wanted her to look at him with unconditional love, to accept him with all his flaws and promise to be his forever.

He rolled onto his side, away from prying eyes, and, at last, asked God for forgiveness…and another chance with Lily.

When he awoke from a deep sleep a few hours later, the hospital was dimly lit. Only a few of those wounded in the recent engagement were still there, joined by one or two others with seasonal maladies. He roused himself, sat up and threw his legs over the side of the bed. One thing had become clear to him in the night. Self-pity would ill serve him; it was the resort of a coward. What had happened to him in the past was unchangeable, but perhaps the future was still in his hands. His immediate goal was to recover his strength. Then to pursue Lily with all his heart. That was a battle too important to contemplate losing.

The next afternoon Lily was surprised and pleased to find Caleb sitting at a small table reading and looking rested. She had fretted through the night about the physical and emotional strain to which he had subjected himself, both walking outside and then sharing his horrific memories. Unspeakable as his descriptions were, she knew there were many more wrenching details he could have shared, more than any woman could possibly imagine. The self-control it took for most of these battle-scarred soldiers to function as well as they did was admirable. Beneath that veneer, Lily suspected that what they most needed was understanding and tenderness.

She approached Caleb and stood over him. "What are you reading?"

When he looked up at her, she saw none of the fatigue of the previous afternoon. "I'm boning up on *Paradise Lost.* Remember, you promised me a discussion of Milton's version of Eve's fall."

"Be that as it may, I've had quite enough of serpents lately."

"But the one in the poem talks."

"He talks, yes, but as a tempter. Oily he is. Can you really blame Eve for biting into the apple?"

"You women always fall for a glib tongue."

She was about to whack him with her handkerchief when she noticed the mischievous grin on his face. "Sir, I think you are teasing me, and, in truth, that is welcome. You must be on the mend."

"I hope so. I've lost too much time here."

"Your body needed that time," Lily reminded him.

He sobered. "As did my soul."

It was his only reference to their conversation of the previous afternoon. She could pursue that train of thought, but that choice was best left to him. "Healing can't be rushed."

"I've heard you say that before, Miss Kellogg."

She smiled. "It's sound advice."

"And I will heed it, though with a strong dose of impatience." He pointed to the vacant chair across the table. "Do you have time to sit for a spell or is duty calling you?"

She glanced around the room to satisfy herself that there were no pressing needs among the patients. "I would like that." She sat down. "Especially because I have received a letter that might interest you." She reached in her apron pocket and pulled out a piece of paper. "This is from Moses."

"Please, read."

"'Miss Lily, you bin good I hope. Ole Massa snake bin keepin' in his hole?'"

Caleb winked at her. "If only Moses knew. Those snakes follow you like bees to honey."

"Let's not talk about it." Lily smoothed the wrinkled page and continued.

"My post is Fort Sill in Injun Territory. It's hot, missy. Like burning coal cinders. Officers keep us busy, but they a good lot, by and large. I hope you safe. I don't forget how nice you be to me."

Lily folded the letter and returned it to her pocket. "It's signed 'Your true friend, Moses.'"

"Your kindness and generosity of spirit obviously meant a lot to him."

"As his bravery and selflessness did to me." She shook her head sadly. "If God created all of us in His image, why can't we get along?"

"I pray unity is God's ultimate plan. Until then, we fight the devil within us, I guess."

Rather than continue with so deep a subject, she attempted to lighten the mood. "Clever, Captain. Now you've brought us right back to *Paradise Lost* and Satan's starring role." She rose and in a mock maternal tone said, "No more, sir, of serpents. This Eve has duties to perform, and they don't include apples."

When she turned to leave, he grasped her by the wrist. "Before you go...Milton also said that we can make a hell of Heaven or a heaven of Hell." His eyes sought hers. "Lily, you have helped make a heaven of my hell." He dropped her wrist, yet she remained rooted to the spot, speechless. "You have restored my trust."

The remainder of the day, she replayed their final exchange, reveling in his compliment, yet feeling both the full weight of the responsibility he had placed in her and her anxiety about fulfilling whatever it was he wanted from her. What had started as friendship and simple attraction had escalated into something else, something she wasn't sure she could handle, at least not without hurting Caleb, who was already so vulnerable. Or was she fooling herself?

* * *

A week later, Fannie stood admiring herself in Effie's full-length mirror while Lily, on hands and knees, measured the hem of the wedding dress. "You are a wiggle worm. Hold still."

"I'm so excited. Lily, I never dared dream of such a splendid gown."

Effie bustled into the room, bearing a small notebook and pencil. "I am off to the sutler's to buy ingredients for the cake. I pray the man has vanilla in stock."

Fannie laughed. "No matter. The wedding will be perfect regardless of what happens."

"How can you say that?" Lily mumbled with pins in her mouth.

"Because I am marrying my Will. All the rest is just, oh, dear, I'm afraid I'm about to make a joke, icing on the cake." Effie hooted and Lily spat pins all over the floor, reflecting that since Fannie's arrival she'd laughed more than she had in a great long while.

After Effie departed, Lily helped Fannie out of the nearly completed gown and folded it carefully. While Fannie dressed, Lily poured two glasses of the lemonade Effie had left for them. They carried the drinks onto the porch where, thankfully, a breeze made the heat bearable. Fannie turned her big brown eyes on Lily. "I know we haven't been acquainted long, but I am so very fond of you. Do you mind if I ask you a personal question?"

"There are no secrets between true friends. Please."

"How do you feel about Captain Montgomery?"

"Caleb?" Lily blushed. "He is a fine man and a good friend."

"That's the way Will feels about him, too. He says he's never had a better comrade." Fannie pursed her lips as if weighing her words, then went on. "He's in love with you, you know."

Lily gaped. "Love?" Yet even as she expressed doubt, she was overcome by a certainty she had avoided acknowledging. "Surely you are mistaken."

"I think not. Will came to that conclusion even before I arrived. I, too, have seen how the captain looks at you, the way his eyes follow you as you move around the hospital." She shook her head decisively. "If Will and I are any judge of such matters, the man is totally besotted."

Lily set the cold glass of lemonade on the porch railing and then wrapped her arms around her waist in a futile attempt to contain her emotions. "No, no."

Fannie quirked an eyebrow. "Come now, my friend. Surely you have noticed something."

"I fear I have no experience with matters of the heart."

"Well, you better be getting some, because, my dear, I think that horse has already left the barn."

Lily rocked back and forth nervously, trying to recapture her moments with Caleb. Any single one of them could be considered innocent. But taken as a whole? And then…the kiss. "What do I do?"

Fannie smiled as if at a wayward child. "What do you want to do?"

Lily had never felt so at sea. "I don't know."

"But you admit it is possible that Caleb could be in love with you."

Helplessly, Lily nodded.

"What about you? Are you in love with him?"

The thought was preposterous. Granted, she had enjoyed the fluttery feelings of attraction and admiration. But love? No serpent of Milton's had ever planted such seeds of confusion as Fannie just had. "I…I can't be."

"Why ever not?"

"Because I'm leaving soon." Lily rushed on to avoid thinking about the shocked look on Fannie's face. "I'm visiting my aunt in St. Louis. It's my dream come true."

Fannie folded her hands in her lap and didn't speak for some time. "Only you know what's best for you. I could tell you not to go, not to turn your back on love, but I won't."

"Perhaps I will find love in St. Louis."

"Perhaps," Fannie said unconvincingly. "May I ask a favor? Please consider your future carefully. Caleb is a fine man whose like you may not find again." She rose from the chair then and came to kneel at Lily's side. "Whatever happens, I am your friend, Lily, and I want only what makes you happy. Forgive me for upsetting you."

"In speaking your mind, you have only done what true friends do."

"I, too, had an important choice to make about whether to come here and marry Will. In my confusion, I learned that all I could do was turn that decision over to God."

"You truly believe God knows what is best for us, that He will provide an answer?"

"I wouldn't be here if I didn't."

Just then Effie came striding toward them, a huge grin on her face. "Vanilla," she shouted triumphantly. "I have it!"

The day then became so busy that it was only that evening in bed that Lily could permit herself to consider the huge questions Fannie had raised. The more she thought about Caleb, the more wide-awake she became. Could it be? She couldn't deny that he often had sought out her company. Protected her from danger. Offered gestures of affection. Was that love?

And what of her feelings? Others could have attended to Caleb after his wounding. The truth was that not only had she stayed by his side to nurse him, but no force, however powerful, could've dragged her away.

All of that aside, he had opened his soul to her, an act of such vulnerability that it had brought tears to her eyes. Yes, there was no doubt. He trusted her.

She lay awake until dawn, her conscience stabbed by the biggest question of all. Was she capable of shattering the trust of a man whom she, indeed, might love in return?

Chapter Eleven

Over the next few days, Lily found it difficult to act natural around Caleb. Ever since her conversation with Fannie, she was self-consciously aware of his eyes upon her, and she found herself overanalyzing everything he said to her. Her friend seemed so sure of her observations, but, then, Fannie knew about love—what it looked and sounded like. Lily, on the other hand, had no experience to guide her. She would like to believe Fannie was embellishing the situation, but deep down, Lily knew something was different about her present relationship with Caleb, and that knowledge both thrilled and troubled her.

Fortunately, as of the day before, Lily didn't have to interact with him at the hospital. Her father had dismissed him to his quarters and ordered his duties curtailed. Now she saw Caleb only by chance across the parade ground or among other people. It seemed to her that he, too, might be experiencing the new awkwardness between them. Perhaps he regretted confiding his battle stories.

Lily, blessedly, had other thoughts to occupy her mind. Fannie and Will's wedding was to be the next Saturday, and the women of the fort were in a frenzy of baking and decorating. The officers and their families plus the men

of Will's troop were invited guests. Among those newly
assigned to Fort Larned was a violinist who would provide the service music. Other musicians among the men
would play for the dancing to follow the ceremony. Caleb
had agreed to move in with a couple of bachelor officers
so the newlyweds could have privacy. Fannie could hardly
contain her excitement, and Will walked around grinning
like a well-fed puppy.

The night before the wedding, a hard rain fell, bringing pleasant temperatures the following morning and renewing the drooping vegetation. By noon, all the ladies
were dressed in their Sunday best while the soldiers had
donned their least threadbare uniforms. The commissary
was festooned with gaily colored ribbons collected from
hope chests and sewing baskets, and two vases of wildflowers decorated the front of the room.

At precisely one-thirty, the chaplain, a gnomelike man
with a cherubic smile, stepped up to face the congregation. Lily waited in the back with Fannie, radiant in her
new gown, and Major Hurlburt, who would stand in for
her father. Effie had arranged Fannie's hair in a ringleted
upsweep, and from her sparkling eyes to the tip of her
toes, the bride was, quite simply, breathtaking.

Lily smoothed her own full blue skirt, then handed
Fannie the small white Bible she had chosen to carry. Just
as the violinist began "Sheep May Safely Graze," Fannie
drew Lily close in an embrace. Lily had just time to say,
"Much joy," before it was her turn to process toward the
chaplain—and Caleb, who stood beside Will. Fans rustled
and heads turned as she made her way down the aisle. Not
daring to look at Caleb, she kept her eyes lowered until
she took her place at the front.

Then Fannie made her entrance on the major's arm, and
whispered exclamations filled the room. "What a beauty!"

and "Lucky man, that." Effie beamed, as if she single-handedly had produced this vision of a bride. Will had eyes only for Fannie. As Lily pivoted to face the chaplain, Caleb caught her attention and smiled. Despite her efforts to remain calm, her trip-hammer heart betrayed her.

Will earnestly repeated his vows, clutching Fannie's hand as if he would never relinquish it. "For better for worse, in sickness and in health, to love and to cherish, until we are parted by death." What depths of love it would take to sustain such devotion. A sudden image of her parents surfaced. They had lived that promise. As her mother had known, life could be hard. How much more difficult would it have been without love?

Lost in such musing, Lily was deaf to the chaplain's words until she roused to hear, "I now pronounce you man and wife. Those whom God hath joined together, let no man put asunder."

Will traced a finger down Fannie's cheek, then turned and offered her his arm. Suddenly wistful, Lily bowed her head. "Lily?" Caleb materialized at her side. "Shall we?"

They followed the bride and groom out into the sunshine. Before others departed the building, Will enfolded Fannie in his arms and kissed her with enthusiasm. The bride's lilting laugh provided a grace note to the nuptials, Lily thought. As the newlyweds began greeting their guests, an aura of happiness enveloped them, and, looking on, Lily knew this was what Fannie's certainty looked like.

Caleb smiled down at Lily. "I doubt my friend could be any happier."

"Nor the bride any lovelier."

He lowered his voice. "No lovelier than her maid of honor."

Lily was loath to look up, afraid what his eyes might reveal...and hers. "You've just never seen me so dressed up." She disengaged her arm from his and twirled about, showing off her dress.

"Your gown is pretty," he conceded, "but I was talking about the woman wearing it."

She had thought to deflect his admiration, but he had countered her ploy. "You flatter me, sir."

"Whoa. I thought we had pledged honesty to one another. Flattery is not among my weapons of choice."

"Then I must do as my mother always taught me in the face of a compliment."

"And what is that?"

"Say, 'Thank you.' So, Captain Montgomery, thank you."

"You deserve compliments, Lily. For your beauty and for your character."

"Surely you are still ill, and it is your feverish brain talking."

He threw back his head and laughed. "No, I am not ill, but I think I have found a way to get you flustered. That's an achievement. You're not usually so flappable."

"And you like getting me flustered?"

"Of course. I spent years teasing a younger sister. Surely I can't let all that experience go to waste."

She mustered a begrudging grin. "There will be food going to waste if we don't join the bride and groom at the table."

The post cooks had roasted a pig for the festivities. In addition to the tender pork, the serving table was laden with baked beans, potatoes, fresh vegetables, cole slaw, melon slices and a tempting assortment of desserts made by the women. Caleb, Lily and the Hurlburts sat at a table with the bride and groom. Dancing followed, and it was comical to watch some of the soldiers dancing with one another.

Lily had been concerned about Caleb's stamina, but he insisted on dancing both with Fannie and with her. When he took her in his arms, she couldn't look at him, but instead concentrated on the feel of his palm on her back, guiding her across the floor. Relaxing into his grip, she felt as light as a butterfly. The Hurlburts glided past, and Effie called out, "You two put the rest of us to shame."

Caleb spun Lily around and then whispered, "We are pretty good together, don't you think?"

Lily gazed up at him, but lost in his twinkling eyes, forgot what she had intended to say.

"I'll take that as a 'yes,'" he said.

Where had she lost utter control of the situation? In the romance of the wedding? The contagious joy of the celebration? Or something else altogether? The magnetism of the handsome captain?

When the music ended, Caleb escorted her to her seat, but soon relinquished her to others seeking a dance partner. Throughout the afternoon's festivities, Lily was aware of Caleb's beaming approval, as if they were a couple and he was merely indulging the other men.

By early evening, the party wound down, and accompanied by noise makers, applause and laughter, the guests escorted Fannie and Will to their quarters. Watching as Will lifted Fannie with his good arm and carried her over the threshold, Lily uttered a silent prayer for their happiness.

Beside her, Caleb sighed and Lily sensed melancholy come over him. She touched his arm. "Already missing your bunk mate?"

"Walk with me?" He tucked her arm in his and began strolling toward the cemetery. "Bunk mates come and go. No, I was just remembering." They walked a few more paces before he spoke again. "I was almost married once."

Curiosity won out over discretion. "What happened?"

He chuckled wryly. "It's not a very original story. Rebecca and I were young, we were engaged to be married, and then the war came."

Lily said nothing, waiting for him to continue.

"I marched off with my fellow soldiers, she promised to be true to me, and many, many months passed. More than either of us had imagined. The thought of her was part of what kept me going."

Lily dreaded hearing the rest, even as she knew he needed to tell it. "But something happened?"

He barked bitterly. "Oh, yes. My best friend happened. It seems while I was off fighting a war, Rebecca took a fancy to Abner. After all, he was right there at home with her. A heart condition prevented him from serving the Union."

"How hurt you must have been."

"Hurt. Angry. Ashamed." They had reached the cemetery bench. "Sit with me, Lily. I want to tell you something."

As she settled on the bench, she reflected that she had never seen Caleb so serious. He picked up her hand and held it tightly. "After I lost Rebecca, I swore off women. I threw all my strength and effort into being the best army officer I could be. I enjoyed the camaraderie of my fellows and satisfied myself that happiness did not depend upon having a sweetheart. That was a lie. There comes a time for most men, I believe, when they miss the companionship and love of a woman." He swallowed, then turned to look directly at her. "That time has come for me."

Lily desperately wanted him to stop with those words just as she equally desperately wanted to hear what he would say next. She sensed they were teetering on a precipice in their relationship, and she wished she could halt time.

"You, Lily," he said, "you have made the difference."

She knew he was waiting for her to comment, but for the life of her, she couldn't think. "I…I don't know what to say. I'm flattered, naturally, but—"

"You don't have to say anything now. But I couldn't continue holding in my feelings. We pledged honesty." His voice fell to a whisper. "I'm in love with you, Lily Kellogg."

Her breath caught in her throat. This couldn't be happening. This was not the plan. Yet at the same time, as she gazed into his eyes, so full of both pain and love, she wanted only to make him complete. "Honesty…" She thought about the importance of what she said next. "You are dear to me, Caleb, and I am honored by your declaration. I know little of love. It would be premature for me to respond."

He raised her hand to his lips and tenderly kissed it. "You need time."

"I do. You have given me much to consider." She struggled to go on. "My fear is that I will hurt you."

He stood and pulled her to her feet. "That is a risk I am willing to take. I have said what I needed to say. Now then, may I escort you home?"

They walked in silence most of the way to her door. Never had Lily known such conflicting emotions. Worst of all, she had not been totally honest with him, and she hated herself for that. She had not told him about St. Louis.

The next day as Caleb went about his duties, he found himself second-guessing yesterday's conversation with Lily. He hadn't really expected her to swoon at his feet, yet he had hoped for something more promising than her careful response. While it had been a huge relief to unburden himself to her, he had been perturbed by her concern about hurting him. He didn't need more rejection, but why had she so immediately considered that possibility?

In fairness, perhaps he was rushing things, but with his army stint drawing to a close in a month, he had little time for courtship. He grinned at the irony of that word—exactly what Will had accused him of and now here he was, knee-deep in it. He wanted to paint for Lily the vision of their home amid the beauty and sweep of the Flint Hills, of children growing up with the freedom of wide-open spaces, of a lifetime of love and devotion. The challenge was having so little time to persuade her.

He drew up short in his thinking. He didn't want to have to persuade her of anything; he wanted her to embrace the future he hoped for them. Ultimately, however, her decision was out of his control. If they were meant to be together, then it would happen.

To that end, before supper, he made his way to the hospital. He had already observed Lily walking toward her mother's grave site and hoped to catch Ezra Kellogg alone. The surgeon was in his office, bent over a book. Caleb tapped on the door. "Could I have a word, sir?"

Ezra closed the book and took off his spectacles. "Of course. Are you having difficulties, son?"

"I fatigue more easily and still haven't full use of my shoulder, but that's not why I'm here."

Ezra pointed to a chair. "Have a seat. What can I do for you?"

Caleb sat down and considered how to phrase his request. "It surely has come to your attention that Lily and I have been spending considerable time together. She is a talented, compassionate nurse. Beyond that, I find her to be a woman of character and grace of whom I am quite fond." He felt beads of perspiration forming on his brow and decided to cut to the chase. "I have come seeking your permission to court Lily."

Ezra stared across the desk at him as if searching out his hidden flaws. "'Fond,' are you?" The word sounded somehow tainted in the surgeon's mouth.

Caleb rubbed his palms on his thighs. "That is not quite accurate." Lily's father was not making this easy. "I am in love with your daughter."

Caleb detected the suggestion of a smile in the man's gaze. "Then why didn't you say so in the first place?"

"What is in my heart didn't make it to my lips, but my feelings are no less genuine for my dissembling."

"Does she reciprocate your feelings?"

"I don't know. I certainly hope so. I have expressed my love for her, but I didn't feel it appropriate to ask for her hand until I spoke with you."

"Admirable."

Was the surgeon playing with him? Thus far Caleb had no sense of the man's reactions. "She asked for time."

"Time, yes. Never good to rush into these things."

"Ordinarily I would agree. However, I will be mustering out of the army sometime around mid-August."

"Does Lily know that?"

"Not yet. I respect her need for time. I don't want my leaving to pressure a response from her."

Ezra pulled out a handkerchief, picked up his eyeglasses and proceeded to clean them. Caleb waited, trying to conceal his discomfort. Finally, the surgeon spoke. "My daughters are dear to me, and I want them to be loved and cherished. You, Captain, are a worthy gentleman, but I will neither encourage nor discourage your suit. Like all girls, Lily has ambitions and dreams for herself on which may well depend her future happiness. If you fit into those plans, I would be pleased. Meanwhile, you have my permission to press your suit." The surgeon rose and extended his hand across the desk. "Best wishes, son."

Caleb thanked the man for his support and made as hasty an exit as was prudent. He hadn't achieved a ringing endorsement, but he admired the surgeon's commitment to his daughters' well-being.

Walking back to his quarters, Caleb was stunned to realize he lacked an important piece of the puzzle. Ezra Kellogg had referred to Lily's ambitions and dreams. The more he thought about that statement, the more Caleb realized he hadn't the least notion what Lily's ambitions and dreams were.

"I thought I'd find you here." Fannie plopped down on the ground beside Lily. "You come here often, don't you?"

"I hope it doesn't seem morbid, but I feel my mother's presence here." Lily patted the mown grass of the grave.

"You were close?"

"Very. Only now that she's gone do I realize how many lessons she taught me."

"Like?"

"Like doing for others. Like how the power of love helps get folks through hardships. Like the need to appreciate each and every day on this earth."

"A wise woman. I've certainly been appreciating the past two days since the wedding." Fannie's face lit up. "I have officially begun my life as Mrs. William Creekmore."

"And?" Lily leaned forward, as if to tease details from her friend.

"And...I am so blessed. Oh, Lily, you can't imagine how glorious it is to lie in the arms of your beloved and know it will ever be thus in this lifetime."

Lily shivered. Why couldn't she so readily identify her

feelings for Caleb? Did Caleb feel about her the way Fannie did about Will? "I am happy for you."

"Thank you, dear friend. I would wish this same happiness for you." Fannie cocked her head inquiringly. "Do you have anything to tell me?"

Lily's blush gave her away.

"You do! I knew it!" Fannie scooted closer. "Tell me."

Lily felt sudden panic. She hadn't intended anyone to know about Caleb's profession of love. She could hardly find words. "I don't know where to begin."

Fannie covered Lily's hands with her own. "At the beginning, of course, but before you start, please know I will keep any confidences to myself." Then she sat back, permitting Lily time to gather her thoughts.

"Oh, Fannie, I'm so confused."

"Caleb?"

Lily nodded. "We had such a fine friendship."

"Had?"

"We could talk so easily, we both enjoy literature…"

"And he's handsome."

"Yes, that, too, but mainly I just enjoyed his company. Then when he was injured—"

"You could hardly leave his side. Did you think no one else could nurse him satisfactorily?"

Lily chewed her bottom lip. Why had she been so devoted a nurse to Caleb? "No, but—"

"It wasn't only about your patient. You needed to be with your man. That was obvious to all of us in the hospital."

"But he's not my man!" Lily's emotions were spiraling out of control. Why was everyone forcing her to deal with her feelings about Caleb?

"Perhaps not. He would like to be, though, wouldn't he?"

Lily hung her head, all the fight draining out of her.

"Yes," she murmured. Figuring she might as well go on, she added, "He told me he is in love with me."

Rather than giving a hoot of triumph, Fannie squeezed her hands, then, relinquishing them, sat back. "Now what?"

"I wish I knew. I don't want to hurt him. I really don't, but—"

"You're leaving." Fannie sighed with resignation. "Be sure you know your own heart, Lily. Then follow it, as I did mine, wherever that may lead you."

Lily closed her eyes, wishing she could have Fannie's certitude. "I care a great deal for Caleb."

"But you also have your dream."

"Yes."

"Pray, Lily. God will guide you." Fannie gathered her skirt and stood. "Take some time here with your mother." Then she slipped away, leaving Lily no more certain of her feelings than she had been before talking with Fannie.

Later that evening while Rose was visiting with Virginia Brown, Ezra and Lily sought the cooler air of the front porch. They sat in companionable silence for some time, Lily playing and replaying events of the past two days, no nearer to reaching any conclusions.

"Are you still determined to go visit Lavinia?" The creak of Ezra's rocker filled the silence.

"She says she will send tickets."

"Daughter, that wasn't my question."

"I think I'll go."

"That doesn't sound definitive. What's the problem?"

How could she answer without giving away more than she cared to? She simply shrugged.

"Your mother would be able to get it out of you."

"I miss her."

"As do I." He rocked awhile. "Since Mathilda isn't here,

I guess it's up to me to ferret out the cause of your lack of enthusiasm. Caleb Montgomery. Am I right?"

"Papa, I don't know what to do." Even to her own ears, her voice sounded strangled.

"One thing you mustn't do is toy with that fine young man's feelings. He has asked my permission to court you."

Lily's heart sank. She'd had no idea Caleb would take such a step so soon. "He mustn't."

"Too late, my dear. Do you care for him?"

"Yes, but—"

"There can be no *but*'s. Your mother and I knew that. A good marriage is based on unshakable commitment. No matter the challenges, there can be no looking back and asking 'What if?'"

Lily thought she might very well love Caleb. But did she love him enough?

Her father went on. "Would you live to regret giving up your St. Louis experience for a man? For Caleb? Are you willing to risk losing him if you make the trip? These are hard questions, but ones you must answer, Lily. Your mother would ask them, too."

"I know." Even embraced by her father's concern and love, Lily still felt alone. All she could do was heed Fannie's advice. Pray for guidance.

Chapter Twelve

Caleb waited a couple of days, deferring a conversation he and Lily needed to have, one fraught with uncertainty. At the fort, it was difficult to find opportunities for privacy, but the cemetery was a place where few ventured—and one place he knew Lily frequented. As was her custom, after she finished her hospital duties, she ambled toward her mother's grave, seemingly preoccupied. He afforded her a few minutes before he approached her. "Lily?"

When she looked up, he noticed the stress lines creasing her forehead. "Caleb, what are you doing here?"

"Following you." She didn't seem overjoyed to see him. "I believe we have cause to talk more honestly with one another."

Lily glanced around, apparently satisfying herself that they were alone. "Could we walk in the cool shade by the river?"

He offered his arm, and they made their way in silence down the path. To be so near her and yet feel so distant was agony. "I've missed you," he said quietly.

She kept walking, head lowered.

"I hope my declaration has not offended you."

At last, she stopped and gazed up at him. "On the contrary, you honored me."

"I fear I took a great deal for granted. You may know I spoke with your father."

He received a nod of confirmation.

"My intentions are serious. Though it is difficult, I am giving you time. After speaking with your father, I realized I have not been as sensitive to your feelings as I should have been and perhaps have jumped to some conclusions."

"I don't understand...."

They reached the fallen log where they had rested the day of the baseball game. He helped her sit, then joined her, knowing that much depended on explaining himself clearly. "I have selfishly considered my own interests and plans, assuming you might share them. In thinking about it, I wondered if I had ever communicated my dreams or, more important, inquired about yours. I love you, but love can only sustain a relationship when two people have a common vision of their life together. Maybe it will assist your deliberations if we speak more openly about our hopes and expectations."

"You are right." Lily reached down and plucked up a blade of grass, worrying it in her fingers. "I have not intentionally withheld anything from you. I have little experience in matters of the heart and did not recognize the depth of your feelings. Before, there seemed little purpose to be served in baring one's soul. I do not want you to think me idly flirtatious. I enjoyed our times together without considering the consequences. Perhaps I was naive. Now I see that you deserve to know what prevents me from encouraging you further."

As if cold hands had seized his throat, Caleb could hardly find his voice. Where he had sought that very encouragement, he was to be denied it. "I am reluctant to hear what you have to say, but our pledge of honesty compels me to ask you to continue."

"I have plans to leave Fort Larned soon."

She couldn't have said anything that would have shocked him more. "Leave? Why? Where?"

She discarded the blade of grass and laced her fingers together. "My mother's sister Lavinia lives in St. Louis. She is quite well off and moves in fine society. For much of our girlhood, Mother encouraged Rose and me someday to visit her and learn city customs and experience the many opportunities available there. Although that is not something Rose wants for herself, such a visit has been my longtime dream."

His heart sank. How could the Flint Hills compete with the sophistication of the city?

She went on. "You have come into my life when I am at a crossroads. I have every reason to believe that any day now I will receive tickets from Aunt Lavinia enabling me to go to St. Louis to spend a matter of months. Yet I did not reckon how difficult it would be to leave you."

Only then did she look up at him, her eyes muddy with concern. Part of him wanted to lash out, to plead his case; but another part recognized her anguish. Her decision was obviously difficult. No wonder she needed time, but was time on his side? "Is there still hope for us?"

"Honestly? I don't know." She turned away then. "St. Louis is everything I thought I wanted. Until you."

He cupped her head in his hands and with aching tenderness, lowered his lips and found the sweet nectar of hers. He caressed the silky smoothness of her cheek, inhaled the lilac fragrance of her neck and felt an overpowering need to claim her as his own. "Dear, dear, Lily. Above all, I want you to be happy."

"I desire that for you, too, Caleb."

"You are my happiness. I had hoped I could be yours." In the gloaming the hum of insects and the croak of frogs seemed joined in a lament. Neither of them said anything. At last, in a soft voice, Caleb intoned, "'How do I love thee? Let me count the ways. / I love thee to the depth and breadth and height / My soul can reach…'" He circled an arm around Lily's slender waist and drew her close. "When you recited those lines at the poetry reading, that was when I knew I loved you and wanted to spend my life with you. If you are determined to follow your dream, then I must let you go, but I cannot permit that to happen without asking you to listen to my dream and consider altering your own."

Knowing he had so much more to tell her about his plans yet wild with the need to assure himself she would be part of them, he slipped from the log and knelt in front of Lily. He hoped against hope that she would hear and respond to the urgent call of his heart. He picked up her hands and held them in his, seeking in her astonishing blue eyes the response he needed to hear. "Dearest Lily, I ask you before God to become my wife. I pledge you my undying love."

Her eyes filled with tears, Lily shook her head back and forth, gripping his hand as in a vise. She opened her mouth to speak, but no sound came. Adrift, Caleb could only stand, draw her to her feet and enfold her in his arms. Her slight body trembled in his embrace and muffled sobs gave evidence of her distress. How long they stood thus was measured by the cooing of doves and the arrival of the first fireflies of the evening. Finally she stepped away and gazed at him with such love he feared ever forgetting the moment. A glimmer of hope. That was all he needed. Then she spoke.

"If mere sentiment and emotion might be the basis of a decision, I would be moved to accept your proposal. But there is also reason, intellect and a lifetime of expectation to be considered. Caleb, dear, you have already been hurt by one who treated your heart lightly. I cannot, I will not, do that. So I beg of you once more, permit me time. Haste must not be a determining factor. May I have a week to consider your proposal?"

Caleb knew it had been unrealistic to expect an immediate answer, much as he craved an acceptance. Right now, a week seemed unendurable, yet if that week ultimately produced an engagement, the time would pass as a blink of an eye. "A man in love is an impatient creature, but you are worth it, Lily. Take the time you need."

Just when he opened his mouth to tell her he would soon be mustering out and to share his future expectations for the ranch, he heard a familiar voice calling his name. He and Lily drew farther apart and Caleb began to laugh. "It can't be." He yelled out, "Seth?"

Lily looked at him quizzically and then at the broad-shouldered, bewhiskered giant lumbering toward them, his arms extended. "They told me you might be here, brother." Then Caleb was enveloped in a bear hug.

Extricating himself, he turned to Lily. "I've told you about my big brother, Seth, and for some reason, here he is. May I present Miss Lily Kellogg."

Seth picked up Lily's hand and bent over it. "My pleasure, ma'am." Then he examined Caleb's expression, turned back to Lily and said, "My pleasure, indeed."

Caleb stared at his brother, dumbfounded at his presence here. "What brings you to Fort Larned?"

"First of all, Sophie, Pa and I have been sore worried since you were wounded, so I came to check on you. Beyond that, I have an important mission the family wants you to undertake after you muster out next month."

"Mus…muster out?"

Both brothers wheeled to Lily, whose eyes flicked from one man to the other. Seth found his voice first. "Why, yes, Miss Lily. Caleb's leaving the army."

"Lily, I'm sorry, I was just now getting ready to tell you."

"Woo-ee. Old Seth spoke out of turn, I reckon."

Lily dusted imaginary dirt from her skirt and, ignoring Caleb, spoke to Seth. "Welcome to Fort Larned, sir. If you'll excuse me, I'll see myself home. I imagine you two have much to discuss."

She turned and marched toward the fort. Caleb paused only a moment before trotting after her. When he reached her side, he took hold of her arm, which she promptly jerked away. "Please, Lily. I was on the brink of telling you all about my plans and about where I would take you if we married and—"

"So much for honesty" was all she said, but even without those words, her withering look doomed him.

Once out of sight of the brothers, Lily picked up her skirts and ran toward home, blinded by angry tears. How dare Caleb withhold such information, assuming she would just go along with any plan he had in mind? For a moment back there, all she had wanted was to fall into his arms, cover his face with kisses and swear her eternal love. To say, "yes," for pity's sake. To scuttle any plan for St. Louis. How could she have been so misguided and besotted?

She dashed through the front door and raced up the stairs, intent upon avoiding her father's startled look and Rose's well-intentioned inquisition. Throwing herself on the bed, she beat the pillows with her fists. Sweet talk, that's all it had been. She had actually believed she had fallen in love with the man—a man she had thought honorable. Yet all along, he had concealed any talk of his future, the very future he had the gall to invite her to share. Spent, she rolled over on her back, dried her tears and focused on calming her rapid breathing. Closing her eyes, she kept whispering her renewed mantra, "St. Louis, St. Louis, St. Louis."

Only when she heard the creak of the bedroom door did she look around. Rose and Fannie stood expectantly at the threshold. "Do you wish to be alone?" Rose asked.

Lily knew the story would have to come out eventually. Much as an incision needs to be made and poison purged, she saw no reason to postpone the inevitable. "It's all right. Come on in."

Fannie went to the washbasin, poured some water and dampened a cloth. "Here," she said, handing it to Lily. "Lay this on your forehead. You are overheated."

The contrast of the cool, damp towel made Lily aware of the oppressive heat in the tiny room. "Thank you."

Fannie perched on the side of the bed, and Rose pulled a chair close. "Sister, we are concerned for you. When I saw how upset you were, I summoned Fannie. We don't mean to intrude, but if we can share your burden, whatever it is, we want to do that."

Lily didn't know where to begin or how to express the conflicting emotions raging within her. "I feel like such a fool."

"How so?" Fannie asked.

"It is surely Captain Montgomery who has put you in such a state," Rose said.

"Caleb." Lily could hardly say his name for the huge

lump in her throat. "I…I was falling in love with him." Even to her own ears, her voice sounded tinny.

"Was?" Fannie's eyebrows shot up with the question.

"This evening he asked me to marry him."

"Surely that didn't come as a surprise," Rose said.

Lily looked at her sister. "I know you like him, but I cannot marry him."

"Did you tell him that?"

Lily mentally reviewed the conversation. "Actually, no. I asked for a week to consider his proposal."

Fannie leaned forward. "But you've already made up your mind?"

"How could I not when I learned he has not been totally forthcoming with me? Rose, you remember when Effie talked about marriage and the importance of communication, of not keeping secrets?"

Rose nodded.

"You will understand, then, how surprised I was to learn this evening that Captain Montgomery is shortly to leave the army. And for what? That is also a piece of information he has not shared. How could he expect me to traipse off into the unknown like some beleaguered pioneer woman?" She shook her head vehemently. "No, I am not such a fool."

"Sister, you speak of openness. Does Caleb know about your desire to visit St. Louis or have you kept that to yourself?"

Lily shrugged. "I kept putting it off. I finally told him tonight."

"Dear, I believe communication works both ways." Rose shook her head sadly. "Do you love him?"

Lily groaned. Her sister *would* have to ask that question.

"I doubt you would be so upset," Fannie interjected, "if

you had no feelings for Caleb. Perhaps there is a reasonable explanation for his withholding his plans. It could be the proposal just popped out of his mouth, or maybe his future is still somewhat indefinite, or—"

"Or he asked me to share my dream, but for unknown reasons failed to share his own. Whatever his vision, mine is firmly set. I am going to St. Louis."

Fannie picked up her hand and gently massaged it. "This is anger and disappointment talking, Lily. Caleb has given you a week to make your decision. I know you are hurt right now, but I urge you to use the next few days to consider what your life would be like without him. Whether the charms of St. Louis are strong enough to overcome your feelings for the man. There is nothing to be gained by an impulsive reaction. Take the time, dear friend. Take the time."

Rose nodded in agreement. "This decision is too important to hurry. Consider, too, that there may be things you don't know that Caleb has been trying to share."

Lily gritted her teeth against the memory of his words: *I was just now getting ready to tell you...* Was that true or merely his way of placating her? "I'm so angry."

Fannie smiled in understanding. "Of course you are. You're feeling betrayed. So often in relationships such schisms are a result of miscommunication. If there is any chance you love him, you will need to confront him with your concerns and hear him out."

Lily wilted under the sympathy and love of her sister and friend. "I don't know if I can do that."

"You must," Rose said in a big sisterly tone that left no room for argument.

Lily sighed. Much as she hated to admit it, Rose was correct. The nature of her relationship with Caleb needed to be settled once and for all. "All right," she said in capitulation. A knowing glance passed between Fannie and Rose, as if to say, "Mission accomplished."

Seth sat on the top step of the barrack porch watching Caleb pace. The brothers had not spoken on their way back from the river. Seth had draped an arm around Caleb as they walked, but seemed to be waiting for him to initiate the conversation that would explain the upsetting events of the past few minutes. What words were there to justify the botch he had made of everything? Or to find the sense in Lily's St. Louis plan? Whether through oversight or assumptions, neither he nor Lily had been as open with the other as they should have been. He didn't know much about love, but Rebecca had surely taught him that honesty was at the heart of any lasting relationship. Why, he hadn't even told Lily about the ranch and how he pictured their life together. No, he'd asked her to take him on faith. Dumb!

"You're wearing out the floor," Seth muttered at last. "I'm a pretty good listener, you know."

Heaving a deep sigh, Caleb collapsed onto the step beside his brother, head down, hands clasped between his knees. "How are Pa and Sophie?"

"Not so fast. They're fine, and there will be time enough to tell you about them. But I recognize a dodge when I see one. What is going on with you and Miss Lily Kellogg?"

Caleb shrugged helplessly.

"That bad, huh?" Seth stretched out his legs, then continued. "Spit it out, Captain."

"I thought I was on the verge of something wonderful. A man doesn't like to have the rug pulled out from under him twice."

"Forget Rebecca. She's not worth talking about. Has this Lily betrayed you, too?"

"Not like that."

"You're pretty sweet on her, then?"

"I asked her to marry me."

"Oh." Seth raked a hand through his curly hair. "Yep, that qualifies as 'pretty sweet.' What was her answer?"

"That's just it. She hasn't said no, yet, but she might as well have. She has plans to leave the fort for a long visit with an aunt in St. Louis. A rich aunt. More fool me, I proposed without knowing about that. Seems her dream has always been to go to the big city and hobnob with the swells."

"Can you change her mind?"

"I'll try, but I'm not optimistic about my chances. Besides, what if I succeed and later on she resents me for interfering with that dream?"

Seth seemed to be considering Caleb's words. "That is a risk, all right. But if she's worth fighting for—"

"She is." A hole as big as the prairie opened in Caleb's heart. He dared not consider a life without Lily. "I will fight, but…"

"If the good Lord wants you two together, He'll figure a way."

"That's putting powerful pressure on Him."

Seth grinned. "He can handle it. His shoulders are broad. Cast yourself on Him."

"If only it were that easy."

"It is." Seth put an arm around him and drew him close. "Besides, you're going to St. Louis, too."

Caleb reared back. "What're you talking about?"

"When you leave the army, there's no sense you coming to the ranch right then, not when we need you in St. Louis to order supplies and make contacts with bankers and livestock dealers. What do you say?"

"I'll do what's needed for the ranch, though personally I fail to see how being in St. Louis will matter if Lily turns me down."

"Patience, brother. We none of us knows what the future holds. That's in God's hands."

Caleb wished he shared his brother's unwavering faith, but right now his future was in Lily's hands, and that didn't feel good at all.

Lily watched out the window two days after the debacle at the river as Caleb rode out with a small contingent of troops. She could tell he was still favoring the side of his wound. She had tried her best to stay mad at him, but now she worried whether it was too soon for him to be on active duty. Then her mere concern made her angry all over again—at herself for caring. In her hand she held a note delivered a few minutes ago by a young private. She had read it twice, shaking her head at the sheer folly that characterized her relationship with Caleb. Despite herself, she unfolded the page and scanned it once more.

My dear Lily,
I could not leave today without attempting to set things right between us. I should have told you I would soon be leaving the army, but truth to tell, after meeting you, I had not anticipated that severance with enthusiasm, since I knew it would remove me from your presence. In a very short time, you have endeared yourself to me in the ways of which I have already spoken. It was never my intent to be dishonest with you.

You were justified to accuse me of not sharing my dreams before asking you to be my wife. The urgency of my love for you overcame reason. Let me share those dreams with you now.

I have saved much of my army pay to join with my father and Seth in buying land for a cattle operation in southeast Kansas in an area called the Flint Hills. Sophie, Pa and Seth have been there for some months and have succeeded in getting the necessary fencing and buildings in place. Despite their labors to that end, my dream is still incomplete. I long for a family of my own. At the heart of that family is a woman to love and to cherish as my wife. That woman, dearest one, is you. However, all I can do now is ask for your forgiveness for my oversights and shortcomings and hope that you will give this letter prayerful consideration.

In humility and love,
Caleb

Stuffing the note in her pocket, she put on her bonnet and circled the parade ground, deep in thought. She couldn't deny her feelings for Caleb. He was everything she should want in a husband. He was a noble and ambitious young man, who shared her values, and a treasured companion. The fact that she melted when he held her hand or kissed her was a delicious bonus and a reason, out of all proportion to common sense, to visualize a happy life with him.

If only…

But the Flint Hills? Another wilderness just like the one she was fleeing? Full of the same heat, drought, prairie fires, wild winds and blizzards? Not to mention vermin and snakes? All of that coupled with her memory of the settler's wife who died in childbirth caused her stomach to clench.

More than ever she wished for some master puppeteer

to pull the strings of her destiny. Anything but having to make decisions for herself.

So intent was she that she barely noticed a platoon of mounted soldiers nearly on top of her. Jumping aside, she watched them pass. The beasts towered above her, and she had a sudden sense of her own insignificance. Self-pity was unbecoming. She had to be prepared with a decision when Caleb returned.

Then as if Mathilda Kellogg was suddenly whispering in her ear, Lily remembered the familiar words with which her mother ended every prayer. *Thy will, not mine, be done.* She would open her heart to God and await His direction.

Chapter Thirteen

Wincing with every jolt of the trot, Caleb bit back a moan as the cavalry made its way over stony ground. He'd been medically cleared for duty, but this sortie had tested him. They had accompanied a wagon train safely through territory where scouts had earlier sighted small bands of Indians and were now on their way back to the fort. Each hoofbeat sent pain radiating across his chest and down his arm.

It hadn't helped that the night before his nightmares had recurred in full fury. Already agitated about Lily, the dream had left him exhausted and frustrated. What had seemed so simple and beautiful several days ago— declaring his love to Lily—had turned to disappointment, but more than that, to hurt and the sense he'd made a fool of himself by trusting a woman again. While he hoped his note to Lily would cause her to see their relationship and future in a clearer light, he wouldn't permit himself to hope.

Bucephalus clattered over a dry streambed, sending shocks through his system, but that was nothing compared to the emotional pain of potentially losing Lily.

Seth's arrival had been a tonic and had given Caleb a

glimpse of his promising future. The basics for a working ranch were in place, and now it was a matter of establishing the herd and deciding on markets for the livestock. Caleb wished he could have responded to Seth's glowing plans for the ranch with equal enthusiasm. Although he would enjoy the change of pace from the army, he feared the most important element of his future might be missing. Lily.

Never having been married, Seth had given what encouragement he could to Caleb's suit, but had spent most of his visit going over the list of supplies and equipment he wanted Caleb to purchase in St. Louis. Rightfully so. The ranch was, after all, their primary focus.

Suddenly Bucephalus shied to avoid a huge anthill, and Caleb nearly lost his seat. Unsettled. That was him. In another day or two, his fate would be sealed, one way or the other. He couldn't remember ever feeling so helpless.

Late in the afternoon Lily stood in the door of the hospital watching the cavalrymen return to the fort, their faces shadowed with trail dust. At the front rode Caleb, his hat pulled low over his eyes, his features drawn as if in pain. Sighing, Lily put words to her concern—had this ride come too soon after his recovery from the shoulder wound? When he dismounted to salute the colonel, she noticed his fleeting grimace. Surely he would seek medical attention if needed.

She had other worries. Advice had rained down from all sides, including Seth. She had been surprised when he sought her out shortly after Caleb left. His had been a persuasive argument.

"Miss Lily," he had said turning his hat in his hands, "might I have a word?"

She had offered him a seat in one of the front porch

rockers, then taken another for herself. Even though he was larger than Caleb, he had the same curly hair and warm hazel eyes. "How may I be of help?"

He cleared his throat nervously. "I reckon I shouldn't be interfering in your business, but Caleb is my business. We've been best friends since we were pups, especially after our mother died. He was always the smart one, his head forever stuck in books. I admire him mightily. If I could've, I'd have protected him from these past years in the army." He hesitated. "He's seen terrible things."

"I know. His are experiences no man should have to endure, but, alas, so many had no choice."

"Then you'll understand, ma'am, why his happiness is important to me and his pa and sister."

"Caleb has told me how close you all are."

"True, but it hasn't been the same without him. We're mighty pleased he'll soon be joining us in God's beautiful country."

"Your ranching enterprise sounds quite ambitious."

"We have big plans, and Caleb will play an important part in achieving success. He's a good man, you know."

Lily lowered her eyes. "Yes, he is." In that moment her heart swelled with affection for the brother so devoted to Caleb.

"I don't exactly know how to put this." He tugged at his cuff as if buying time. "He's powerful in love with you, Miss Lily."

Lily blushed, unable to speak.

"I don't want my brother to get hurt. He would be a fine husband for any woman, but he doesn't want just any woman. I do believe if you turn him down, that'll be the end of courtship for him." He hurried on, as if racing to complete his spiel. "You would like our family. Why, you and Sophie? Shoot. You'd be sisters in less time than it takes to skin a rabbit. And Pa and me? Why, we have pined to have another woman about the place. Our ma was special. I think you are, too. With all respect, ma'am, please give Caleb a chance. He truly was trying to tell you all his plans when, like a big galoot, I interrupted." He stood and clapped the hat on his head. "I expect I've said all I came to say, and I'll be leaving for home tomorrow. I hope I haven't overstepped my bounds by speaking with you, but I love my brother and wanted to do all I could to reassure you that he is the finest man I know. There. That's all."

Lily would like to have put the man out of his misery with the answer he had come to solicit and he had certainly made some telling points, but she was still of two minds about her future. "Seth—may I call you Seth? You have done yourself and your brother proud. I promise to consider what you have said. You are absolutely correct— Caleb is a fine man who doesn't deserve further hurt. However, there are many factors at play, and I'm doing my utmost to consider what will be best for both of us."

"Thank you. That's all I can ask." He tipped his hat. "I hope to see you again someday."

Then, without a backward glance, he had lumbered off.

Watching now as the soldiers dispersed, Lily saw Major Hurlburt and Caleb walk toward headquarters, deep in conversation. Every now and then Caleb made a grab for his arm; it was then she knew that he was, indeed, in pain. Many men might have asked to be excused from duty for medical reasons. Not Caleb. It wasn't in his nature to shy away from a fight.

Her father had already gone home for dinner when Lily finally finished remaking the beds of two soldiers who had been dismissed to their barracks. Her back ached and the stifling heat rendered her clothing uncomfortable. Before leaving, she splashed cool water on her face and wrists. She knew she was delaying, finding distraction in her duties. Tonight she faced the difficult task of deciding once and for all where her heart lay.

She had prayed for guidance, even going so far as to ask God for a sign to help with her decision. However, she had not counted on His surprising efficiency. When she entered their home, her father stood near the kitchen table beside Rose. As Lily approached them, she was discomfited by their wary expressions.

Then she saw it. Lying on the table. A flat package. Addressed to her. Color flooded her cheeks. A package from Aunt Lavinia. She couldn't move.

Rose came to her side. "Aren't you going to open it?"

Her father eased himself into a chair and sat, hands folded in his lap, head bowed.

"Yes," Lily said, untying the string enclosing the parcel. She was all thumbs and the knots were proving difficult. Finally she succeeded in unwrapping the contents and spreading them across the surface of the table. An itinerary. Money for travel clothes and stagecoach fare to Independence. Tickets for passage on a riverboat down the Missouri. And a letter from Aunt Lavinia.

She crumpled into the chair beside her father. "I'm really going, aren't I?"

His Adam's apple worked and all he could do was nod. Looking up, Lily watched Rose turn toward the stove, but not before a tear ran down her face.

Lily knew she should be ecstatic. Lying before her were the means to achieve an ambition she had cherished since childhood, the fulfillment of years of daydreams and fantasies. Yet the hurrahs that should be bursting from her mouth were nothing more than sawdust. She had never been so confused in her entire life. Any decision would be the wrong one. *Thy will, not mine, be done.* How was she to know the difference?

After Rose went to bed and her father left for his nightly hospital rounds, Lily sat at the kitchen table, bent over two letters, one of which would seal her fate. The first from Aunt Lavinia, the other, Caleb's. She moved the lantern closer and read, for the fourth or fifth time, words that had etched themselves on her heart.

I long for a family of my own. At the heart of that family is a woman to love and to cherish as my wife. That woman, dearest one, is you.

She caressed the note with her fingertips before laying it aside and returning to her aunt's message, one replete with enticements she had long envisioned.

My darling niece,
We are back from Newport—a charming summer retreat among the most genteel families. How I wish you could have enjoyed our pastimes—sailing, lawn tennis and first-rate evening amusements. I am confident that day will come for you after you make a fine marriage. Already I have identified some up-and-coming young men for you to meet. What fun we shall have picking among them!
 I have booked river passage for you on the *Mary McDonald,* due to arrive here in mid-September. The trip will be arduous, but with what a loving welcome we will greet you! It will be a joy to show you the sights and have you as my companion for the theater. Mr. Dupree has agreed to squire you to

lectures by noted area intellectuals since that is not my cup of tea.

All of this, of course, will be preceded by dressmakers', milliners' and cobblers' appointments and a tutorial concerning the local social customs. By coming here, you will not only bring me much pleasure, but you will also honor your mother's fondest wish. From her letters, I know how Mathilda yearned for you to experience the opportunities and culture available here.

Awaiting your arrival with love,
Aunt Lavinia

Lily extinguished the lantern. She could no longer confront the words tugging at her as if she were a rag doll being contested by two children. But these were not children. They were two loving human beings, both committed to her happiness. Childless Aunt Lavinia, offering her a Cinderella transformation, a fairyland of diversions and fulfillment of both her own and her mother's aspirations. And Caleb…offering her the uncertainties and hardships of the prairie, the promise of a home and family and…his heart. No closer to a decision than she had been all evening, she buried her head in her arms, willing a lightning bolt to etch the answer across the night sky.

"Lily?"

She must have dozed, because when she looked up, her father was standing over her, his hand resting gently on her shoulder. "Papa…what time is it?"

"Just after eleven." He sat down at the table, reaching out to cover her hand with his own. "Can't sleep? What's fretting you?"

"I'm so confused."

He patted her hand. "Big decisions, daughter. Do you want to talk about it?"

She had talked with others until she was exhausted by the effort, but this was her father who had never done anything but love her. She nodded.

"Well, then, let's lay out both cases. What compels you to go to St. Louis?"

She ran through all the reasons she had amassed through the years, including her longing for intellectual stimulation and her antipathy for frontier living. She ended with what was, for her, the most binding emotional argument. "It was what Mama wanted."

"And young Captain Montgomery?"

"He would take me to the very prairie I mean to escape."

"One's environment can be important," her father said noncommittally. "What else?"

"He yearns for a wife and family. He is a hard worker and a good man."

"You make him sound like a paper cutout." In the moonlight, he studied her face. "What are you holding back, Lily?"

She looked away from her father's probing eyes, her chest constricted by what she couldn't bring herself to utter.

"Lily? No running away. Not when you have such an important decision to make." He withdrew his hand and leaned forward on his elbows, repeating his question. "What are you holding back?"

Finally she met his eyes. "He loves me and I don't want to hurt him."

"I agree that he is very much in love with you. What about you? Do you love him?"

There it was. *The* question. "I don't know."

"I think you do know." He paused to let his words penetrate. "What is holding you back?"

"Oh, Papa." She stood and began pacing the room. "I'm afraid. I'm afraid if I don't go to St. Louis, I will one day regret that I didn't and, worse yet, resent Caleb for frustrating my dream. I'm afraid of the harsh life I might lead as the wife of a cattle rancher. I'm afraid I will be disloyal to Mama. I'm afraid of making a mistake I can do nothing to rectify, not without involving too many other people."

"The best decisions never arise from fear, daughter. They result from love." He rose, rounded the table and held her in his arms. "Here is what I have learned. Love must be grounded in truth and in the desire to put another before oneself, but there are no certainties. Love is a huge risk. You must be sure you take it with the right man." He held her close and she could hear the steady beat of his heart. "One last thing. Your mama is no longer here, but I can tell you with certainty what she most wanted for you. Your happiness. She would approve whether you go to St. Louis or marry Caleb so long as you are happy."

Lily was overcome by the depth of her father's love for her and hers for him. No matter what she chose to do, leaving him and Rose would make any decision bittersweet.

"Now, child, let's retire for the evening." With a pat on her shoulder, he was gone, and shortly, she followed him upstairs.

Will Creekmore sidled up to Caleb after the morning briefing. "You all right, Montgomery? I notice you favoring your arm."

"Still feeling a bit rocky, but I'll be fine."

"I don't reckon the latest mission helped any."

Caleb laughed mirthlessly. "We army men do what we must."

"Not much longer for you. When do you leave?"

"Around the middle of August. It feels strange. This—" he gestured around the fort "—has been my entire adult life."

"You'll be a fine rancher. After a bit, you won't miss the army."

Caleb nodded, but knew he would never forget where he had been and what he had done in the line of duty.

"Maybe it's none of my business, but Fannie and I wonder how you plan to leave things with Lily."

"I've laid my cards on the table. Now it's up to her."

Will gave him a two-finger salute. "We're rooting for you, Cap." Will proceeded across the parade ground toward his home, leaving Caleb standing alone, staring up at the flag flapping in the breeze. Across the way he heard a hammer clanging on an anvil in the smithy's shop, the raucous shouts of the hostlers outside the stables and the playful whinnying of horses. Saw the line of peaceful Indians, settlers and soldiers coming and going from the sutler's. Smelled the aroma of fresh-baked bread from the baker's oven. All of it familiar and soon to be forever left behind.

Seth's visit had provided an incentive to prepare himself for the next chapter. His brother's excitement about the ranch was contagious, and being with Seth had made him long for his father and sister. In some ways he wished he were going straight to the Flint Hills, but being assigned the St. Louis trip on ranch business made him feel useful and needed.

His daydreaming came to an abrupt end when a sergeant approached, saluted and handed him an envelope with the single word *Caleb* inscribed on it. As he wandered toward the stables to check on Bucephalus, he opened the envelope and unfolded a small scrap of paper. "Please meet me tonight after supper in the cemetery. Lily." He stopped in his tracks. The barest of messages, couched in the most neutral of tones, saying nothing to give him hope. He had no means either to make time fly or to affect her answer. The day simply had to be endured.

Lily excused herself from supper, offering no explanation. Before she met with Caleb she wanted time with her mother. The earth was still warm when Lily sank to the ground beside the grave. When the time came, how difficult it would be to leave this sacred spot. Yet more enduring than this place were the memories of her vibrant, loving mother which would accompany her wherever she went.

"Mama," she murmured. "It's time for me to go—either to St. Louis or to marry Caleb. How I wish you were here to advise me. I think I know what I must do. Please help me to go forth with courage and hope and live each day fully, as you taught us to do." Her mother's *Amen* came in the rustle of wind through the grasses and the repetitive song of a whip-poor-will.

She stood, adjusted the skirt of her best dress and waited, hands patiently folded, for Caleb to arrive. She had not spoken to him during this long week, their only communication being the exchange of notes.

Then she spotted him, striding toward her, dressed in his official "best," his polished buttons, shiny boots and clean-shaven face a testimony to his care in preparing to meet her. He approached, stopping several feet from her. His was an arresting presence—so straight of posture, his broad shoulders a bulwark of strength. Nerves threatened to undo her. "Good evening, Caleb."

"Lily," was all he said, and on his lips her name sounded like a prayer.

"Shall we walk?"

He put an arm around her waist. "It's what we do, isn't it?"

Without a word, they made their way toward the river. Now that he was here by her side, her heart fluttered like a hummingbird's wing. Every thought, every argument, every emotion she'd experienced in the past seven days seemed centered in the sensation of being nestled against him. "I noticed you were favoring your shoulder when you returned from the last mission."

"Ever the nurse, aren't you?" His smile looked forced rather than teasing. "As you've pointed out, healing takes time."

"Lots of things take time."

He stopped walking and turned to face her, his expression solemn. "Like decisions?"

"Like decisions."

Neither of them spoke for a long while, their eyes locked in a communication beyond the power of words. Lily wished this moment would never end, because to end it would set a course from which there could be no return.

Caleb lifted his hand to her face, his fingers moving lightly as if memorizing her features. "Nothing has changed for me, Lily. I love you and pray you return that sentiment. These days of waiting have been agony."

Her lips trembled under the butterfly-wing touch of his thumb, and her body quivered, racked by a storm of indecision. But no. She had made up her mind. Inhaling deeply, she forced out the words. "You honor me with your love and with your proposal. I have considered both long and prayerfully."

"And…?" In his eyes she read the pain of one facing an executioner.

"Caleb, I cannot marry you." She watched him bite

his lower lip, then stare over her head at some point on the far horizon.

"You're going to St. Louis to live in your aunt's world."

On his lips, the words sounded like a renunciation of all that she held dear. "I must. Please let me explain."

"What's there to explain? You have the chance to move in social circles I could never offer you, with opportunities beyond my power to provide. You have been clear with me that such an adventure is what you have always yearned to experience. I suppose I can understand that life on a ranch in the middle of nowhere can hardly compete."

Lily knotted her fingers in anguish. "It's not that. Your offer to share your dream, even if it is vastly different from mine, touched my heart. And I know you meant to tell me all about it before Seth arrived, but, Caleb, what if I gave up my dream for yours and ultimately came to resent you? I don't want a life where I'm constantly second-guessing my decisions."

"Nor do I. If you cannot give yourself to me unreservedly, as I do to you, then we are doomed." He kicked the toe of his boot into the dirt. "What kind of man would I be if I stood in the way of your dream?"

"What kind of man will you be, anyway?"

He shook his head, and she couldn't bear to meet his eyes. "A broken one without you." A tinge of bitterness crept into his tone. "But again, healing takes time and, somehow, I will heal."

"It isn't that I don't care about you." Even to her own ears, that sounded weak.

"I suppose there is no need to prolong this conversation. I would prefer we try to end as we began, as friends. Further talk might make that impossible. Please, though, permit me to satisfy myself by asking one more question."

"Of course."

Quite unexpectedly, he drew her to him, so close she could feel the heat rising from his body. "We've always pledged honesty. Now, Lily, tell me you don't love me."

Surely he must hear the crack of her heart and sense the anguish of her soul because, God help her, she could not utter those words.

Caleb never knew how he held himself together to escort Lily in silence to her home. Foolishly, he had believed that she had come to love him as he loved her. All his pipe dreams of making a home together and fathering her children had gone up in a puff of smoke. He knew he would never be the same, nor would he ever stop loving her. It had been one thing to lose Rebecca to another man, but to be rejected for himself was a hurt beyond describing. Yet, loving Lily, he could hardly stand in the way of her happiness. Reaching her porch, he took a deep breath and forced himself to say, "I shall love you till the day I die. I hope your dreams come true. I wish you only the best."

"Thank you, Caleb. Your understanding means a great deal." She laid the flat of her hand against his heart. "Honestly, I cannot say that I don't love you. I very well may. What I *do* know is that when I commit to a man, it will be unconditionally and forever."

"I appreciate your honesty." Before he turned to go, he captured her face between his hands and kissed her with all the regret and love warring within him. "Be happy, Lily." Then he walked swiftly away before she might hear the unmanly sobs gargling in his throat.

As he strode across the parade ground, a long-forgotten memory came to him. He and his mother in their garden, hunkering beside a bird, struggling to fly. "Oh, poor thing. Look, Caleb. Its wing is broken."

"Can we fix it? Please, Ma. It can't fly."

His mother had studied his crestfallen face and then scooped the tiny creature into her apron. "All right, son, we'll do our best, but you have to understand one thing."

Elated that they would try to save the bird, he had scarce heard what she had said next. "We can nurse the bird, but it will never be ours. We will fix the wing so the bird can enjoy what it was born to do. Fly. We cannot keep creatures unless we give them freedom."

Now her words came back to him like a clarion call, and he understood them as never before. Lily could never be his until she flew away to freedom. All he could do was let her go. And pray.

Chapter Fourteen

For Lily in the ensuing days, it was as if she was experiencing everything for the very first time—and the last. Why hadn't she paid more notice to the sheer gold of the sunflowers as they followed the sun across the sky or to the flutelike trills of the bold meadowlark perched on a nearby post? Never before had Rose's biscuits and honey tasted so satisfying, nor the chorus of male voices singing camp songs from the barracks sounded so hauntingly melodic. As departure approached, she gathered such memories into her heart. Bittersweet memories.

It pained her to observe Caleb going about his business, never glancing in her direction. However, there was nothing more to be said. She had hurt him, and for that she was regretful. Occasionally she succumbed to second thoughts, but then chastised herself. She had charted her course and was determined to take full advantage of the journey upon which she would soon embark. Another letter had arrived from Aunt Lavinia, enclosing a beautiful invitation to an early fall garden party at the home of a neighbor. The elegant engraving abraded Lily's finger, a tactile reminder of the wonders awaiting her.

She had been filling her days instructing Fannie concerning hospital procedures. Worried about Papa being shorthanded, she had been relieved when he solicited Fannie as her replacement. Fortunately, Fannie was proving an apt pupil.

The two sat in front of the apothecary's chest, Lily introducing Fannie to the properties and uses of the medicines stored there—from quinine for malaria to home remedies for coughs and catarrh. "Once you begin administering these, you will have no trouble remembering their uses," Lily reassured her friend.

Fannie looked up from the notebook in which she was inscribing Lily's instructions. "I'm excited to have this opportunity. Besides, it will help pass the time."

"It does do that. Daily fort life can be dull."

"With the help of this hospital work, I have not yet been bored."

"Spoken like a true newlywed."

Fannie turned to Lily, her eyes sparkling. "I pray it may always be so. With my Will, I am confident it will be."

Lily suppressed the flicker of envy that caused her to look down at the bottle of iodine she held in her hands. "You are truly blessed."

"Indeed."

Lily sensed Fannie had been about to speak of Caleb, but had censored herself. She stood to replace the iodine in the cabinet, but that action served for naught because the question tumbled out, anyway. "How is he?"

Fannie did not pretend ignorance. "Caleb goes through the motions of work, Will says, but mainly keeps to himself. I've often seen him entering the library in the evening. No doubt you would like me to say he is fine, but that would be an untruth. The man is pining." Fannie closed her notebook. "Perhaps you would prefer that he pine, since that offers strong proof of his affection for you."

"I need no proof of that," Lily whispered. "I know I am walking away from a wonderful man."

"It is not for me to judge. You are my friend, and I trust you to know what is best for yourself."

"Can one every really know that?"

"I know. Will is best for me." Lily saw the concern for her that Fannie could not conceal. "One day, you, too, will know beyond any doubt what makes you happy." She snapped the notebook open. "Now then, tell me about belladonna."

For the next hour, they applied themselves to the lesson. When they finished, Lily patted her friend on the shoulder. "Good work. I feel so much better about leaving Father."

"You worry about him."

"I can't help it. Ever since my brother and then Mama died, he has aged rapidly. I think he's tired."

"And grieving."

"That, too. Leaving him and Rose for so long will be hard."

"Try not to fret. I will write frequently, keeping you posted on things, including your father's well-being."

"Thank you, Fannie. I am blessed to have such a friend as you."

Fannie leaned over and hugged her. "Let us vow always to be close."

"I am counting on that," Lily said, suddenly envisioning the miles and miles she would soon put between herself and everyone she loved. She would need all the courage she could muster.

With only two weeks left of his army service, Caleb found himself slowly transitioning out of involvement in strategic planning. At loose ends, he often found refuge in the library, but not even *Moby Dick* with its vivid descriptions of whaling could capture his attention. More often than not, he simply sat in a chair holding his open book, wishing for the hours and days to pass until he would no longer be tortured by proximity to Lily. Yet, paradoxically, the thought of being separated from her was devastating.

Just before taps one evening, the library door opened, and he was surprised to see Ezra Kellogg. "I thought I'd find you here," the older man said.

Caleb remembered his last conversation with Ezra. How different he had felt on that occasion when he'd been given permission to court Lily. Now he couldn't imagine what they could possibly have to discuss. "I enjoy the quiet." Caleb pointed to a chair. "Please. Sit."

Ezra had the grace not to mince words. "I am sorry that Lily's decision has probably disappointed you."

"Thank you." Caleb didn't trust himself to say anything further.

"You must be wondering why I've sought you out."

Caleb shrugged.

The surgeon leaned forward in his chair, pinning Caleb with his piercing blue eyes. "I have a favor to ask, one that I have no expectation you will want to fulfill. Yet please hear me out."

Caleb sat back and folded his hands. "I'm listening."

"If I had any other recourse, I would not presume upon your good will. From young Creekmore, am I correct in understanding that your brother has asked you to go to St. Louis on ranch business?"

Caleb had an uneasy suspicion where this conversation was headed. "Yes."

"Difficult as it might be, I am asking you to consider accompanying Lily on her trip there."

Caleb felt blood suffusing his cheeks. He wanted to

slam his fist on a table or stalk out of the room. How dare the man suggest such a thing!

Ezra held up his hand. "Before you say anything, just listen."

Caleb waited. He figured silence was his most gentlemanly response.

"Lily has never traveled by herself. You and I both know the possible perils for a single woman in a stagecoach or on a riverboat. I am concerned for her safety. She is headstrong enough to think she can handle the exigencies of such a journey."

Caleb closed his eyes against images of foul-mouthed frontiersmen and coarse, beefy sailors—all of whom would salivate over a beautiful young woman.

"I have no one else to ask. Lily is precious to me, and I'd like to believe to you, as well. There is no denying the awkwardness and, dare I say, the pain of such an arrangement." The man took off his glasses and swiped at his eyes. "It is difficult enough to let her do this thing without also wondering each hour if she is safe."

Caleb gritted his teeth. He couldn't imagine a worse torture than spending days on end with a woman he loved who could not return that sentiment.

"If you care about her, as I know you do, surely you see the wisdom of traveling together."

"I'm not sure I can make such arrangements at this late date." The minute the words came out of his mouth, Caleb knew he'd capitulated.

"I have telegraphed the steamboat line to secure your passage. Your river voyage will be at my expense, sir." He paused. "As for the stagecoach, perhaps the ranch can cover that cost. If you agree to help Lily, you might have to spend a few extra days here after you muster out."

"When is she leaving?"

"August 20." Caleb half listened as Ezra outlined the plans in more specific detail. Every fiber of his being cried, "No!" Why was he even contemplating such a masochistic endeavor?

Lily. The love of his life. That was why. "Against my better judgment but out of concern for your daughter, I will accompany her to the wharf in St. Louis."

Ezra slumped in relief. "I, sir, will be forever in your debt."

The morning before she was scheduled to leave, Lily sewed the final button on the jacket of her new traveling costume—a serviceable blue, matching her bonnet. Her trunk was packed, despite the fact Aunt Lavinia would probably cringe at her unfashionable wardrobe, and she had made a list of the items she would carry in her reticule. Snipping the final thread, she sat back, running her hands over the bodice of the jacket. How many days would she alternate between this and her only other travel ensemble? Now that her departure was imminent, she was filled with a cascade of emotions—excitement, anxiety, nostalgia, homesickness—and a number of questions. How difficult would it prove to be on her own? To leave her beloved father and sister? To say goodbye to her mother's grave site? She swallowed threatening tears. To travel for three or more weeks with Caleb?

She stood, shook out the jacket and moved to the ironing board. The iron heating on the stove hissed when she tested it. Spreading the jacket on the board and bending to the task, she remonstrated with herself. She had formulated her dream, and with Aunt Lavinia's help, she was on the verge of realizing it. Now was not the time for faintheartedness. Upset as she had been when her father gave her the news that Caleb would travel with her, she acknowledged grudgingly that his presence would help secure her safety until she reached St. Louis. However, it would not ensure a relaxed trip.

The day passed in a whirl of last-minute details. The Hurlburts were entertaining the family for her final dinner at Fort Larned. Before dressing for that occasion, she made a final visit to the cemetery. The setting sun cast burnished rays of light upon the grave, and the familiar cooing of doves produced a plaintive requiem. Lily stood, rapt, staring at the chiseled name on the stone. *Mathilda.* In a moment of clarity, she realized that no matter how far from this place life took her, her mother's influence would accompany her. She placed a hand on top of the grave marker. "Mama, Papa told me all you ever wanted for me was to be happy. I intend to do that by taking full advantage of new opportunities. Thank you for your love and example." Then, oddly, she found herself smiling, as if her mother had touched her in blessing.

The dinner party was a time of forced gaiety, involving the major and his wife, Fannie and Will, Ezra and Rose… and Caleb. As a result of the cavorting butterflies in her stomach, Lily picked at her food, knowing full well she would think of this sumptuous spread many times as she sampled the fare at stagecoach way stations. Adding to her nervousness were the veiled looks passing between Effie, Fannie and Rose and then redirected to her, as if she were a patient who required observation for an undetermined illness. No clairvoyant, she nevertheless knew exactly what they were thinking. How could she launch into this adventure and turn down a man as fine as Caleb? She had ultimately given up trying to explain. She was moving on to the "beat of a different drum," as Mr. Thoreau had put it.

Before the party broke up, Effie pulled Lily aside and

wrapped her in a motherly hug. "We will miss you more than you know," she whispered. Then she pulled away, held Lily by the shoulders and added, "Whenever you find a man suitable as a husband, remember the importance of honesty."

Lily nodded. "No secrets, right?"

"Open communication. Trust."

Lily embraced the older woman again. "Thank you. I shall miss your counsel."

"And I, your sunny, generous nature."

Later, snuggled under the light sheet next to Rose, Lily realized she would probably never again share a bed with her sister. Starting the very next night, she would find herself alone for the first time in her life. Her new reality came crashing down and she moaned softly.

"Lily?" Rose turned to face her. "You can't sleep, either?"

"No. So many thoughts are running through my mind."

"I can't believe the time is finally here."

"Nor can I. Before, such a trip was a fantasy."

"Papa and I will miss you so."

"And I you." Even on the eve of her trip, Lily found it difficult to imagine a life without her family.

"I've cried all the tears I have within me, but I want you to know that Papa and I will be fine. We will be praying for the fulfillment of your dreams."

"When we meet again, Rose, I shall have so much to tell you."

"I will count the days." Rose laced her hand through Lily's. "I love you, sister."

"I love you, too." Somehow in the silence, Lily managed to calm her racing heart and fall into a peaceful slumber, her fingers still entwined in Rose's.

* * *

Caleb had been part of too many leave-takings to watch Lily bid farewell to her family. Instead, he busied himself loading their trunks on the stagecoach. Insofar as possible, he planned to keep his distance from her, staying just close enough to protect her from unwelcome attentions. Surveying the fellow passengers, he saw only one other woman, a toothless crone headed for Council Grove, and four men, from their Western dress, obviously veterans of the trail. He would need to keep his eye on them, particularly the one ogling the assembled women, spitting tobacco indiscriminately and turning the air blue with oaths.

The driver bawled out the order to leave. Lily threw herself into her father's arms, her "Oh, Papa!" moistening every onlooker's eyes, including, to his chagrin, his own. With the halfhearted effort of a jaunty salute, he hauled himself onto the top of the coach. If he could maintain this seat for the trip to Independence, he could avoid all but the most cursory conversation with Lily. The passengers began taking their seats, but Lily lingered until she was the last one to climb into the coach. Then, with the crack of the driver's whip, the vehicle lumbered onto the trail, jostling passengers and careening from side to side as the horses picked up speed.

From his perch, Caleb watched the buildings of Fort Larned grow indistinct until the only landmark remaining was the towering flagpole with the colors flying in the stiff breeze. Unexpectedly he felt a lump rising in his throat with the reality that the painful first chapter of his adult life had closed. Too much conflict, too much blood, too much guilt. He had hoped to end his career with the promise of a new life with Lily. Now, somehow, he faced that next chapter even more alone than he had been when he had marched to war with his comrades from Jefferson

City. He pulled the brim of his hat lower over his face, resigned to the long, challenging trip.

Lily had only thought she knew discomfort before. Miserable August heat, clouds of dust, mingled odors of unwashed bodies and the nausea-producing motion of the lurching coach caused her to pray constantly for deliverance even as she knew she faced more days on the trail. Alighting at night, she hoped for relief, but the inns along the way were primitive and the food so unappealing she could scarcely eat, even though she knew she must. It was only at meals that she saw Caleb, who hovered close by to spare her the conversation of trail-hardened men. Her fellow passengers were an odd lot—the old woman said nothing, one of the men hummed under his breath in a sleep-inducing monotone, two engaged in hotly contested card games and the fourth made her miserably uncomfortable by staring at her over the edge of the newspaper he pretended to read.

Arriving finally at an inn offering a bath, Lily could not wait to divest herself of her soiled clothing and cleanse away the grime of the trip. Afterward, she felt minimally refreshed and was pleased to find in her reticule a small vial of eau de cologne. Dabbing a drop behind each ear, she felt feminine for the first time since leaving home. She combed her newly washed hair into a chignon and went downstairs for a supper no better than the others along the route. For once, she beat Caleb to the table, but she was not without company. The unpleasant newspaper reader sidled up next to her and sat down. "How you doin', purty lady?"

She inched away from him, not daring to look into his lascivious face. "Middling."

"A lady such as yourself shouldn't be on the trail all by

her lonesome." He bit into a hard biscuit and continued talking, spewing crumbs across the table. "Might need a man to escort you. I'd be just the fella. Wouldn't let nobody hurt ya."

Lily froze, her spoonful of beans halfway to her mouth. She'd heard another man talk like this once before. Ingratiating. Sly. Contemptible.

"Cat got yer tongue?" The man leaned forward and circled her neck with his rough hand, his foul breath hot on her face. "Yer not only sweet-smellin', yer purty, too."

Adams! Without even thinking, she sprang to her feet, spilling her meal across the table and onto the floor. "Stay away from me!" She ran for the door, only to be swooped into Caleb's arms as he entered the tavern.

"Go to your room, Lily. Lock the door." Caleb set her down and strode toward the offensive passenger. As she darted up the stairs, she heard scuffling and then Caleb's commanding voice. "If you ever touch that woman again, even look at her, I will do to you what I have not hesitated to do to my enemies in battle. Are we clear?"

Lily could not make out the man's answer, but she sank, trembling, onto the cornhusk mattress, grateful beyond words for Caleb's intervention. Again. Whatever their current relationship, he was still her knight in shining armor.

A light rap sounded on the closed door. She moved cautiously and put her ear against the wood. "Lily? Are you all right?"

Relieved, she opened the door a crack. "I am fine, thanks to you. You seem to make a habit of saving me."

Caleb stood with his hands behind his back, worry etched on his face. "I'm glad I was here. I have put that man on notice. Furthermore, he and I will be trading places. Tomorrow he will ride topside, and I will join you in the coach."

Her heart gave a lilt before catapulting back down. She would be grateful for his protection, but having him by her side for the upcoming miles would pose challenges. She could not permit herself to get too comfortable with him or put too much reliance on his good will. "I shall welcome that change. He was a most disagreeable companion."

"That's putting it charitably," Caleb muttered. Then he seemed to draw himself up. "I bid you a good night."

"It is already good. You have been a source of great help. Thank you." She gazed up at him, at once wanting to prolong their conversation, but knowing she must end it. "Good night, Captain."

He nodded, then turned to walk away, but not before she heard him correct her under his breath. *"Caleb."*

The paddleboat *Mary McDonald* was a pleasant surprise to Lily, outfitted with the latest furnishings and amenities and carrying genteel passengers in the cabins near hers. The dining room sported crystal chandeliers, and the tables were covered with sparkling white linen and silver place settings. A string trio played in the background while the diners feasted on delicately prepared dishes, a far cry from the tasteless fare of her thirteen days on the trail. Still, the slow-moving boat, maneuvering the snags and shoals of the river with care, offered little relief from the heat. During the day she often sat on deck. She and Caleb had been seated at the same dinner table, so perforce, they were speaking often.

Three days before their docking in St. Louis, he sought her out on the deck. "May I sit?"

She waved vaguely at the vacant chair next to her. "Of course."

He settled beside her and pulled a book from his pocket.

"I found this volume in Independence and thought you might like it."

He handed it to her. *"Little Women?"* She couldn't hold back her smile. *"I've read about Miss Alcott's work."*

"It gives a different view of the War between the States. It is a touching story about a mother and her four daughters and the challenges that faced the families of soldiers."

She cradled the novel to her chest. "I will begin posthaste in order to finish it before we dock."

"No need. It is yours." He studied the passing shoreline as if to avoid looking at her. "An appreciation for literature is one thing we have in common."

She remembered fondly their discussions of poetry. "Thank you. I shall look forward to the story."

He stretched out his legs and folded his hands across his middle, seemingly engaged by the passing scenery. A puff of black smoke snorted from the stack and the boat shuddered as the paddle wheel began turning faster. Lily opened the book and tried to read, but lack of concentration caused her to go over one sentence four times. What was the matter with her?

Then Caleb put it into words for her. "We have only three more days together." Lily waited for him to go on. "I long ago decided that there is no purpose to be served by taking one last opportunity to press my case, nor to upset you by an emotional plea." After a slight pause, he turned to her. "But, Lily, you are my friend. I hope I am that to you, as well. I confess to having avoided you for much of the trip. Frankly, being near you is, in some ways, painful. However, I would like to propose that we spend this remaining time enjoying each other's company so that we may part from one another with mutual affection."

It was as if Caleb had read her mind. Even though her life was soon to take off in a dizzying direction, she craved the reassurance of his company and his steadying influence. Truth to tell, the nearer the boat approached its destination, the more edgy and insecure she felt. She had not seen Aunt Lavinia since childhood, nor, despite letters from her through the intervening years, could Lily picture with accuracy the grand life she was about to enter. "I should like that very much."

"Perhaps we could revisit our unfinished yet lively debate about Milton's poetic vision of the Garden of Eden."

"Let's do. Pray tell, of what value was poor Adam to the curious Eve?"

Their animated conversation began, continued during a promenade around the deck and concluded only when the dinner table conversation involving other passengers shifted to the latest news about railroad expansion across the West and the very recent introduction of reliable passenger service to those parts.

Rocked in the easy motion of her berth later that night, Lily smiled with the recollection of their stimulating conversation and in anticipation of future such dialogues with learned St. Louisians. Caleb's dedication to educating himself made him a stimulating and humorous partner in discourse. She would concentrate on those qualities and not on his mischievous eyes or his hearty laugh. And certainly not on the quivery feeling she had in the pit of her stomach every time he looked at her.

The closer they churned toward the wharf, the more boats of all sizes crowded the two rivers joining forces in St. Louis. Smoke belched from stacks, bells sounded warnings and rivermen's raucous cries filled the air. Caleb stood at Lily's side on the rail, watching the beehive of human activity around them. Or in Caleb's case, pretending to watch. All of his senses were centered on the beautiful young woman beside him who so filled his every waking thought. Out of the corner of his eye, he tried mentally to capture the exact hue of her honey-spun hair, the apricot glow of her cheeks, the insouciant turn of her mouth, the expressiveness of her long fingers, knowing even as he did so, that the image would fade like an old tintype.

Beside him, he could sense her breath coming in short gasps as tension stiffened her body. Before them spread an incredible sight—wagons, carriages, omnibuses weaving through a crowd of pedestrians of every race and nation; men of color, their bodies gleaming with sweat, hauling thick hawsers or hoisting bales of goods on their shoulders; huge warehouses lining the docks alongside taverns spilling noisy men onto the streets. "This isn't Fort Larned," he said in wry understatement.

Lily clutched his arm, her eyes widened in surprise. "Caleb, what have I done?"

He wondered that himself, but his role was to smooth her transition. "This is no place for a lady. Your aunt will soon whisk you off to their lovely, quiet residence."

She continued to hang on to his arm while the paddleboat nudged the dock, the porters began offloading baggage and the first passengers disembarked. She spoke, but in the whistle from the stack, he hadn't understood her. He leaned forward to hear her repeat herself. "I don't want to go."

"Faint heart, my lady? That will never do. You are experiencing a momentary loss of courage. I know you better than that. You are setting forth on a mission, the culmination of your dreams. Now then, take my arm and we'll find your aunt." Never had such cheering words been spoken with less sincerity. All he wanted to do was pick her up and carry her off, to save her from… What? He sighed. He couldn't save her. He was setting her free.

They made their way through the crowds to a place where a stack of baggage from the *Mary McDonald* awaited claiming. He had just located her trunk, when he heard a shrill voice. "Lily? Lily Kellogg?"

Lily stood on tiptoe and waved her hand. "Here I am, Aunt Lavinia."

With the dignity and command of a general, a woman dressed in a full-skirted emerald gown of flounces and appliqués and crowned by a large feather-covered hat parted the proverbial seas to reach Lily. "Niece, at last." She enveloped Lily in an embrace, and then stood back to study her. "You are lovely, my dear. I shall enjoy choosing a wardrobe to put you à la mode. You will be the talk of St. Louis."

Caleb hung back. He could hardly imagine Lily would want such recognition, but perhaps he was mistaken.

"Aunt Lavinia, I would like to present my friend and escort Captain Caleb Montgomery."

The woman's eyes swept over him in both inspection and dismissal. "Your service to my niece is appreciated, sir." Then she turned to Lily and pointed at the ground. "Are these your things?"

"Yes."

"My driver will gather them." She looked around, turning up her nose in distaste. "Let us remove ourselves from this disgusting place and wait in the carriage." She encircled Lily's waist. "Come along, now, dear. You're almost home."

Before Caleb could gather his wits to tell Lily goodbye or once more let her know that he would always love her, the formidable aunt had ushered her through the crowd toward a handsome carriage. Caleb stood motionless as if

the ground had collapsed beneath him, unaware of anything but Lily's fleeing back and the glint of her golden
hair. Then, slowly, he made his way to a vantage point
where he could watch her approach the vehicle that would
carry her away from him forever. Lavinia Dupree had a
death grip on her niece's arm, but he noticed Lily dragging her feet. Then just before she entered the carriage,
she turned her head, somehow finding him in the crowd.
Her eyes met his, and then she smiled—so wistfully that
even from that awful moment, he mined a nugget of hope.

Chapter Fifteen

Lily dipped her pen in the inkwell and then set it down. The blank sheet of stationery on the desk stymied her. How would she ever be able to describe for Rose and her father the grandeur in which she found herself? Her fantasies had been one thing; the reality was quite another. From the moment she sank into the lush carriage cushions at the wharf until she cast eyes on the Italianate facade of her new home, she had entered a world beyond her imagining. Stately elm trees shaded the avenue, lined with other equally imposing residences set back from manicured lawns. A housemaid, dressed in a black uniform and starched white apron, had greeted them at the door to relieve Lily of her hat and reticule. In that first moment, she could hardly take in the furnishings—marble floors, Chinese vases, silk tapestries, gilded mirrors—and everywhere elegant tables and chairs, artfully arranged on thick Persian carpets. The air itself, fragrant with floral potpourri, seemed rarefied.

Glancing around her ornate bedroom, hung with velvet drapes, she marveled at the poster bed, chiffonier and dressing table, all delicately painted in gilt and ivory. What would Rose make of this room? Even after two weeks, Lily was having difficulty falling asleep in the commodious bed. Fort Larned seemed very far away, indeed. Despite her sumptuous environment, the city was noisy and confusing, and she struggled to keep homesickness at bay.

Procrastination would get her nowhere. With a sigh, she adjusted the blotter under the stationery, picked up the pen again and began writing.

Dearest Rose and Papa,
By now you will have received my first, abbreviated message announcing my safe arrival in St. Louis and thanking you for taking the precaution of engaging Captain Montgomery to accompany me.

It is time for a more leisurely epistle in which I recount "Lily's Grand Adventure," not unlike that of Gulliver, who also entered strange, new lands. Aunt Lavinia has been most generous, transforming me from a rather drab personage into a belle (those are her words).

Once more Lily set aside the pen. Her family would be distressed to know the means of that transformation, beginning with consignment of most of her clothes to the rag bin. Since her arrival she had been prodded by corsetieres, measured by shoemakers, draped by dressmakers, coiffed by hairdressers, topped off by milliners and subjected to milk baths, hand creams and cucumber facials—all in the name of fashion. Her reading of *Godey's Lady's Book* had ill-prepared her for how exhausting the pursuit of style and beauty could be.

You would not recognize your prairie flower, decked out in crinolines, satins, laces and dancing slippers. At last, Aunt Lavinia has pronounced me fit for polite company. Yet there is much I still must learn to prevent embarrassing myself in society. I hasten to assure you that every minute here has exceeded my expectations. Despite that, I miss you both more than I even imagined and pray nightly for your health and well-being.

She concluded with a cursory description of the house and a mention of the garden party which would serve as her introduction to the Duprees' coterie. Blowing on the page to dry the ink, she slipped it into the envelope she had already addressed and rose to deliver it to the mail stand in the front hall.

Reaching the bottom of the stairs and depositing the letter, she decided to go to the library in hopes of finding something to read. The room was dark, and high shelves laden with books dwarfed her. Crossing to the window, she pulled back the drapes to let in the sunshine. Studying the spines of the volumes nearest the light, she didn't hear Lavinia enter.

"Child, whatever are you doing in here?" Her aunt stood in the doorway, her brows elevated in surprise.

"I am hunting for a book to amuse or educate me."

"Amuse? Educate?" Lavinia made the words sound like blasphemy. "Libraries are for men. No point to fill your pretty head with tedious ideas, especially not on a lovely autumn day like this. Repair with me to the morning room, and I shall fill you with all the latest gossip, a better education for society than any treatise in that library. Then this afternoon, you may accompany me on my weekly social calls."

Wisely, Lily did not argue even though she longed to point out that many modern women were becoming more broadly educated. Caught up in Lavinia's wake from that moment on, it was only that night in the solitude of her bedroom that Lily had time to reflect on the strange episode in the library. Never in her life had she been discouraged from reading. Quite the contrary. Apparently, though, it was not an activity smiled upon for women in this milieu. Lily was dumbfounded. Were females supposed to park their brains at the door? Rely upon men for news and intellectual stimulation? For the first time she began to wonder what she had bartered away for her St. Louis adventure.

His business in St. Louis concluded after a couple of weeks, Caleb was set to embark upriver late in the afternoon for Independence and then on to the ranch by horseback. He had been able to negotiate some favorable terms and delivery dates and felt satisfied with the contacts he had made. After the relative quiet of Fort Larned, the hubbub of the city was a constant assault on the senses. Outside his hotel window, heavy conveyances rattled past at all hours, hawkers selling wares shouted their spiels and from the riverfront came the never-ending noise of gears grinding and whistles screaming. The heavy smoke settling over the town made him long for prairie breezes.

Yet desirable as leaving this place might be, the idea set him on edge. Once he departed St. Louis, whatever chance he had to see Lily again departed with him. All morning as he set about packing his belongings, he fought with himself. He had seen Lily's aunt and her carriage. *Opulent* was the only word for the life Lily had entered two weeks ago, the life, he reminded himself, that was the fulfillment of her dream. Why couldn't he leave it at that? Walk away into his own new life?

Against all reason, he couldn't forget her farewell smile,

rather like that of a home-loving waif being packed off to boarding school.

Finally, with no chores left to accomplish and several hours yet to kill before boarding the boat, he acted on an impulse that even he knew was the height of folly. He hired a horse-drawn cab and gave the driver the address Ezra had provided him.

"That's a posh part of town, sir. Old families with piles and piles of money. Some made honest, some on the sly."

"Drive on." Caleb didn't relish the man's opinions, which only confirmed his own.

Once they arrived in the "posh part of town," Caleb wondered what he'd been thinking. That he'd somehow spot Lily strolling down the street? That he would pound on the Duprees' door and demand an audience? Or did he simply need to torture himself with a glimpse of her fashionable world?

"We're here, sir." The driver slowed the horse to a walk, then gestured at a huge stone residence. "This be old man Dupree's. He's got more money than he can count."

"Stop." Caleb studied the place, the likes of which he had seen only in travel books. The heart seemed to drain out of him. Lily had most definitely arrived. Just as he leaned forward to ask the driver to move on, the front door of the mansion opened. At that same moment, the Dupree carriage rounded the drive. Lavinia sailed forth and stood waiting imperiously. But following her…it couldn't be. A fashion plate in an elaborate full skirt topped by a crimson pleated jacket with wide sleeves stepped out, pulling on lacy gloves. Yet the tilt of her head and the spun gold of her hair left no doubt. His Lily. *No, no,* he corrected himself grimly. Just Lily, his lost love.

The ballroom glittered in the reflected light of crystal prisms dangling from massive chandeliers. In keeping with the season, the refreshments were displayed on sideboards decorated with cornucopias overflowing with fruits and vegetables. Behind a screen of potted plants, a small orchestra played, and whirling about the parquet floor were men in evening dress coupled with women in a kaleidoscope of colorful ball gowns. Uncle Henry and Aunt Lavinia had spared no expense in making this event memorable. Lily's head swam with the many people to whom she'd been introduced, including an outrageous number of unattached gentlemen. She danced now with Lionel Atwood, whose father was an important St. Louis financier. Thanks to the dance master Aunt Lavinia had engaged for her, Lily could make conversation without undue worry about the placement of her feet.

"Miss Kellogg, what are your impressions of our fair city?" Atwood had an athletic, rapierlike body, a chiseled face, dark hair and a waxed mustache in which he took obvious pride. Lily found him quite handsome, more than some of the other men clamoring for her attention.

"It is a wonder, sir. I am enjoying discovering more about it."

"Splendid." He led her on a dizzying series of steps, ending with a flourish near a secluded alcove just as the music stopped. "St. Louis must provide a welcome contrast to the frontier."

"Certainly there are many more amusements here." He would not make her disparage her upbringing.

He smiled down at her. "Of which I hope to be one. I am most eager to hear about the red savages and why our army has not yet succeeded in subduing them." He sniffed. "It's a national disgrace."

She thought of the times she had watched the troops ride out and of Caleb lying wounded in the hospital. "It is not as easy as it might appear from a distance."

"With your permission, I should like to call one afternoon this week. Perhaps then you can tell me more."

Lily had no sense that she would be able to bring truth into play, given the man's preconceived notions. She was grasping for a delaying tactic, when Aunt Lavinia swept up to them. "Lionel, Lily. How lovely your names sound together."

Lionel smiled smugly. "I was just asking Miss Kellogg if I might call on her this week."

There was no mistaking the gleam in Aunt Lavinia's eyes—this was good news to her. "But, of course, my dear boy. Just send your man around with a note so that we may properly receive you."

Lionel picked up Lily's hand and bent over as if to kiss it. Yet his lips hovered above it. "I shall eagerly await our conversation." He straightened to his full height and then excused himself, leaving the two women alone.

Lily felt Aunt Lavinia's fingers digging into her arm. "Well done, Lily. I do believe you have enchanted the most eligible bachelor of the season." She gazed out over the crowd, crooning softly, "What a match that would be!"

The rest of the evening passed in a daze. Never had Lily imagined so elegantly dressed a crowd or been the object of such attention. It was both heady and daunting. By evening's end, more than one of the young men had mentioned calling on her. Yet it was difficult to assess the difference between their genuine interest and social duty. Courtship here apparently involved both a language and an etiquette, the permutations of which seemed beyond her grasp.

In the wee hours of the morning when the last guests had finally departed, Lily escaped to her bedroom where the maid assisted her out of her gown and took down her hair. When the young woman picked up the silver brush,

Lily reached for it. "It's late. Go on to bed. I'll do it." The maid's surprised look let Lily know she had made yet another gaffe, but she craved solitude in which to reflect on the evening. That was not to be. With the merest rap on the door, Aunt Lavinia, clad in her dressing gown, breezed into the room and took the chair nearest Lily.

"You were a sensation, my dear." Aunt Lavinia's eyes glittered with approval.

"If in any way that is so, the credit goes to you. I can't thank you enough for all you have done for me."

"It's as Mathilda would've wished."

At her mother's name, Lily stopped pulling the brush through her curls. "I do not want to disappoint her—or you."

"With no daughter of my own, having you here and being able to introduce you to the best people is quite special. And what Mathilda wanted for you." Then her aunt stood, came close and picked up the brush. "Let me," she said, smoothing the hair off Lily's forehead. "As you can see, I am surrounded by every object money can buy. Henry has been quite indulgent with me and I am grateful to him."

Lily waited, sensing that words were being left unsaid. Though polite and deferential to one another, Lily had seen little affection pass between her aunt and uncle.

"He knows how dear your mother was to me and will spare nothing for you to have a lavish and successful season."

"Successful?"

Aunt Lavinia maintained even brushstrokes. "Of course. Finding you the most advantageous match."

Lily had a sudden impression of herself as chattel.

"You have made a marvelous first step. Lionel Atwood would be a most suitable husband. His prospects are boundless."

What about the museums she had yet to see? The lectures she was to attend? The public library she might now be forbidden to visit? "Husband? It's too soon. I had thought to do and see so much and—"

"Nonsense. There will be time for other pursuits after you are comfortably settled. If a wife is discreet, a man generally will overlook her intellectual pretensions." She set down the brush and patted Lily's head. "For now, you just concentrate on your young men. Particularly Lionel. Henry would be so pleased with that alliance."

Once her aunt had left the room, words, none of which made any sense to Lily, whirled about her—*successful season, advantageous match, prospects* and, worst of all, *alliance.* Is that how the Duprees saw her? As their representative in an *alliance?*

One word, she noted, had never been uttered. *Love.* It seemed to Lily a rather important oversight.

Throughout the month of November and into early December, hardly a day had passed without a social engagement of some kind—teas, concerts and balls. At first each new event had delighted Lily whether it was sitting, breathless, in a theater box, thrilling to an opera singer or dining on a sumptuous seven-course dinner served by footmen. No matter what surprises her social schedule presented, she would never become accustomed to the elaborate ritual of her toilette. Aunt Lavinia had made it clear that a lady never received company nor left the house until dressed in the appropriate gown and with every hair in place. Some mornings Lily longed to throw on an old gingham dress and tuck her hair into a bun as she had done every day of her adult life up until now.

Among her suitors were several socially charming yet intellectually dull fellows, but, gradually, Lionel Atwood had outpaced them until it was obvious he regarded himself as the front-runner for her affections. She had no trouble understanding why her aunt and uncle favored him. He was polished and urbane—a Harvard graduate and heir to his father's banking and financial empire. The mystery was why he preferred her. Following their several conversations about the settling of the West, Lily suspected she presented a novelty—an unpolished gem. Just last night in his carriage returning from a play, he had said, "Surely those barbarians have no understanding of civilization."

"It depends upon what you mean by *civilization,*" she had countered. "While we might regard their living conditions as primitive, Indians have every bit as much sense of family as we do, as well as strong tribal loyalty."

"But aren't they filthy?"

"No more so than anyone who lives close to nature. The buffalo hunters, for instance."

"That's different."

Lily failed to see how, but kept that opinion to herself. "Some are talented craftsmen. Their beadwork and pottery are exceptional."

"Perhaps they should pick up their tepees and go someplace where they can indulge those pastimes and quit harassing our supply routes. The government is supposedly in the process of relocating these people. Not quickly enough, apparently."

Helpless to overcome his disdain, Lily could at least attempt to ameliorate it. "Had you been at Fort Larned these past few months, you would have witnessed the noble efforts the military is making to control the situation."

"Too bad they didn't employ the same strategy as at the Battle of the Washita River."

Lily's mouth went dry. From Caleb, she knew what a ghastly chapter that had been in military history—and how scarred he was by the event. "Sir, in the interests of friendship, I believe we should find another subject to discuss. That battle was a massacre, and those who fought it must live forever with their shame."

Lionel turned to look at her in the faint light of the passing streetlamps. "Whose side are you on?"

"I don't see why I must pick sides. There is good and evil in all of us."

He had patted her hand. "My dear, you are such an idealist." It didn't sound like a compliment.

Recalling the conversation the next morning, Lily tried to rationalize Lionel's remarks. He shared the prejudice of so many of his class, especially those geographically removed from the problems of the West. He had no experience with the complexities of subduing a people spread over thousands of miles who were doing nothing more than protecting and defending lands they regarded as their own. More almost than his ignorance of the realities, she was bothered by his condescending attitude, as if she could have nothing of value to contribute to the topic.

Yet the man had his redeeming qualities. He was unfailingly solicitous of her and seemed to take pride in entering a room with her on his arm. He was generous with gifts of flowers and jewelry and had helped to ease her into several challenging social situations. There was much to like about him, and she promised herself to focus on those qualities.

He was picking her up this morning for church. Lily enjoyed this element of St. Louis life. Sunday services at the fort had been hit-and-miss, dependent upon the presence of a chaplain or the availability of the commanding officer. The Duprees and Atwoods attended a large

Episcopal church with beautiful stained-glass windows and a massive pipe organ. If grandeur had anything to do with God's favor, and she doubted it did, this congregation was blessed.

Standing at Lionel's side as they sang the opening hymn, she could almost picture herself as his wife. He tucked an arm around her waist and his pure tenor soared with the words, "Faith of our fathers, living still…" The sermon was uplifting, and the formality of the service impressive.

Outside the church afterward, she asked Lionel how long he had been a member.

"Since childhood."

"Religion must be an important part of your life."

"In what way?"

She opened, then closed her mouth. Had he not understood the simple question? To cover the awkward silence, she stammered, "Well, in all ways. Providing support in challenging circumstances and comfort in times of distress or grief."

"I'm sure it offers those amenities for many."

Amenities? Blessings, rather. "But for you?"

"I enjoy the aesthetics and the associations I make with the people."

"Membership is beneficial for your business, then?" Only with great restraint did she withhold her sarcasm.

"That's a bit crass, Lily, even if there is an element of truth in it. Let me reassure you that the Lord is still knocking at my door. I just haven't quite let Him in, yet."

Lily sighed with relief. She couldn't fault him for resisting God's call so long as he was receptive to it. Admittedly, she herself was not without an occasional question.

During the drive home, he took the liberty of holding her hand. "I presume you know how very fond of you I am."

Lily lowered her head to avoid his direct gaze. "You have been most courteous in escorting me about the town."

"It's more than courtesy, my dear. I enjoy showing you off." He tilted her chin so she could not avoid his chocolate-brown eyes. "You are quite beautiful, my dear. Any man would be proud to have you on his arm."

Here it was. All the sophisticated flattery and flirtation she had so long imagined, falling from the tongue of a handsome man practiced in the art. "Lionel, you make me blush."

"That is one reason I am so fond of you. You have none of the pretense or coyness of other women, whom, to be frank, I find boring."

"I often feel like a sparrow among the peacocks."

"Nonsense." He raised her gloved hands to his lips. "You are a rare, exotic bird, whom I treasure."

Oddly, her heart continued to beat at its normal rate. Her breath came easily. Why wasn't she ecstatic with joy to have such a sought-after bachelor singing her praises?

"May I?" And before she could stop him, he leaned forward and brushed his lips across hers, his mustache tickling her skin. He leaned back, then, smiling at her. "As delicious as I imagined."

She couldn't have written the dialogue any more effectively had she been Miss Austen or Miss Brontë, yet strangely, it had none of the power to move her as the novels had. The question boiled down to this: Could she will herself to love Lionel Atwood?

Astride the bay gelding he had bought in Independence, Caleb stared across the snow-covered Flint Hills, marveling at the sheer expanse of land. Three nights before, a powerful north wind had swirled down upon the ranch, bringing with it the first blizzard of the season. Only today was he able to make his way into the Cottonwood Falls post office where a week's worth of newspapers and mail had accumulated, including a letter from Will Creekmore.

Caleb had hoped Will's message would include word of Lily, but, instead, it was primarily an account of the diminishing number of military engagements at Fort Larned and one sentence extolling Fannie's virtues as a wife. He hadn't really expected Will to comment about Lily, nor, did he suppose, would it have made any difference. He guided his mount around a drift even as he reproached himself for letting Lily creep into his thoughts, as she did so maddeningly often. Foolishly, he had expected the change of scenery to help. He knew he needed to give her up, but knowing that didn't make it easier.

After stabling his horse, he walked toward the ranch house, a two-story frame-and-stone dwelling Seth and his father had built. The front porch had a sweeping view to the southwest. The rear was sheltered by a low hill and several cottonwoods and elms. Caleb stepped into the warm kitchen, eased out of his boots and laid the mail on the rough wooden table.

Sophie, her freckled face flushed, stood at the stove, stirring a delicious-smelling batch of beef stew. "Anything for me?"

"What were you expecting?"

She pursed her lips as if deep in thought. "Oh, maybe a billet-doux from the marquis or a proposal from the duke."

"Will you settle for the *Kansas City Times?*"

She faked a pout. "You're no fun."

"No, I guess I'm not." He'd intended the words jokingly, but they came out flat.

She set the spoon on a rest and turned to face him. "We

need to talk. Sit down there—" she gestured at the table "—and have a cup of coffee with me."

He wanted to slither away, but he knew his sister. She was a woman on a mission. She served him, then sat down across from him. "You know I love you."

"I do. However, I sense a *but* coming."

"But—" she grinned by way of emphasis "—you've got something on your mind and whatever it is has stolen away my brother. You remember him? The kind, funny, lovable fellow I adore?"

He made a play of looking around the room. "Hmm. He doesn't seem to be here."

"Well, I want him back." She reached across the table and captured both his hands in hers. "You may not want to talk about this with Pa or Seth, but I can be relentless. I've waited long enough for you to broach the subject. Your time's up. Tell me about her."

He was trapped, not only by Sophie's hands, but by her penetrating look. His sister had always known him better than anyone else. "It's that obvious?"

She looked at him as if he'd just asked the world's dumbest question. "Spit it out, brother."

He disengaged from her grasp and, with a sigh, leaned back in his chair. "Her name is Lily Kellogg."

"Seth told me about her. Said you'd asked her to marry you. That's serious business. Where is this Miss Kellogg who has stolen your heart?"

Slowly, reluctantly, he told her about Lily's dream of visiting St. Louis and his final, heart-wrenching view of her outside the Dupree mansion.

Sophie's eyes never left his face. When he finished, she nodded several times. "You love her still."

It wasn't a question. It didn't need to be. Sophie listened with her heart. "Yes."

"Did you have reason to believe she could return your affection?"

"Once I did."

Sophie picked up her coffee cup and stared into it, as if it were a divining pool. "You were right to let her go."

His head snapped up. "How can you say that?"

"She had to try it."

"It?"

"The fancy life in the big city. She would never have been happy wondering if she had missed out on that adventure."

"Small comfort," he muttered.

She eyed him over the top of her cup. "I believe it is. Now listen to me, Captain Caleb Montgomery, stormer of fortresses and leader of men, are you surrendering or is she worth fighting for?"

His sister had always had a strong will, and he felt himself being propelled along by it. "I will never love another woman the way I love her."

Sophie whooped, set down her cup and gave the table a tattoo with the flat of her hands. "Aha! I thought so. Your Lily must be quite a gal. So count me in!"

"For what?"

"Our strategy. I'm tired of you moping around here. You are going to win her back, and I am going to help with the battle plan. 'Faint heart ne'er won fair lady.'"

Caleb felt his face relax into a smile. Sophie was a force of nature and he trusted her mightily. He couldn't explain it, but once again a ray of hope lightened his gloom. He corrected himself. More than hope. Determination.

Chapter Sixteen

Dressed in a plum-colored afternoon dress, Lily sat by the cozy fire in the parlor awaiting Lionel's visit. Ever since the New Year's ball held in his parents' home, he had grown increasingly attentive, squiring her to a concert by a noted tenor and treating her to several drama productions. She exulted in each exposure to such cultural events. Yet the highlight had come not with Lionel, but rather with Uncle Henry when he escorted her to a scientific lecture concerning Charles Darwin's controversial *On the Origin of Species*. There was no particular in which her fancies had gone unmet. She should be basking in contentment, but despite all she had been given and had experienced, she was aware of a void that went beyond missing her family.

In such moments she often thought of Caleb. Wondered what he was doing. If he was happy. At the same time, though, she recalled the brutal conditions on the frontier, especially in this season of icy blizzards and bone-chilling temperatures. Surrounded by creature comforts, her every need anticipated and met, she dismissed such idle speculation. She had made her choice.

In the distance she heard the butler greet Lionel and

stood to welcome him. He entered the room, cheeks pink from the cold, and went to the fire to warm his hands before turning to clasp hers. "Let us find hope in the words of John Keats. 'If Winter comes, can Spring be far behind?'"

"Shelley," Lily found herself saying before she could stop herself.

"Shelley? My dear, you are mistaken."

Lily knew she was not and dared to correct him again. "Percy Bysshe Shelley. 'Ode to the West Wind.'"

Cocking one eyebrow, Lionel released her hands and laughed. "Silly goose. Who went to Harvard, you or me? I remember well. John Keats penned those immortal words." He ushered her to a love seat. "Never mind—" he sat beside her "—spring will bring not only temperate climes but beauty."

Lily did not appreciate being patronized, but decided pressing her point would gain nothing. She couldn't help thinking that Caleb would have known the difference. "Do you think it will snow soon?"

"I pray not. The town comes to a standstill, especially if there is ice." He leaned forward ingratiatingly. "Before that happens, I want to take you to an exhibition of paintings opening at my club Saturday."

"I should like that very much."

"I will call for you at two and perhaps we can stop afterward for an early supper at a highly recommended new café." He leaned forward and kissed her cheek. "I so enjoy showing you off."

She stifled the feeling of being objectified. After all, she had always dreamed of a man who would appreciate her and court her with devotion. She smiled coquettishly. "I shall do my best to live up to your expectations."

He beamed at her. "You always do. Few men can boast of having such a beauty on their arms."

"And what of brains?" she urged.

Again, he laughed. "Brains? What need have you of those pesky things? Leave that to me. Men are trained for the intellectual side of life. Women have their place in the home and as complements to their husbands."

Lily winced. She knew that such role expectations existed in society and had even seen them acted out by her aunt and uncle, but she had never before heard them so baldly expressed. Could she be the mere ornament of a man? But what was the use of confronting Lionel now? She usually enjoyed his company and thrived on the fascinating places he took her. Theirs was a relationship of mutual benefit. It wasn't as if they were engaged, she reminded herself.

"Lionel, you are somewhat old-fashioned, I suppose."

"Spoken like a freethinker, which I devoutly hope you are not."

"No, not a freethinker, but I do enjoy a spirited discussion of contemporary issues."

"At the appropriate time, my dear. In private."

It wasn't exactly like being muffled. Perhaps he would be open to serious conversations so long as others were not involved. She mentally shook her head. She was a long way from home.

After Lionel departed, Lily retreated to her room and picked up the most recent letter from Fannie. As she read, a wave of homesickness caught her by surprise.

Dear Lily,
I have much to tell you, but first, I hope you know how much all of us miss you. Yet we revel in your accounts of the places you are going and the sights

you are seeing. It is a joy to picture you in your fine gowns living in the comfortable home you describe. How generous of your aunt and uncle to treat you with such affection!

Your father and Rose are in good health and spirits. Will and I continue to thank God for our blessings. Indian activity has subsided during the winter, so we are able to spend more time with one another. Yet the weather has taken its toll on the men, and I am very busy at the hospital. But, oh, Lily, how I love learning about medicine and being of help to your father, so devoted to his patients.

Lily laid the letter aside and gazed out the window at the bare branches scraping against the mansion's exterior. An ache of longing filled the pit of her stomach. The hospital. Once, she had felt useful, valuable. Her next thought struck her with the force of a blow—when had she experienced that kind of fulfillment here in St. Louis? She had been so caught up in the whirlwind of Aunt Lavinia's social agenda that she had not taken time to reflect on what she might be missing. In memory came the sights and smells of the hospital, the gratitude of her patients, her sense of satisfaction in her duties.

How could any number of exhibitions of paintings with Lionel compare?

Saturday morning as Lily was getting dressed for her outing with Lionel, Aunt Lavinia entered the room, shooed the maid away and perched on the crewel-covered bench at the foot of Lily's bed. "Tell me, dear, how are you enjoying our winter pastimes?"

"From *The Taming of the Shrew* to yesterday's band

concert, I count myself among the most fortunate of young ladies, thanks to you."

"It is you who have given us the pleasure. I know Mathilda would be enormously pleased with how you are blooming in this setting." With her bejeweled fingers, she adjusted the large cameo hanging from her neck. "She would be pleased, as well, with the attentions of Lionel Atwood."

Intent on inserting her earrings, Lily waited, sensing her aunt had more to say.

"He seems very fond of you."

"He has been most kind."

Lavinia cleared her throat. "Perhaps he is more than fond."

Lily wheeled around. "Whatever do you mean?"

"I wasn't going to tell you, but perhaps it will be helpful for you to know. He has spoken with Henry."

Lily drew a quick breath. "'Spoken?' Surely you can't be serious…"

"Yes, I believe he intends to ask you to marry him."

Lily gasped. "No. I mean, we hardly know each other that well."

Lavinia waved her hand in dismissal. "You know him as well as any bride can know her intended before the wedding. My dear, any true marital relationship develops after courtship. Most brides take their husbands on faith."

Lily was appalled. *Take a husband on faith? It sounded no better than an arranged marriage.* "Aunt Lavinia, I am at a loss for words…"

"How many young women of your set will envy you your good fortune in bewitching Lionel. Why, I can see it now. A late-May wedding. The peonies will be in bloom and roses, too. A reception in our garden, and—"

"It's too soon." Lily could scarcely breathe. "I need more time with Lionel. I must sort out my feelings."

Lavinia rose to her feet. "Nerves, dear. We all have them, but, rest assured, you could not make a more promising match. What a delight it will be to host your wedding, and, of course, we must invite your father and sister."

"Stop!" Lily tried to soften the panic in her voice. "Lionel hasn't even proposed yet."

Lavinia smiled confidently. "He will." Her aunt stood, kissed her on the top of the head and repeated the ominous words. "He will."

After she left the room, Lily sat, hands folded in her lap, studying her reflection in the dressing table mirror. She hardly recognized the woman staring back—hair curled atop her head in the latest Parisian fashion, diamond earrings twinkling in the morning light, the rich peacock-blue fabric of her dress showing off her tiny waist. She glanced at her hands, pale and smooth, her nails buffed just so. Nothing about her reflection recalled the dedicated nurse enduring the hardships of life on a military outpost. She turned away from the mirror and stared into space. Did she even know who she was anymore?

The day was bitterly cold, but clear, and the bare mounds of the Flint Hills stretched to the horizon. Caleb and his father worked side by side digging stones for a pathway between the house and barn. The team of horses hitched to the wagon waited patiently as the men slowly hefted flat rocks onto the bed. Near noon, Caleb watched his father remove his hat and wipe away the sweat on his brow. The man was no longer young, but still worked like a strapping lad. "Let's stop for lunch, son," he said.

From the wagon seat, Caleb retrieved the packet containing slices of fresh baked bread slathered with apple butter, beef jerky and a chunk of cheese and settled on a nearby boulder next to his father. They ate in silence until his father spoke matter-of-factly. "You're having the nightmares again."

Caleb lost his appetite. When he had first returned home, the dreams came intermittently, but had ceased in recent weeks until the night before when they had returned with a vengeance. "I had hoped no one noticed."

His father chewed on his jerky. "I reckon you came by them honestly. A man can't witness what you undoubtedly have and remain untouched."

Fleeting images of bloodshed passed through Caleb's mind. "I can't forget."

"Nor should you. I had hoped, though, that you would find peace with regular physical exercise here in God's country."

"I'll be fine."

"Are you so sure? Sophie tells me you might have something else on your mind. *Someone.*"

Caleb grimaced. Count on Sophie to spill the beans, although he suspected Seth also might have blabbed. "I'm dealing with it."

"Heartbreak is a difficult thing." His father gazed beyond the wagon, seemingly in another world.

Minutes passed while Caleb worked up the nerve to ask the difficult question. "Why didn't we ever talk about Ma?"

His father's jaw clenched. "I couldn't, son. Maybe it would've helped us all if I'd been able to." His gnarled hands restlessly folded the oilcloth that had held their food. "But, you see, a part of me died with her. I loved that woman beyond reason. Nothing in my lifetime will be worse than losing her, except now if I lost one of my children. I have tried to be the best father I can be to Sophie. She is precious to me, but everytime, *everytime* I look at her, I see your mother and remember that awful night when she breathed her last."

Caleb studied his father's face, set like the very rock upon which they sat, and he understood that the man's tears had been there all along, dammed up by his need for control. "She was a wonderful mother."

"And a blessing as a wife." Then his father wrapped an arm around Caleb's shoulders and uttered words Caleb knew he would never forget. "Son, if you have found that kind of love, go after it. Your agitated spirit will never find peace until you become one with the woman God has sent you to love. Never mind where she is or what has come between you." Then his father abruptly stood and finished in a husky voice. "If you love her, fight for her, son. Whatever it takes."

Caleb got to his feet and breathed in the pure fresh air of the prairie. *Whatever it takes*. He knew now, more powerfully than ever before, that Lily was his other half, and fight for her he would, no matter what the challenges. Come spring and better weather, his and Sophie's plan had to work.

The art exhibition was breathtaking. So engrossed was Lily in examining each painting in detail and then standing back to admire the totality of the artist's concept, that Lionel grew impatient, often withdrawing his watch from his vest pocket to study the time, as if by that act he could hasten their departure. They had arrived at his club at the height of the showing, but now the crowds had dwindled and winter dusk was settling in.

"Could we go now, Lily?" He stood with his back to the wall, ignoring the art on display. "We will be late for our supper at Café Maurice."

Lily took one last glance at the remarkable painting before her, then faced him. "I'm sorry, Lionel, but this afternoon has been a sheer delight. Such talent beggars the mind."

Lionel concealed a yawn. "So glad you enjoyed it, my dear. Now let's be off."

In the carriage Lily shook off the sense that Lionel had been bored. Perhaps she had lingered a trifle beyond the hour he had expected to leave, but it had been difficult to tear herself away. "Thank you for a lovely afternoon and for being patient with me."

"The art I studied today wasn't a framed piece on the wall. I had the leisure to study you."

She blushed with the thought that she had been the object of such scrutiny. "Sir, you are quite a flatterer."

"Flatterer? I think not." He gathered her gloved hand in his. "Would that I might always have the pleasure of your beauty." He sank back on the cushion, a satisfied smile on his lips. "One day soon, perhaps."

Lily froze. Was he referring to an imminent proposal? *Not today, oh, not today.* "I hope you do not regard me merely as a possession to be acquired."

He laughed then, a sound that relieved her tension. "Hardly. There is your lively spirit to be taken into account, as well. In short, Lily, you intrigue me."

She had never thought of herself in that light. For an uncomfortable moment, she recalled this morning's reflection in the mirror—a young lady of fashion, bedecked in the best money could buy, prepared to set forth on a romantic conquest. What did that woman have to do with Lily Kellogg? In a flash of insight, she realized that the Lily in the carriage was an actress playing a part on the stage of St. Louis.

When they arrived at their destination, the carriage

drew to a stop and Lionel handed Lily down. The sidewalk bustled with people going home from work, and the street was crowded with carriages and wagons. The setting sun created a glare, and the cold caused Lily to gather her mantle about her. Across the way she noticed several former slaves unloading barrels and crates from a dray and carrying them into a dry goods store. Just then, their driver yelled, "Runaway, runaway!" Lionel grabbed Lily and pressed her against the side of the carriage.

The rattle of wheels, the cries of bystanders and the neighing of horses filled her ears. Careering down the street toward them came a wagon drawn by frightened, out-of-control horses, their nostrils flaring, their eyes white with panic. People ran for cover and other vehicles drew to the side. Now the wagon was upon them, and Lily felt the swoosh of the horses as they passed and heard the crack of the driver's whip. Then she heard a sickening thump, and all the breath went out of her. The wagon was long gone, but lying on the street was a limp body. A barrel rolled and bounced in the silence that had fallen over the onlookers.

Without a second thought, Lily tore herself from Lionel's grasp, ignored his "Lily, get back here now!" and raced for the victim, who had been unloading the dray. "Don't touch him, miss!" cried one; "Leave him be," yelled another. No one approached to help her. Heedless of her fancy gown, Lily knelt beside the man, feeling for a pulse. With a spasmodic jerk, he gasped for air. He was alive, but Lily didn't like the looks of the head wound gushing blood onto his black skin. She lifted her skirt and ripped a strip of cloth from her petticoat, then folded it and applied pressure to the wound. "Call a doctor," she shouted to Lionel. Instead, he rushed forward and tried to pull her from the man. "Come away, Lily. This man is beneath you. Leave him. Someone will attend to him."

"He could die," Lily muttered, squirming away and renewing her efforts to help the victim.

"Let him," Lionel said. "This has nothing to do with us."

Lily looked at Lionel as if she had never seen him before. "It has everything to do with us. He's a human being."

Lionel's dark eyes burned with a banked fire. "*Now,* Lily. We're leaving."

Ignoring him, she leaned over her patient and spoke softly in his ear. "Stay with me. You've a nasty wound, but we're taking care of you."

Lionel backed away, and out of the corner of her eye, Lily noticed that still no one had come to her assistance. She glanced around at them. "What's the matter with you people? Somebody help me."

After long minutes, two strong lads approached. "Doctor's comin', miss. We'll take him to the saloon, lay him out on a table. This is no place for the likes of a lady."

She rocked back on her heels, uttered a short prayer for the victim and then stood. "Thank you. Keep pressure on the wound."

Oblivious to the blood splattered on her dress and gloves, she watched the two carry the man off. Why had others ignored the situation? Didn't they see his blood was as red as theirs? She nearly wept with the injustice of it all, and thoughts of Moses threatened to break her completely apart.

Finally, utterly spent, she turned toward Lionel, who waited stony-faced beside the carriage. "Get in," he barked.

He helped her in, pulled himself up and gave orders for

the driver to take them to the Duprees'. Hell would freeze before Lily would utter the first word to him.

After several miles, the silence unbroken except for the clop of hooves and the creak of leather, Lionel finally spoke. "What in the name of God were you thinking?"

"It was exactly in the name of God that I *was* thinking. A life hung in the balance." She sighed sadly, knowing that nothing she said would touch him.

"Who do you think you are? Florence Nightingale?"

"As a matter of fact, yes. I am a nurse."

"Not here, you're not. Do you have any idea how you've humiliated me? Demeaned yourself?"

"What? By trying to save a life?"

"Ladies of your social class are not nurses, and they most certainly do not touch strange men, especially of the ilk of that no-account."

Why had she even tried to get Lionel to see reason? Was he really that caught up in status and prestige? Worse yet, were the social mores of his class such that human life was inconsequential? She could see no point in prolonging their conversation. She didn't know with whom she was more disgusted. Lionel or herself. When had she lost sight of what really mattered? It certainly wasn't finery and balls and palatial houses. Nor, God help her, one's social standing.

Lionel held himself still as a graven statue until they mercifully arrived in front of the Dupree mansion. Stiffly, he did her the courtesy of escorting her to the door. There he dismissed her with one curt sentence. "You have gravely disappointed me, Miss Kellogg."

Lily waited until the door closed behind her, then sank to the cold marble floor, shuddering with the enormity of the events of the past half hour. The accident had happened in a split second, but the ramifications reverberated in her head like thunder. Anger, indignation, bafflement—it was all overwhelming. But in no corner of her brain could she rationalize that she should have acted differently. A human being was hurting and needed help which was not forthcoming from others. In no world could she have stood idly by and watched the man suffer. If Lionel was horrified, so be it.

In another part of the house she could hear the tinkle of goblets, the clink of silverware and the quiet shuffle of servants moving between the kitchen and dining room. Dinner. The aroma of roast beef wafted under her nose, and a spasm of nausea caused her to get to her feet and flee to her bedroom. There, she threw herself across the bed and lay in the dark, a whirl of questions giving her no peace. How could she have seriously entertained Lionel Atwood's attentions? Today's actions would surely dash Aunt Lavinia and Uncle Henry's plans for her. She smiled bitterly. The much anticipated *alliance*. How would they react? Would they share Lionel's disappointment in her? It seemed that her every basic instinct was at war with the society in which she found herself. The society she had coveted.

She rolled over on her back, shielding her eyes with her forearm. There was one silver lining. For the first time since arriving here, she had done something truly useful. She had once more become a nurse. In that same act, though, she had also been confronted by the bigotry that surely could play no part in God's plan. Yet all in all, she felt more alive, more herself than she had in months.

There came a light tap on the door, and her maid called out, "Miss, are you all right? Is there aught I might do for you?"

Lily raised her head to be heard through the door.

"Please ask my aunt to come to my room at her convenience." It was best if Aunt Lavinia heard the story from her rather than from Lionel. Lily knew the conversation would not be pleasant, but better to get it over with as soon as possible.

She stood up, then glanced down at her dress, which bore mute testimony to the violent scene in the street. The maid had gone, but Lily had spent years dressing and undressing herself and managed to step out of the bloodstained gown and slip into a robe. Near the window were two chairs. Lily sat down in one to wait, all the time wondering what she had found so appealing about St. Louis society that she had left her family, denied Caleb and abandoned the nursing that gave her life purpose. She had some serious thinking to do.

She was so engrossed in her thoughts that she didn't hear Aunt Lavinia knock and only roused when she heard, "Why are you sitting here in the dark?"

Lavinia moved to the bedside table and turned on a single gas lamp.

"I have something to tell you. Please, come sit with me."

Lavinia, her brow furrowed quizzically, took the chair across from Lily's. "Are you ill?"

"No." Lily fingered the silken tie of her robe. "I have done something I believe to be right, but which I fear will be upsetting to you." Then drawing a deep breath, she launched into details of the accident and her own part in tending to the former slave's wound.

Lavinia listened without interruption, although Lily observed the sag of her aunt's shoulders when she described the victim. "Oh, child" was all she managed when Lily concluded with Lionel's unforgiving reaction. "I'm afraid you have jeopardized your chances with Lionel."

"I have no doubt of it." Lily raised her head in defiance, far more concerned about the fate of the victim than Lionel's pique. "Mr. Atwood and I come from two different worlds, and I have concluded I have no desire to be any part of his."

"But surely—" her aunt sputtered the words "—you understand that it is not merely Lionel of whom we speak. Hobnobbing with inferiors is just not done. Touching such a person, bloodying yourself—why, it's unthinkable behavior. If word of this gets out, you will become a social pariah."

Lily gritted her teeth. She had not realized how ingrained the mores of Lavinia's class could be. "I know you're disappointed in me. I am grateful for all the many opportunities you have provided, but I fail to understand people who put self-perceived propriety above human decency."

Lavinia heaved a sigh. "My, you are your father's daughter."

"And proud of it."

Lavinia sat back in her chair, hands folded in her lap, deep in thought. Finally she spoke. "Lily, I love you. I always will. Yes, you have embarrassed Henry and me, and I have no doubt rumors of your outrageous behavior will spread. However, we will hold our heads high and proceed as if nothing has happened. Perhaps other swains will appear. It will take time for gossip to die down. Meanwhile, I ask you to act with decorum and abide by the customs of polite society." She leaned forward and fixed a piercing gaze on Lily. "Do I have your promise?"

Once again this day, Lily felt as if she were sacrificing an essential part of herself, but after all the Duprees had done for her, it was fair of them to ask. "Yes, Aunt Lavinia."

Even as she uttered the word, Lily knew the time would come when she could no longer stay in St. Louis. Worst of all, she was slowly coming to the realization that she had burned the only bridge that really mattered—Caleb.

Chapter Seventeen

Lily slit open the envelope the maid had deposited on her desk and withdrew a card laced with pink satin ribbon. Beneath the words Happy Valentine's Day, a rosy-cheeked cupid holding a bow and arrow smiled up at her. The verse read, "When Cupid's arrows pierce your heart, / You'll know my love though we're apart." On the back was a note in her sister's spidery handwriting. "I miss you and hope you are finding true love in St. Louis."

Lily clasped the card to her chest, a surge of homesickness and guilt sending an ache throughout her body. If Rose only knew. Lily had utterly failed in her ambition to become a sophisticated, sought-after young lady. It was no surprise that Lionel had dropped her, barely acknowledging his acquaintance with her when their paths crossed, and word of her serious faux pas had obviously spread. The only person now who could remotely be called a suitor was a doughy-looking young man with rosy cheeks and plastered blond hair whose father owned a brewery. As for her would-be female "friends," now only their mothers called on Lavinia, always ready with an explanation why their daughters had been unable to accompany them.

Lily set the card back on the desk, acknowledging that essentially she was a social outcast. All the more reason why she longed for her sister's comfort and reliability and her father's steadfast devotion. Like a bird in a cage, she was without options. Her father had decided to leave the army in the upcoming summer and set up a small medical practice, but had not yet decided where to relocate. Until such time as those plans solidified, Lily was stuck in the luxurious prison of the Dupree mansion.

Odd. At one time she had thought of Fort Larned as a prison. She had chafed under the wilderness hardships, barely tolerating the extremes of weather, the wild winds, gritty dust clouds and vermin of all descriptions. Yet she couldn't help thinking that instead of finding her niche here in the city, she had merely traded one wilderness for another—this wilderness characterized by snobbery, hypocrisy and indifference to human suffering.

She had never felt so alone. Oh, Uncle Henry and Aunt Lavinia cared for her, but they no longer sought out places to take her to show her off. The family's social outings had been curtailed, and Lily knew she was the cause. It was Aunt Lavinia's way of "lying low" and waiting for the gossip to subside. Lily shook her head. And all because of one humanitarian impulse on her part, an impulse she would act upon again in the same manner.

What would Caleb say about her actions? Would he, too, condemn her impulsivity, or would he join her to relieve another's pain? In her heart, she knew the answer. The two of them had often discussed God's role in human suffering. She was coming to believe that much of human struggle was self-inflicted. God didn't start wars; mankind did. Nor did God create barriers between different kinds of people. It was up to each person to exercise free will and make loving, compassionate choices. For the first time that day, Lily smiled. Maybe, just maybe, by going to the poor man's rescue as he lay in the street, she had pleased God.

Fierce March winds swirled around the ranch house and sleet clacked against the windowpanes. Seth rose from his chair to set more logs on the fire while Sophie and Pa bent over the chessboard, locked in fierce competition. Caleb moved closer to the flame, the better to read Mark Twain's *The Innocents Abroad,* travel adventures that sometimes made him chuckle aloud. He had needed laughs during these short winter days and long nights when, more often than not, he fell into bed exhausted from his labors. His nightmares had subsided, perhaps as a result of fresh air and hard work. Between them, he, Seth and Pa were creating a cattle operation that held great promise. Yet while it was a blessing to be with his family, something was still missing, and he intended to do something about that.

"Mate!" Sophie cried in triumph.

Pa grunted. "Well, I'll be hornswoggled if this polly-wog didn't beat me."

"I would never count her out," Caleb said.

"It doesn't hurt that she has us menfolk wrapped around her little finger," Seth agreed.

Sophie batted her eyelashes. "My, how you do go on."

Caleb studied his sister, suddenly struck by the fact that she was no longer all tomboy. She still had a head of flyaway red curls, but her body was more womanish and her freckles seemed to have faded some. How had he not noticed? He figured soon they'd have to be protecting her from the area bachelors. How many such single men were even now clustered around Lily, beguiling her with sweet talk and showering her with extravagant gifts? He closed his book in disgust. He could not let himself think like that. He had to remain positive.

Sophie set the chess pieces back in their box and then turned her chair to face Caleb. "I reckon now that spring is soon upon us that it's time we told Pa and Seth about our plan."

Caleb's stomach churned. To say it out loud might sound foolish and make him out to be some wild-eyed Don Quixote on a futile quest. "Maybe."

"No 'maybe' about it. We are all in this together." She glanced around at the men, then grinned impishly. "Raise your hand if you want to make Caleb happy." She glared at Pa and Seth until slowly each raised his hand. "And in one word, what will it take to accomplish that?"

Caleb blushed mightily when all three shouted, "Lily!" He had hoped that, by and large, he had concealed his longing for her.

Then Sophie launched into the details of their scheme, which filled Caleb with hope while at the same time scaring him with its finality.

Sophie leaned forward and placed a hand on his knee. "Truth to tell, we're doing this as much for ourselves as for you. Your hangdog lovesickness needs a cure. Sometimes you're not exactly pleasant to be around."

Seth nodded vigorously. "I love you, brother, but sister has the bead on you. I met your Lily, you remember, and I can understand how you could be right fond of her. But you're a soldier, so forward, march!"

Pa got to his feet. "Gonna check on the livestock," he said, putting on his coat.

"I'll come with you." Caleb needed air...and the reassurance of his father's counsel. As they strode toward the barn, trailed by a pair of mixed-breed ranch dogs, neither said a word for the howling of the wind.

Inside, the odors of hay and warm animal flesh greeted them. Holding his lantern high, Pa moved from stall to stall, Caleb trailing him. "All's well," he said, coming to the end of the barn.

"Is it?" Caleb faced his father. "Is what Sophie and I are proposing crazy?"

Pa set the lantern on the floor, sat on a wooden crate and gestured at a nearby hay bale. "Sit."

Caleb did as he was told, then waited for his father to speak.

"When I first met your ma back there in Missouri, I was barely eighteen, wet behind the ears and awkward as a newborn calf. Everytime I saw her, my throat would get all tight and I couldn't get a word out. Even then I knew I was meant to be with her, to be her man. So I kept hangin' around. To this day I don't know what she saw in me, but together we were somethin'. More than either of us could have been on our own. That kind of completion, son, that's love. That's what your mother and I had, and that's what I want for all you children." Then he stood and led the way to the barn door where he paused and turned to Caleb. "I love you, son."

Caleb embraced his father, so choked up he could barely get out the words. "I love you, too, Pa."

Lily stepped around the piles of dirty snow lining the sidewalk outside the church. A charcoal haze hung over the city, and looking around, she noticed the bleak window-eyes of the brick row houses across the street. An unseasonal late March storm had taken the city by surprise. It was hard to believe spring was just around the corner. Sometimes she doubted that even flowers would perfume the air, so often befogged with smoke. St. Louis was not the alabaster city of her dreams, but a gritty, noisy mecca of commerce.

"Lily, dear, do come on. We shall be late for the restaurant." Aunt Lavinia stood by the carriage, her expression one of disapproval.

Lily hurried toward her, aware that once again she had disappointed her aunt. No matter what she did these days, she seemed to fall short. Just an hour ago as she was entering the church, Lionel had cut her dead and behind her she had heard Aunt Lavinia's tsk-tsk. Throughout the service, she was aware of thin-lipped dowagers studying her from beneath their bonnets and prissy young ladies studiously ignoring her. How long could these people censure her? She wasn't sure she wanted to know the answer.

Somehow Lily endured lunch at the highly touted restaurant, where elegance of food presentation outweighed taste. Other than these Sunday outings, she contented herself with the piano, needlework and reading. Although Aunt Lavinia had never again spoken to her about the sanctity of Uncle Henry's library, by tacit agreement, Lily was permitted to peruse the volumes stored there. With each advancing day, her restlessness grew, akin to that she had experienced at Fort Larned. Then, that restlessness had had a foreseeable end—her visit to St. Louis. Here? Nothing. At least not until her father and Rose were settled and she could join them. She steadfastly refused to name the other cause of her restlessness. Even saying Caleb's name filled her with fierce longing and unutterable regret.

Riding back home in the stuffy carriage, Aunt Lavinia and Uncle Henry were silent. Lily studied them, noting how apart they seemed—like a pair of bookends separated by their individual busy lives. They were civil to one another, and each seemed proud of the other, but where was the joy? Why, even their bedrooms were separate. Was this what marriage was like? Giddy first love replaced by tolerant acceptance?

Fortunately when they returned home, Aunt Lavinia withdrew to her boudoir with a headache, so Lily was free to curl up in her room with the delightful new book she had just started, *The Innocents Abroad.* Mr. Twain had such a droll way of poking fun. She almost laughed aloud as she read about the ignorance of the smug, ill-informed tourists. She had just finished a chapter and moved to the window to note with pleasure that the clouds had been replaced with sunshine when her maid knocked and entered. "Miss, you have a gentleman caller."

Please, not the brewmaster's son, she thought to herself. "I am not expecting anyone."

"He said as much." The girl screwed up her face. "But then he added the strangest thing."

"What was that?"

"Well, miss, these are his very words. 'Ask Miss Lily if she needs to be saved from snakes.'"

Lily's hand flew to her heart and fireworks exploded in front of her eyes. "Caleb? Caleb?" She nearly knocked the maid down as she ran past her, into the hall and down the stairs to the foyer, where she stopped cold, questioning the evidence before her eyes. There stood a handsome young man with warm hazel eyes, curly hair and broad shoulders dressed in a dark brown suit. Once more she croaked, "Caleb?"

He never stopped gazing at her as he crossed the floor, took her in his arms, folded her against his chest and whispered, "Lily, my dearest Lily."

So long as he lived, Caleb would never forget this moment. Holding her, breathing in her lilac scent, feeling the wisps of her gold-spun hair tickle his cheek, hearing her whisper his name over and over again, he gave a mental nod to his father. Lily Kellogg completed him.

After moments when nothing sounded but the steady ticktock of a grandfather clock from the next room and the two remained locked in an embrace, Lily finally stepped back, her blue eyes luminous with tears. "I can't believe it." She clasped his shoulders as if to assure herself he was real. "How did you get here? When? Oh, my, I'm flustered with so many questions."

He looked about, then said, "In a house this big, could we locate a quiet corner where we might talk?"

A joyful giggle escaped her. "I imagine we could find one." She pulled him along after her. "Oh, Caleb, there's so much I want to know."

"And so much I want to tell."

After they were settled on the love seat in the parlor, she covered his hand with hers. "I've missed you."

"And I, you." He wanted a few minutes to savor his welcome before he presented his case, so he bought time by telling her about the ranch and giving an account of his travels.

When he finished, Lily said, "This is a delightful surprise. Are you here on business?"

"Yes, but not the kind you mean." With one finger, he reached out and tilted her chin, so she was looking straight at him. "I've come for you."

Her eyes widened. "I don't understand."

"Every hour without you has been torture. That day you left me on the wharf and climbed into your aunt's carriage was the lowest point of my life. Yet I knew you had to come here—" he gestured around the opulently appointed room "—and see for yourself. What I'm hoping is that your curiosity has been satisfied in a way that has given you much pleasure, but that you might now be ready to entertain a marriage proposal."

Her hand fluttered to her heart. "I don't know what to say."

"Hear me out, dearest. I cannot give you what you have here. If it is culture, fine clothes and posh society you crave, then you must deny my suit. What I *can* offer is a promising young cattle business, a welcoming family and…my heart. We once talked of dreams. Here is mine. You by my side, a home of our own and children to cherish."

"You honor me. I don't deserve a second chance." She threaded her fingers together in her lap.

"I sense some reservation."

She nodded almost imperceptibly. "I don't know where I fit. I've learned I'm not cut out to move in these rarefied circles, but I don't know where I *do* belong." She raised her head and in her eyes, he read both pain and honesty. "Kansas was difficult for me. The constant spring winds grated my soul and there was no keeping up with the dust. The scorching heat and the freezing cold brought unrelieved misery. I don't know if I can go there again, even with you."

"You forgot to mention the snakes," he said dryly. He slumped. There was no way he could alter the forces of nature. "That's the choice, isn't it? I'm committed to the ranch and, frankly, to what I see as the beauty of the Flint Hills. I love you, but I don't want you to marry me because you have no other options. Even though I didn't want to lose you to St. Louis, I knew you had to have the experience so that if we got together later, you wouldn't resent me for holding you back. I feel the same way about our potential marriage. If you say yes, you must say it with the conviction that you will never blame me for the place we live." He paused to get a breath. "It's all or nothing, Lily."

"Would it be ironic to say I need time to think?"

He tried to keep bitterness from his laugh. "I expected as much." He rose to his feet.

"Must you leave so soon?"

"I have accomplished what I came to do. I'm needed at the ranch and must hasten home. Walk me to the door?"

She gripped his arm and suddenly she seemed frail to him. "You really came all this way just for me?"

"I'd walk the world for you, Lily."

They had reached the front hall. "What happens now?"

"You do whatever thinking you need to do to come up with an answer."

"How will I get in touch with you?" There was a frantic edge to her voice.

He reached in his jacket pocket and pulled out an envelope. "This is a letter for you from my sister, Sophie. You will find our address enclosed." Just as he handed it to her, he sensed another presence. Looking up the stairs, he saw Lavinia Dupree standing on the landing.

"Who is this gentleman, Lily?" She began her descent. "I hope you have not been entertaining him without my permission."

Caleb bit his tongue and bowed slightly. "We met on the wharf, Mrs. Dupree. I am Caleb Montgomery, retired captain of the United States Army."

"I remember now. You escorted Lily on her trip to St. Louis." She looked from Caleb to Lily. "But what on earth are you doing here now, young man?"

"I have come in the expectation that Lily might agree to become my wife."

If the situation hadn't been so serious, Caleb would

have laughed aloud at the way Lavinia drew back in horror, her bosom heaving. "Lily!" was all she could manage.

"The captain was just taking his leave, Aunt Lavinia. You and I will talk later. Right now, I am walking him out to his cab." Without a backward glance, Lily sailed defiantly out the door.

At the cab, he held her once more, shielding her from the cold. "Please, Lily, give us a chance." He uttered a silent prayer, then said, "I asked you this question months ago, and I ask it now for the final time, because after today, you will see me again only if it is your choice. Here is that question." He stepped back to plumb the depths of her eyes. "Can you say in all honesty that you don't love me?"

She drew a gentle hand across his cheek. "Dear Caleb. It is a valid question. And you will have an answer."

He hoisted himself into the cab. Unable to say goodbye, he simply said, "Until we meet again."

Clutching Sophie's letter, Lily dashed by her aunt with a curt "Not now," and headed for the privacy of her bedroom. In the past hour she had run the emotional gamut from surprise to delight to confusion and loss. It was hard even now to believe Caleb had actually been here, that he had made a difficult journey simply to see her, that he had persevered in his proposal and then left as unexpectedly as he had arrived. His appearance seemed incongruous, his simple clothes and unaffected air at odds with the grandeur of the place. Oddly, he had seemed more at home, more comfortable than the preening Lionel ever had. Caleb displayed a confidence that went far beyond others' opinions of him.

Why hadn't she let him sweep her off her feet, rescue her once again? It would've been so easy to tell him she loved him, to say "yes," but she had decided long ago that she would never promise herself to a man, to Caleb, unless she could do so without reservations. He deserved that. If she were to join him in the Flint Hills, she would have to embrace his world rather than criticize it. Both the wilderness of Fort Larned and the alien wilderness of St. Louis society had been difficult. Was she brave enough to face yet another on the prairies of Kansas?

She also had Aunt Lavinia and Uncle Henry to consider. They had been more than generous to her and, indeed, had fulfilled all her dreams of city life. If she accepted Caleb's proposal, would that be a slap in the face to them? Their world was far different from anything she had experienced before, and she didn't want to hurt them, but the fact was, this was not her world.

Then there was Caleb. So steadfast, so true. She could never doubt his love. He had demonstrated it again and again. Yet in his final words to her, she recognized he was losing patience. She would not have another chance. Sitting by the window, she picked up Sophie's letter. Caleb had always told her she would like Sophie, and as she read her words, Lily knew he had been right.

Dear Lily,

I know this is an irregular way to introduce myself, but I want to offer you some food for thought. It is not my intention to meddle in your business, though perhaps I am. My brother is very dear to me, and when he suffers, I suffer. And he is suffering. From love of you. I don't suppose I need to catalog for you his fine qualities, though I will mention one. Devotion. If you should accept his proposal, you would never have cause for distrust. He will cherish you beyond measure.

As for Pa, Seth and me, we would welcome you

warmly and embrace you as sister and daughter. Personally, I long for the kind of friendship we two women might enjoy on the prairie.

Yet Caleb has told me about your reservations. Leaving all that is familiar for a strange place which, like Fort Larned, is subject to the extremes of weather and climate might prove difficult. That we cannot change. But I can assure you that we will do our utmost to make you comfortable. And think of the garden you and I could create! Oh, and I promise to take care of any menacing snakes.

Lily stopped reading, picturing in her mind Caleb's family and his irrepressible sister. Already Lily felt a bond of sympathy with this plucky young woman who seemed to make the best of life and cared so deeply. Sophie's next words bowled her over.

Here is my proposal. Seeing is believing, they say. Why don't you come try us out? Caleb will send money for you to take the train to Kansas City where I will meet you and accompany you on to Cottonwood Falls and the ranch. Spend time with us, with the Flint Hills and, above all, with my darling brother. Then make your decision. Because I warn you—unless you want to experience the wrath of Sophie, don't marry my brother unless you love him unconditionally. Here's what I think: How could you not?
With high hopes,
Sophie

The generosity and enormity of Sophie's offer stunned Lily. Yet it made perfect sense. She didn't have to commit to the unknown. She would have the chance to experience the Flint Hills wilderness. And the lure of Caleb was intense. When he had driven off in the cab, a wave of loneliness had engulfed her.

She reread the letter, smiling at the exuberant, nononsense tone. Lily knew she would treasure Sophie's friendship, particularly after the affectations of the young ladies she had met in St. Louis. She sat a bit longer pondering the events of the day and praying for guidance. Then, knowing she could delay no further, she made her way to her aunt's room.

Lavinia sat at her dressing table, trying on and then discarding jewelry. Holding two necklaces, she turned to Lily. "Which do you think? The topaz or the amethyst?"

"They're both exquisite."

"The amethyst, I think." Lavinia fastened the gem around her neck and then said with asperity, "What exactly was that about this afternoon?"

Lily sat down on a nearby slipper sofa, clasping her icy hands in her lap. "You heard him. Caleb Montgomery has asked me to marry him."

"What kind of prospects does he have, pray tell?"

"He owns a ranch in Kansas, along with his father and brother."

"A ranch!" Lavinia couldn't have sounded more shocked if Lily had told her Caleb was a pirate. "Lily, dear, that will never do."

"Perhaps it will."

"Are you out of your mind, child?"

"I love him, Aunt Lavinia. He's been the only one ever since I met him. I admit that, like you, I am hesitant about what life on a ranch would be like, but his family has kindly invited me to visit so that I can make my own determination."

"It's out of the question." Lavinia's jowls quivered.

"His sister will accompany me on the journey from Kansas City, and Caleb is paying for my travel."

"This is crazy talk. I forbid you to go."

"I am of age, Aunt Lavinia, and not a captive here. I am going."

Lavinia threw up her hands. "You're just like your mother."

"Whatever do you mean?"

"No matter how I tried, there was no talking her out of marrying Ezra, nor dissuading her from traipsing about the country with him. She would have followed that man into the jaws of hell."

"That's the kind of love I hope to find. Why is following my heart wrong when it feels so right?"

"There is much more to what you call love, my dear, than feelings."

"What, for instance?"

"Knowing your situation is secure. Never wanting for fine things. Moving among the best people."

"Forgive me, but that sounds more like a business relationship than a marriage."

Lily noticed her aunt's fingers trembling. "You are so naive," she rasped. "I shouldn't be surprised. Your parents were the exception to the rule."

"Rule?"

"That few marriages are made in heaven." Lavinia lowered her head, pleating and repleating the folds of her skirt.

Lily waited, not knowing what to say but sensing a kind of cataclysm within her aunt.

Then Lavinia leaned back in her chair and fixed her eyes on Lily. "You're determined?"

"Yes."

"Then I will not argue further." She seemed to wilt

with that concession and sat wordless for a time. "I only hope you know what you're giving up."

Lily admitted she'd disappointed her aunt, but there was no turning back. "Thank you for all you and Uncle Henry have done for me. I shall always be grateful."

"You have made us very happy." The older woman fiddled with the amethyst, and Lily was shocked to see her eyes glaze with tears. "It isn't always so with Henry and me."

"But you are adored, Aunt Lavinia."

"Oh, yes. 'Adored.' But am I loved?" She shook her head sadly, and Lily heard bitterness tinge her aunt's voice. "There is a gulf between being adored and being loved. I have been pampered and appreciated, but loved? I think not."

Lily was appalled by both her aunt's confession and by the forlorn look on her face. Gone was the confident woman in control. "I had no idea."

"I don't intend to shock you, but marriage is a complicated arrangement. I settled, Lily, and to all outsiders, it must look as if Henry and I are devoted and content." She leaned forward and grasped Lily by the shoulders, her words falling with the force of a hammer. "Don't settle, Lily, whatever you do. Don't settle, as I did. Go." She waved her hands in dismissal. "Go find your Caleb."

Chapter Eighteen

Excited by the novelty of railroad travel, Lily watched the countryside roll by at astonishing speeds, green trees and fences blurring with the expanse of the Missouri River. The staccato rhythm of the wheels on the railroad track sang an insistent song: *Ca-leb, Ca-leb, Calebcalebcaleb.* Following his St. Louis visit, a flurry of correspondence had ended in the arrangements for this day. With the recent advances in rail transportation, he had not wanted to wait for her to make the slower river voyage. This very evening she would alight in Kansas City to be greeted by Sophie. In mere hours she would be lifted from Aunt Lavinia's world into Caleb's. She gazed at the distant riverbank. Could his world become hers?

Pondering that question, she recalled Aunt Lavinia's final words to her on the train station platform. "Be open to all the possibilities, Lily. As I know all too well, no joy is to be found in stubbornness, nor, as your mother proved, is there any hardship love cannot overcome."

The acrid cinder odor and the swaying motion of the train did nothing to ease the nervousness that had settled in her stomach. Yet it was a good kind of edginess, born out of anticipation and hope. She reached in her pocket and withdrew an oft folded and refolded letter from Caleb, the first after he received word she would come visit.

My dearest Lily,
You cannot know with what elation I received your recent letter. You are coming! My family thinks I've gone daft with the excitement of it. Although I harbor high expectations, let me assure you that I know the visit in no way entails a promise of any kind on your part. Yet I long to share with you the special nature of my home and pray that you will be able to see it through my eyes. Once again, let us be honest with one another, for we cannot go forward with secrets or reservations.

I am counting the days until I see you, beloved.
Yours devotedly,
Caleb

During the train trip Lily prayed for the openness Lavinia had urged. If only she could embrace the Flint Hills wilderness the way she longed to embrace the man she loved... She was realistic enough to know that happiness would result only from a shared vision of their future. She laid her head back and, rocked by the motion of the train, allowed her eyes to drift shut.

She was awakened by the soft voice of a porter. "Ma'am, Kansas City be the next stop."

Every nerve in her body came alive as she fumbled with her hat pin in her haste to ready herself for meeting Sophie, who also had been corresponding with her. The train slowed, snorting and puffing its way to the depot, then hissed to a stop, throwing Lily forward in her seat. A small crowd waited on the platform, and as Lily scanned those greeting the passengers, she saw her—Sophie! Tou-

Into the Wilderness

sled red curls, just as Caleb had described, a trim, shapely body clad in a simple dress and a smiling face dusted with freckles.

No sooner had Lily stepped off the train than Sophie came running toward her and engulfed her in a hug. "You have to be Lily! I'd have known you anywhere. Welcome, welcome! We are all so delighted that you agreed to come."

"I am grateful for the invitation."

Sophie pulled away and stood beaming at her. "How I wish Caleb were here to share this moment, but very soon I shall witness your grand reunion." She clasped Lily around the waist. "Now then, let's gather your bags and catch a cab to the hotel. We'll spend the night and then tomorrow get on the stage and then…"

Lily couldn't help smiling, pulled along into the future by Sophie's chattering account of their plans.

Clutching a bouquet of lilacs, Caleb paced the boardwalk outside the general store in Council Grove, willing the arrival of the stagecoach from Kansas City. Nearby loomed the towering oak tree that gave the town its name. Under its shade the Osage Indians had signed a treaty granting right-of-way for the Santa Fe Trail. The town bustled with Saturday business. Loafers gathered on corners to jaw and spit tobacco, while children darted in and out among the men and women intent on their shopping. Caleb thanked God for this mild, sunny May day to welcome Lily. Now that his and Sophie's plan was in full swing, he was questioning it. So long as Lily hadn't yet rejected the Flint Hills, he could live in his dream, but if she did…?

From the edge of town, came the excited cry, "Stage is a'comin'!" Heeding the announcement, small boys ran to greet the coach, now visible and rumbling toward its stop in front of Caleb. First out was a large, stern-faced woman, taking her sweet time. Then he saw his Lily—her bonnet slightly askew—her eyes searching the onlookers. He stepped forward just at the moment she spotted him. He would never forget her gasp of pleasure nor the sunshine of her smile as he handed her the bouquet and drew her into his embrace. Their simultaneous "Lily" and "Caleb" mingled in his ears as he held her, still trying to convince himself she was actually here.

"Hey, brother. What about me? Do I count?" Sophie's teasing giggle caused him to reach out and gather her into the hug.

After retrieving their baggage, Caleb led them down the street to the hotel he had booked for the night. "You two freshen up and then we'll have dinner. We need to get a good night's sleep before we set out for home."

"How far is it?" Lily asked.

"About nineteen miles. The ranch is just this side of Cottonwood Falls. We'll have a long day."

"With our chatting, it will pass in a flash," Sophie said, linking her arm through her brother's. "We'll give Lily a regular tour."

"I'll look forward to that." Lily beamed up at him, her eyes dancing. "I'm so happy to be here." Then under her breath so only he could hear, she added, "With you."

Caleb had not exaggerated. It had been a long day riding through the rolling hills, but he and Sophie had entertained her nearly the entire route with amusing stories of their childhoods, recitals of their neighbors' backgrounds and a botany lesson concerning the area flora. Finally, they started up the road to the Montgomery Ranch. Sophie raised her arm and pointed. "There," she said with a contented sigh. "That's home." The last rays of the setting sun slanted across the meadow highlighting a two-story stone house sheltered by a hill and overlooking a prairie panorama. Beyond it was a huge stone barn and corral.

Lily sensed Caleb studying her for a reaction. She touched his arm. "It's far grander than I had imagined." Knowing they were nearing the barn, the wagon team broke into a trot. As they approached the yard, Lily noticed the colorful flower garden bordering the front porch and the large vegetable patch a few steps from the kitchen door. The Montgomerys had obviously worked hard to create such a welcoming home. The last of the day's sunlight reflecting off the tall, narrow windows was like a whispered blessing.

Seth and a tall, weathered man came outside the barn, both waving their arms aloft while two dogs danced around them. Lily was seized with momentary jitters. She had met Seth, but she so wanted to make a good impression on Caleb's father. Caleb handed the two women down from the wagon bench, setting Lily down gently. "You know my brother, but this is my father, Andrew Montgomery."

Lily felt her hands grasped in Mr. Montgomery's large, worn ones. "My dear, we have awaited your arrival with much happiness."

"Thank you for inviting me."

Caleb's father chuckled, then winked at his son. "What could we do? He held a gun to our heads."

Momentarily disconcerted, Lily wondered what to say, but then when all three Montgomerys laughed, she realized Caleb's father was teasing.

That was by no means the end of the joshing. This family was such a departure from the formal Dupree household that it took Lily a while to relax and relish the give-and-take of an affectionate, happy family. The first time she managed to make a joke, they acted as if she had won a blue ribbon at the county fair. In the first few days, she and Caleb walked or rode horseback around the countryside, lush with blue-green grasses undulating in the wind.

Awakening one morning late into the second week of her visit, she was charmed by the melodies of a variety of birds, all trying to outdo one another. She had attended several concerts in St. Louis, but none had brought her the pleasure of this natural symphony. Gathering the blanket around her, she went to the bedroom window and opened it to a breeze fragrant with dewy grass, honeysuckle and wood smoke. Caleb had been gentle with her, giving her time and space to adapt to this new environment. She was grateful to Aunt Lavinia for once again calling in the dressmaker, this time to equip her with a wardrobe more suitable for the frontier. Already she and Sophie had spent hours together, weeding and planting in the garden and cooking. To her surprise, Lily found she enjoyed the food preparation Rose had customarily done. If she did say so herself, she was turning out light, feathery biscuits the menfolk seemed to enjoy.

One day Andrew Montgomery took her aside and walked her out to a pasture where he explained about cattle breeds and the seasons of ranch life. As they strolled home, he spoke about Caleb. "He is a fine son, a good man. His mother's death was hard on him, and the little I know about his war experiences sounds like it could do a fellow in. You probably are aware, too, that in the midst of that conflict, he got his heart broken."

"I know about Rebecca."

"Well, I reckon that match wasn't meant to be." He stopped walking and faced her. "Lily, I'm hoping this one is. Whatever you decide, though, make sure it's final and forever." He took off his hat, then repositioned it on his head. "Caleb can't take much more sorrow."

Lily nodded, too moved to speak. She guessed Andrew Montgomery also had experienced more than his share of heartbreak.

The second Sunday after her arrival, the men harnessed the buggy for Lily and Sophie and rode alongside them for the two miles to the community church. The white clapboard building with a small steeple surmounted by a simple cross was set on a corner near the general store. Horses, buggies and wagons pulled up to the hitching posts or stopped along the side of the street disgorging whole families of settlers who greeted each other with happy voices or claps on the back. In the first five minutes, Sophie had introduced Lily to several women who clucked over her and smiled their approval. Finally it was time to settle on the plain wooden benches, so different from the carved, high-backed pews of her St. Louis church.

Caleb stood aside to let the two women enter the row first before taking his place next to her. Nestled between the brother and sister, Lily glowed with a comfortable sense of belonging. When they stood for the first hymn, Caleb tucked a hand beneath her elbow and leaned closer to share the hymnal with her. When the congregation began singing and she once again heard Caleb's melodious voice, she could hardly squeak out the words, so perfectly did they pertain to the two of them.

"Blest be the tie that binds
Our hearts in Christian love.
The fellowship of kindred minds
Is like to that above."

With her free hand, Lily slowly withdrew her handkerchief, knowing she would soon need it. Verse two began and Lily couldn't sing at all as her eyes sought Caleb's while he sang tenderly as if only to her.

"Before our Father's throne
We pour our ardent prayers;
Our fears, our hopes, our aims are one,
Our comforts and our cares."

Lily bowed her head and softly blew her nose. *Our fears, our hopes, our aims are one, Our comforts and our cares.* She thought of her friend Fannie who knew the truth of those words, of her father and mother who had lived them and of the man beside her who loved her with all his generous heart. With newfound clarity, she realized she could not go through life without him. She caught her breath, then looked up to find him studying her with blinding affection.

After a picnic lunch on the green beside the church, one by one, the families began hitching up and leaving. On their way back to the ranch, Seth commented about the gathering clouds. "Mighty tall ones. Storm's a'comin'."

Sophie shook the reins, urging the horses into a quick trot. Seth and Caleb rode ahead to check on the stock and get the barn closed. The air carried the metallic hint of rain, and off in the distance a bolt of lightning speared the darkening sky. By the time the others reached the barn, secured the buggy and stabled the horses, rain had started to fall. Sophie and Lily raced for the house, belted by increasingly powerful gusts of wind. Shivering, Lily went to retrieve a shawl. When she came back into the kitchen, Sophie had stoked the fire and put on the kettle for tea.

Caleb was the first of the men to arrive back at the house. "This is going to be a whopper." He stood near the stove, drying his hands. Soon he was followed by Seth and Andrew. When they entered, the fierce wind nearly ripped the door out of their hands. Somewhere close by, Lily heard a loose gate whipping back and forth, and peering out the window, she saw bean plants lying flat, beaten down by the wind and rain.

When the wind died and there was a sudden lull in the rainfall, Andrew moved into the front room to look out to the southwest. "I don't like this," he said. The others joined him. Outside, the sky had taken on a sickly mustardlike hue and the distant clouds were roiling and becoming convoluted as if they were rapidly outgrowing their bounds. Then out of one of the clouds emerged a wide corkscrewlike tail moving like a ravaging beast toward the ranch, accompanied by now deafening winds. Andrew pivoted quickly and shouted, "Cyclone! Get to the storm cellar."

Watching the terrifying cloud-creature advance, Lily went numb. She had never been more afraid in her life. "Lily!" Caleb grabbed her arm. "C'mon." He pushed her in front of him out the back door where his father stood holding open the cover of the storm cellar. From below, Seth reached up and lifted her into the earthen cave, then Caleb and Andrew jumped in, pulling the heavy cover shut behind them. In the dark, Caleb found her and nestled her close, his warmth quelling her trembling. The dank quarters smelled of fresh earth and above them they could hear the thrashing and thumping of a violent wind.

Sophie lighted a candle, throwing shadows into the corners. On each grim face, Lily read concern. What damage might such a storm inflict upon all the work these three had expended? Lily reached out and touched Mr. Montgomery's hand. "Might we pray?" He nodded, managing a half smile.

She sought the words. "Dear God, in Your mercy bless

this ranch and those who have toiled so diligently to produce its bounty. Spare us and this place that we may go out from this shelter to continue the good work You have begun in us." Before she could say "Amen" a particularly loud thump caused her to jump. "Amen," the others echoed. Then they sat quietly, each lost in thought. After what seemed a long time, the winds died. Andrew withdrew his watch and leaned close to the candle, checking the time. "We'll wait five more minutes. Then I'll check outside."

When at last he opened the shelter door, a welcome rush of fresh air greeted them. The men left first, then assisted the women to the surface. Lily gasped. All around them were downed trees, shingles and broken fence posts, but, blessedly, the house and the barn still stood. "Praise be," Andrew muttered.

Before leaving to assist his father, brother and sister with the cleanup, Caleb ushered Lily into the kitchen. "You can help by fixing supper." He lingered there, seemingly reluctant to leave. Then staring at his feet, he said quietly, "I guess your worst fears were realized this afternoon."

She was speechless. He had voiced exactly what she was thinking.

"I don't know how to make it right. You saw what happened, Lily. There's no way I can control events like this. Cyclones, prairie fires or blizzards, it doesn't really matter. Life on the prairie is perilous. The most I can promise is to try to keep you safe." He looked up then, his face pale, his eyes reddened with regret. "I reckon you'll want me to make arrangements for you to leave."

She thought about the inconveniences, the deprivations and the outright dangers. Then about these four dear people who had shown her nothing but acceptance and affection. About the one who loved her. Then a surprising insight came to her. In that storm shelter, she had not been afraid. How could she be, surrounded by the Montgomerys and comforted by prayer? With an ecstatic sigh, she realized *I am home. At last.*

"Caleb, dear, I think that might be a bit premature. I haven't even seen my first snake."

He looked at her with dawning incredulity.

"Besides," she continued, quoting the hymn, "'our hopes, our fears, our dreams are one, our comforts and our cares.'"

Beautiful weather followed the storm—warm days and cool nights with the gentlest of breezes teasing the petals of the roses climbing the trellis beside the back door. Lily and Sophie had toiled in the garden to set things to rights while the men had checked on the cattle, repaired the roof, trimmed tree limbs and sawed broken trunks into firewood. A week after the storm, Caleb approached Lily early in the evening. "The almanac predicts a full moon tonight. Might I invite you for a buggy ride? I have something to show you."

Lily smiled. She had enjoyed watching him these past few days, looking at her when he thought she wouldn't notice as if checking to be sure she was still in residence. "I would like that. Let me get a wrap."

She trembled with delight when he spanned her waist with his warm hands and lifted her onto the buggy seat. He climbed up beside her, gathered the reins and clucked to the horse. She laced her arm through his and snuggled close. Neither the horse nor the buggy occupants seemed in any hurry.

"Where are we going? What is it you want to show me?"

He chuckled, a warm, throaty sound. "There's that curiosity of yours rearing its saucy head. Can't you wait to be surprised?"

She grinned. "It's not easy." She moved away from him briefly. "But I do like surprises, sir."

They rode in silence for several minutes, watching while the fading sun slipped behind the faraway hills. The only sounds were the regular clip-clop of the horse's hooves, occasionally punctuated by the call of a mourning dove. They began an ascent through a patch of trees and emerged on top of one of the lower hills. Caleb stopped the buggy at a point where it faced east. Below, a lazy stream wound its way among the rocks. "Do you like this view?"

"It's beautiful," she said, and in her heart she knew it was so. "Your Flint Hills are beginning to charm me."

He cuddled her closer. "Just you wait," he whispered.

Almost without warning, an orange ball rose in front of them glazing the landscape with moonlight. Lily shuddered with delight. "Caleb, I've never seen anything more lovely."

"I have," he said softly. He turned and gathered her in his arms. "You."

In the pause that followed, she thought she might expire if he didn't kiss her, but then his lips lowered to hers and all the moons and suns and stars in the skies couldn't ignite in her the sheer joy of his kiss. "Oh, Caleb," she murmured when they parted. She drew his face to hers to repeat the bliss.

Abruptly, he leaped from the buggy and came around to her side to help her down, pausing in that effort for yet another kiss. Then he took her hand and walked her a ways down the hill. Locating a flat rock, he sat her down. "It's time," he said quietly.

Lily glanced up at him, dismayed by his serious expression.

"I need your answer, Lily. You have been here long enough to know your mind, and I cannot go on living beside you, all the time wondering whether you will stay. Either you love me enough to endure what you call a wilderness or you don't."

She rose and took both of his hands in hers, gripping with all her might. "I know all about wildernesses now. I've lived in them. Here is what God has revealed to me." She drew in a quick breath. "A wilderness, my dearest love, is any place without you."

He reeled a bit, then cupped her face in his hands, searching her eyes. "Does that mean you can't say you don't love me?"

"I could never say that because it would be dishonest. I, Lily Kellogg, love Caleb Montgomery with all my heart."

She was crushed then in his embrace, and if she didn't know better, she would think he was stifling a whimper. Finally, he whispered, "I've waited so long for you." He drew back and held her by her arms. "Now then, *please,* do me the honor of becoming my wife."

Arms outspread, she whirled around and around, shouting to the moon resting over their heads, "Yes, yes, yes!"

After more kisses, she looked up at him, her expression turning serious. Her next words, she knew, had to be said. "Caleb, before we say anything further, I want you to know that I understand, as much as it is possible for a woman, how your experiences in battle have affected you and how they will always haunt you. You did what you had to do then, but this is a new day. God knows your heart, and I know your heart. You are a good man. On this earth, we will never escape the bad things that happen or fully comprehend God's plan, but perhaps we can agree to live each day in the hope of His grace."

Caleb placed his hands on her shoulders and fixed his eyes on hers. "You are part of His plan. Right now, that's proof enough for me. Faith will grow as, together, we put our trust in Him."

Sensing, the need for a lighter mood, she said, "You mentioned a surprise. Is it time now?"

"Follow me." He took her hand and led her around a large clump of bushes. "There," he said, pointing to a stone foundation.

She walked closer to examine it. "What is it?"

"Our house."

"Our house?" She spun around, her hand to her mouth.

For a brief moment, he looked dubious. "You did say you liked the view."

"Yes, but—"

"Hoping for the best, in my spare time, I've been working on it. Here is where our dream can begin—having babies, raising a family, growing old."

"It's perfect," she said, and knew it was so.

"Perhaps I can make it a bit more perfect," he said grinning mischievously.

"It couldn't be."

"You doubt me, Miss Kellogg? I have one more surprise for you." He reached in his pocket and withdrew an envelope. "Read this."

Had it not been for the light of the full moon, Lily could not have recognized her father's bold hand nor read the astounding message.

Thank you, Caleb, for your kind offer to establish a medical practice in Cottonwood Falls. Rose and I have discussed the situation, so if, as I suspect she will, Lily accepts your proposal, we will make plans to relocate near you later in the summer.

Lily sank to the grass, dumbfounded. Gathering her wits, she said, "You've planned this all along?" She shook her head in bewilderment. "How did you know I would say yes?"

"I didn't, but prayer can work wonders." He held out his hand and assisted her to her feet.

She leaned against him, knowing she would always feel safe in his arms. "Captain, you have thought of absolutely everything."

"Caleb," he reminded her with a lilt in his voice.

She laughed out loud. "Oh, yes, *Caleb.* My darling, dearest man. Caleb." *The love of her life.* It hadn't been an easy journey, but Fannie had been right about love. When a woman knows, she knows. And, thanks be to God, Lily knew.

* * * * *

Dear Reader,

What a blessing it is to write for Love Inspired, a change that has both reinvigorated my storytelling and freed me to explore some of the many ways God acts in the lives of people.

I do not believe it was by accident that several years ago I found myself at Fort Larned, Kansas, a National Park Service Historic Site and a well-preserved example of a frontier fort. In the visitor center, I was captivated by a faded photograph of two young women who lived there for a time following the Civil War with their father, an army chaplain. My imagination rioted: What challenges would an isolated existence among soldiers present to females? How might the men stationed there react to them? Could romance flourish in such constrained conditions? Images of those two young women stayed with me for many months and ultimately gave rise to the characters of Lily and Rose Kellogg. This book is my response both to the uncanny sense of immediacy I experienced at the fort and to my ongoing speculation about the role of women in such a place and time.

Into the Wilderness is Lily's story. Rose's must wait. Lily has her future neatly planned—she will escape to the cultured urban life about which she has long fantasized. Cavalryman Caleb Montgomery, scarred veteran of the Civil War and Indian Territory campaigns, looks forward to leaving the army and establishing a home and family. Their divergent paths collide, thanks to the unexpected power of love. The challenge for both is to determine how God's will and their individual goals can come into harmony.

Certain events in the book can be historically documented—the Battle of the Washita River, General George Custer's service at Fort Larned and the role of the Buffalo Soldiers. Where I have exercised literary license, I have made every effort to depict events in a way consistent with the historical background and setting.

I hope you find promise in the ways in which God works in Lily's and Caleb's lives.

Blessings,

Laura Abbot

Discussion Questions

1. How have Caleb's military experiences influenced his character? What obstacles have they put in his path? In what ways, if any, do those experiences parallel current events?

2. How does the thread of grief throughout the story affect the characters? How do they deal with their grief? What do they learn from their losses?

3. What role do idealized visions play in the story? In your life, where have you found your dreams clashing with reality? What did you learn from such experiences?

4. The Fort Larned of the story presents a narrow, closed society. How does this setting limit the characters and/or affect their behavior? In what ways do they adapt to the situation?

5. How do Effie Hurlburt's gifts of empathy, common sense and leadership affect characters and events in the story?

6. In what ways does Lily defy expectations for young women in her time and place? How does Rose contrast to Lily? Is there someone in your family who is quite different from you? How does that difference hamper or enhance your relationship?

7. Caleb is scarred by events in his past, which both trouble him and yet make him the man he is. How

does he attempt to deal with and rise above those difficulties? How do you manage to overcome past disappointments and hurts in order to flourish in the present?

8. In what ways does St. Louis fulfill Lily's expectations? What are the factors that ultimately disillusion her? What does she learn from her time with the Duprees?

9. It is often said, "God helps those who help themselves." How is this true of Lily and Caleb?

10. Despite their obvious differences, Lily and Caleb have much in common. What factors contribute to that harmony?

11. God often uses other people as his messengers. Can you think of characters in the story whose behavior might have furthered God's will for Lily and Caleb? Can you think of a time in your life when such a messenger influenced you?

COMING NEXT MONTH
from Love Inspired® Historical
AVAILABLE AUGUST 6, 2013

THE BABY BEQUEST
Wilderness Brides
Lyn Cote
When a baby is abandoned on her doorstep, schoolteacher Ellen Thurston fights to keep the child despite the community's protests. Her only ally is handsome newcomer Kurt Lang—but can these two outsiders make a family?

THE COURTING CAMPAIGN
The Master Matchmakers
Regina Scott
Emma Pyrmont hopes to convince single father Sir Nicholas Rotherford that there's more to life than calculations and chemistry. As she draws him closer to his young daughter, Nicholas sees his daughter—and her nanny—with new eyes.

ROPING THE WRANGLER
Wyoming Legacy
Lacy Williams
To save three young girls, schoolmarm Sarah Hansen teams up with her childhood rival. But is Oscar White still the reckless horseman she remembers, or has he become the compassionate cowboy she needs?

HEALING THE SOLDIER'S HEART
Lily George
After his experiences at Waterloo, Ensign James Rowland finds healing through governess Lucy Williams's tender encouragement. However, their different social stations threaten to ruin their happily ever after.

Look for these and other Love Inspired books wherever books are sold, including most bookstores, supermarkets, discount stores and drugstores.

LIHCNM0713

REQUEST YOUR FREE BOOKS!

2 FREE INSPIRATIONAL NOVELS
PLUS 2
FREE
MYSTERY GIFTS

Love Inspired.
HISTORICAL
INSPIRATIONAL HISTORICAL ROMANCE

YES! Please send me 2 FREE Love Inspired® Historical novels and my 2 FREE mystery gifts (gifts are worth about $10). After receiving them, if I don't wish to receive any more books, I can return the shipping statement marked "cancel." If I don't cancel, I will receive 4 brand-new novels every month and be billed just $4.74 per book in the U.S. or $5.24 per book in Canada. That's a saving of at least 21% off the cover price. It's quite a bargain! Shipping and handling is just 50¢ per book in the U.S. and 75¢ per book in Canada.* I understand that accepting the 2 free books and gifts places me under no obligation to buy anything. I can always return a shipment and cancel at any time. Even if I never buy another book, the two free books and gifts are mine to keep forever.

102/302 IDN F5CN

Name _____ (PLEASE PRINT) _____

Address _____ Apt. # _____

City _____ State/Prov. _____ Zip/Postal Code _____

Signature (if under 18, a parent or guardian must sign)

Mail to the **Harlequin® Reader Service:**
IN U.S.A.: P.O. Box 1867, Buffalo, NY 14240-1867
IN CANADA: P.O. Box 609, Fort Erie, Ontario L2A 5X3

Want to try two free books from another series?
Call 1-800-873-8635 or visit www.ReaderService.com.

* Terms and prices subject to change without notice. Prices do not include applicable taxes. Sales tax applicable in N.Y. Canadian residents will be charged applicable taxes. Offer not valid in Quebec. This offer is limited to one order per household. Not valid for current subscribers to Love Inspired Historical books. All orders subject to credit approval. Credit or debit balances in a customer's account(s) may be offset by any other outstanding balance owed by or to the customer. Please allow 4 to 6 weeks for delivery. Offer available while quantities last.

Your Privacy—The Harlequin® Reader Service is committed to protecting your privacy. Our Privacy Policy is available online at www.ReaderService.com or upon request from the Harlequin Reader Service.

We make a portion of our mailing list available to reputable third parties that offer products we believe may interest you. If you prefer that we not exchange your name with third parties, or if you wish to clarify or modify your communication preferences, please visit us at www.ReaderService.com/consumerchoice or write to us at Harlequin Reader Service Preference Service, P.O. Box 9062, Buffalo, NY 14269. Include your complete name and address.

LIH13R

SPECIAL EXCERPT FROM

Love Inspired HISTORICAL

*Oscar White has come to town to tame a horse,
but finds love in the most unexpected of places.*

*Read on for a sneak peek at
ROPING THE WRANGLER by Lacy Williams,
available August 2013 from Love Inspired Historical.*

"They say he's magic with the long reins—"

"I saw him ride once in an exhibition down by Cheyenne…."

Sarah clutched her schoolbooks until her knuckles turned white. The men of Lost Hollow were no better than little boys, excited over a wild cowboy! Unfortunately, her boss, the chairman of the school board and the reason Oscar White was here, had insisted that as the schoolteacher, she should come along as part of the welcoming committee. And because they'd known each other in Bear Creek.

But she hadn't known Oscar White well and hadn't liked what she had known.

And now she just wanted to get this "welcome" over with. Her thoughts wandered until the train came to a hissing stop at the platform.

The man who strode off with a confident gait bore a resemblance to the Oscar White she'd known, but *this* man was assuredly different. With his Stetson tilted back rakishly to reveal brown eyes, his face no longer bore the slight roundness of youth. No, those lean, craggy features belonged to a man, without question. Broad shoulders easily parted the small crowd on the platform, and he headed straight for their group.

Sarah turned away, alarmed by the pulse pounding frantically in her temples. Why this reaction now, *to this man?*

Through the rhythmic beating in her ears—too fast!—she heard the men exchange greetings, and then Mr. Allen cleared his throat.

"And I believe you already know our schoolteacher…"

Obediently she turned and their gazes collided—his brown eyes curious until he glimpsed her face.

"…Miss Sarah Hansen."

His eyes instantly cooled. He quickly looked back to the other men. "I've got to get my horses from the stock car. I'll catch up with you gentlemen in a moment. Miss Hansen." He tipped his hat before rushing off down the line of train cars.

Sarah found herself watching him and forced her eyes away. Obviously he remembered her, and perhaps what had passed between them seven years ago.

That was just fine with her. She had no use for reckless cowboys. She was looking for a responsible man for a husband.…

Don't miss ROPING THE WRANGLER
by Lacy Williams,
on sale August 2013 wherever
Love Inspired Historical books are sold!